Mrs. Quigley's Kidnapping

Jean Sheldon

He who is not contented with what he has,
would not be contented with what he would
like to have.

—Socrates

Prologue

Vagabond shifted from foot to foot, swinging his great head with displeasure as Diana Quigley mounted. Surprised by his uncharacteristic protests, she stroked his neck and tugged the reins softly to direct him toward a familiar grove of trees. "What's the matter, old boy? Don't you want to ride today? I promise we'll keep it short. I need to be at the museum this afternoon for the arrival of some new paintings, one of which looks very much like these woods."

The area surrounding the Quigley estate that so pleased Diana offered more than a pleasant view. It provided sun and soil to a wide variety of plants and trees including century old eastern white pine and craggy black oak that stretched skyward over a hundred feet and beckoned visitors with leaves twice the size of a human hand. Those monuments to nature's patience and endurance offered refuge to white-tailed deer, muskrat, raccoons, mink, screech owls, songbirds, red-tailed hawks, and others. Two-legged visitors found the quiet, natural paths a perfect place to relax and reflect.

But the serenity of that warm August morning in 1968 did little to soothe Vagabond, and minutes after urging him into their private sanctuary, Diana Quigley would regret her failure to understand his warning.

Chapter 1

My name is Matilda Constance Draper. Folks not young enough to call me ma'am know me as Mattie. Like most of humanity, I've seen good times and a few that weren't so good. That's how it goes. At sixty-seven, I'm old enough to know things sometimes happen that I can't control and it's up to me to do the best I can with the changes that come along. I've also learned that if you make friends with pigeons, you have to accept every part of the relationship. As a female private investigator, I learned to deal with my share of crap.

Draper Detective Agency opened shortly after my twenty-seventh birthday, and I kept the heavy oak and glass door swinging for thirty-eight interesting and rewarding years.

Before becoming a PI, I'd tried my hand at a number of jobs, most often involving secretarial work. My problem with that particular profession was that it didn't take long to learn the job well enough to do it in my sleep. Within a few months, my thoughts turned to greener pastures, or at least more interesting places to graze.

What prompted my frequent changes in employment was an eagerness to learn, not, as a few friends and family members have implied, because I couldn't hold a job. If you've ever done office work, you can understand why I needed a change. How many times can you type "Dear Sir or Madam" before you start rubbing your finger against your lips to make strange buzzing noises?

I didn't have the right stuff to sit behind a desk eight hours a day, five days a week. The longer I tried, the unhappier I became. Trouble was I had no idea how to remove myself from the gloomy situation and still keep the landlord smiling. My friend, Frankie Ficaro, himself a private investigator, suggested I try detective work.

Frankie and I had only known each other a few months when we first talked about my becoming a detective. He thought with the way my brain worked I'd be good at finding clues and solving puzzles. Considering the number of jobs I'd had in my short life, I knew I had a knack for working things out. The more I thought about it, the more I liked the idea.

When I was in high school, I read a book called *This Girl for Hire* about a detective named Honey West. I thought being an investigator would be exciting and fun. I just hadn't pictured myself in her shoes, especially since the heels were three inches high.

Frankie said that I'd have an advantage over other new investigators because as a woman I'd be unusual. I was sure he meant unique. He also believed in what he called "a woman's natural nosiness." I told him the word he wanted was intuition. Frankie doesn't always have his finger pressed on the pulse of humanity, but he's a good detective. More importantly to me, he's a good person.

To be honest, my agency might not have made it out of the starting gate if it hadn't been for Mr. Ficaro. When I finally decided to take his advice, I told him I planned to work from my apartment. He didn't think that was a good idea. He said clients needed to feel confident they were hiring a real private investigator. That meant having a real office. He told me about an empty office space between him and a bail bondsman in his building on Ashland Avenue. The PI that previously hung his hat there had finished a big case and made enough money to retire. Frankie said that was a good omen. I agreed.

The entire first floor of the two-story structure housed a currency exchange. Frankie, the bail bondsman, and yours truly occupied the three offices upstairs. The building smelled stale and musty, and enough feet had tramped in with city dirt and grime to make everything a shade or two darker than its original color, including the windows. Radiators clanked and the water pressure suffered more mood swings than my cat, Sebastian, but everything worked well enough. That was what mattered. At least it did to me. The location, a less desirable Chicago neighborhood, made rent affordable. That mattered even more.

Both Frankie and the bondsman put air conditioning units in their office windows. For the first few weeks the racket they made went right through me. Neither of the guys seemed to notice. I couldn't afford an air conditioner, but the icy breeze from my neighbors' units cooled the space and kept my share of the electric bill manageable.

Frankie did more than find me an office. Since his agency kept him hopping, he gave me his overflow, cases he couldn't or didn't want to handle. They were usually small—chasing down a cheating spouse or finding missing animals. I didn't mind, as long as I could work as a PI. Typing an invoice after a case, no matter how small the fee, was a heck of a lot more fun than typing "Dear Sir or Madam."

It wasn't until I completed my first big job that I could afford to have *Draper Detective Agency* painted on the window of my office door. That was the Quigley case and it came six months into my new career. The job did more than put my name on the door. It made me a detective.

Frankie didn't give me the Quigley job, although he did help. By the way things kept happening with that investigation, I wondered more than once if it might end up being my last.

The year was 1968, a hellish time for the United States. We saw the assassinations of Martin Luther King, Jr. and Bobby Kennedy, the war in Vietnam dragged on, and for reasons no one understood, kidnapping became a popular way to make quick cash.

I didn't learn about Mrs. Quigley's disappearance until she'd been gone nearly 48 hours. That was when David Quigley, husband of the victim, showed up at my office. It surprised him to find a woman sitting behind the desk—at least one who wasn't a secretary. He said he thought M. Draper was a man and he wanted a male detective working for him. I didn't take offense. Female investigators were rare, and besides, I wasn't sure if I was ready to handle a kidnapping.

Quigley was a good-looking, well-dressed guy. The way his hands wouldn't stay still told me that he was in sorry shape about something. I explained how I ran a one-woman detective agency and that I had a ninety-seven percent success rate. That was true. I just didn't tell him how many bites and scratches I earned completing those cases.

Frankie must have been listening through the paper-thin walls because he stuck his head in and asked if I'd stop by his office when I finished. He said he was working a new case and needed my advice. Frankie didn't need my help. He wanted me to get the job.

It must have worked, because Quigley relaxed a little. Although I suspected by seeing how he dropped into the chair, it was more that he didn't have the energy to search for another PI. He said one of his associates recommended me and was sure I could find his wife. The words bolstered my confidence enough to make me believe I could do it. That was my first mistake. I hadn't handled a kidnapping, but in my mind, good sense and logic could solve any crime. That was my second.

For the two years since I've retired, I've been telling myself to write this story down. Now I have. The following account of Mrs. Quigley's kidnapping is from my notes and my memory, both of which are slightly worse for wear.

Chapter 2

On August 26, the evening of Diana Quigley's abduction, David Quigley received a phone call instructing him to take the $100,000 ransom to a specified location at a beach in Evanston. The caller warned Quigley that if he involved the police, he could start planning Mrs. Q's funeral. Unfortunately, the local sheriff had installed a listening device on the phone and recorded the call. Mr. Quigley didn't have much choice other than to go along with a poorly thought-out plan. He attempted to deliver the money with Sheriff Brown and half a dozen deputies fumbling around like a bunch of circus clowns. That act nearly got both Mr. and Mrs. Quigley killed because the kidnapper spotted them. After waiting the entire next day and hearing nothing, Quigley decided to hire a private investigator. Me.

The first time I went over my notes, I thought that if Mrs. Quigley had a large life insurance policy, her husband made a good suspect. My early research uncovered a rumor that the business he co-owned, an office furniture manufacturing company, was having money problems. Kidnapping his wife wouldn't solve those problems for Mr. Quigley, but if they found her dead, a big insurance policy could give him extra cash. If he could make it look like she died by her kidnapper's hand, he'd collect on the policy and keep his business, if not his wife, alive.

I kept in mind that he'd been the one who sought me out, but that made me wonder who recommended me. We didn't exactly travel in the same circles. Before I put too much effort into investigating any one suspect, I wanted to meet his business partner, Jeffery Joseph Sumner. I also wanted to see what information the police had gathered. Right after talking to Mr. Q in my office, I went to the Quigley estate. I hadn't expected to find many hot leads lying around overlooked by investigators. At least I hadn't until I met the sheriff and his deputies.

Just prior to my arrival and following the botched payoff, the FBI sent a couple agents to help. They weren't there officially because there was no indication that Mrs. Quigley had crossed state lines, but the more the merrier I thought, so it was all right with me. It meant we'd find Mrs. Quigley that much sooner. My optimism and my ego suffered slightly when I learned that I wouldn't be an active member of their investigation. My request to the local sheriff's department for information proved unproductive and apparently humorous.

When I introduced myself to Lake Oak's Sheriff Brown, he looked me up and down and asked which one of his buddies paid me to pretend I was a private investigator. I showed him my license and convinced him I was a real detective working for Mr. Quigley. All that accomplished was to make him mad. He glared, puffed up his chest, and ordered me to stay the hell out of his way.

One of the things Frankie told me before I opened the agency was that the feds and local law enforcement folks weren't big supporters of PIs. He said they rarely offered help or information. He meant to *male* investigators. You can imagine how they felt about having a woman working their territory.

Once I had a clear picture of my relationship with the sheriff, deputies, and agents, I left them to do their work and tried to do mine. They didn't plan to tell me anything, even if they had anything to tell, but Mr. Quigley agreed to pass on whatever he could. He still hadn't heard from the kidnapper and I expected the call would come soon. At least I hoped it would.

The second name on my list of possible suspects, after David Quigley, was Josh Spencer. He'd been the Quigley's gardener and stable hand for the last three years. That didn't make him a suspect, but the fact that he was the last person known to have talked to Mrs. Quigley before she disappeared did. I found him outside the barn brushing a stately gray quarter horse. As I approached the pair, the horse did a little sideways two-step and I saw he wasn't comfortable with strangers. I stayed back while Josh stroked his neck to calm him.

"Hello, Mr. Spencer. My name is Mattie Draper. Mr. Quigley hired me to find his wife." I didn't wait for the obvious question. "I'm a private investigator. Do you have a few minutes?"

"It's nice to meet you, Miss Draper." His voice was deep, soft, and friendly. "How can I help?" He offered his hand.

I'd done quite a bit of hand shaking in my first six months of business, but Josh surprised me. He didn't give me a weird stare or make a dumb remark, and he didn't hold my hand like it was a limp cloth. He shook it, the whole hand, not just the fingertips. "You're not shocked that I'm a female detective?"

"I've seen stranger things in life than a woman investigator. No offense."

"None taken." I caught myself hoping that Josh wasn't the kidnapper. I liked him. "How did Mrs. Quigley seem before she left for her ride?"

"She was quiet. She usually is. I mean she's pleasant, but not much on small talk. She talked more to Vagabond than to me." He noticed my confusion and explained. "This is Vagabond, Mrs. Quigley's horse." He patted the thick gray neck. "They're good pals. Not too many people can handle this guy the way she can."

"You do all right."

"That's because Mrs. Quigley settled him down and told him he could trust me."

"Did she saddle the horse herself?" I knew a little about horses because my sister, Mary Anne, and her husband, Rick, had a horse ranch. You didn't jump on their backs and take off the way they did in the movies.

"No, I saddled him. She pretty much always rides in the morning. She lets me know first thing if she isn't going out. I didn't hear from her that morning so I knew to have him ready. I brought him from the barn set to go when she came around nine."

"How old is Vagabond?"

"Eight."

The horse stood around fifteen hands and was as fit as any horse on Mary Ann's ranch. "Did she say anything to you?"

"Nothing other than good morning and thanks. I heard her tell Vagabond the ride would be short because she was going to see some paintings. She doesn't need help mounting, so I stayed back and watched her climb into the saddle." He scratched his chin, which struck me as the habit of a much older man. According to my notes, Josh was twenty-five. "I did notice one thing out of the ordinary. I told the police when I talked to them. Vagabond was jumpy. Even when Mrs. Quigley rubbed his neck to calm him, he didn't settle down. Mrs. Q must have thought he was okay because they rode into the woods, but it was almost like he tried to warn her."

I wasn't a big believer in animals communicating with people, although Mary Anne swore they did, and Sebastian always had a lot to say. Unfortunately, I didn't understand a meow of it. "How long did she usually ride?"

"She tried to take a short ride every day—at least 20 minutes or so. On mornings when she didn't have meetings, she'd ride for an hour, sometimes longer. She liked to ride to the lake and read. I didn't give much thought to her not coming back right away. I forgot that she'd told Vagabond they'd keep it short until Mrs. Allen asked me if I'd seen her."

I looked at my notes. "Mrs. Allen, the housekeeper?" He nodded. "You didn't see anyone in the woods?" I wanted to ask if he'd followed her, but decided it might be wise to keep as many people on my side as possible since the police and FBI weren't.

"No ma'am. There was no one around."

"Call me Mattie. Do you mind if I call you Josh?"

"That'd be fine."

"Did you notice anything else unusual?"

"There was a rope tied to two of the trees blocking the path. The police thought it had pushed Mrs. Quigley off the saddle." He sounded doubtful. "It doesn't make sense that Vagabond didn't stop when he saw the rope. He must not have seen it."

"Mr. Quigley mentioned the rope," I said. "You didn't notice anything else?"

"No, not that I recall."

"Do you live here, Josh?"

"In a cabin behind the barn. Would you like to see it?"

"Not now. Thanks. I'm going to take a quick look around. I'll talk to you later."

"I sure hope you find Mrs. Quigley, Mattie. She's a good boss and a good person."

I watched him walk to the barn with Vagabond and decided to inspect the woods where he'd pointed. Mr. Quigley told me that the police seemed sure about the rope catching Diana across the chest and sweeping her from the saddle. Josh didn't share their certainty. She'd have hit the ground hard because Vagabond was a good-sized horse.

The soothing quiet in the woods surprised me. I imagined I could hear the trees stretching their roots and branches to greet the day. I also noticed that the critters quit chattering with my arrival and guessed they were waiting for me to leave.

I grew up in Chicago where noise was as much a part of life as daylight. As I stood in those woods, I found it hard to believe that Lake Oak and Chicago were in the same state, no less separated by only thirty miles. The peaceful environment so calmed me that when an unintended sigh escaped, I nearly apologized for the disturbance.

That brought me back to the purpose of my visit, but unfortunately there wasn't much to see. The sheriff's department must have taken the rope when they checked the area. I found nothing disturbed enough to indicate that someone had pushed or pulled Mrs. Quigley from her horse. The main path split into other trails farther into the woods and they all had enough hoof prints to indicate there had been traffic in the last week or so. The center one, which led to a clearing, was the only one with relatively fresh horse manure. I guessed that was the path that Diana and Vagabond took.

I found more fresh manure in the clearing and wondered why, if the rope had swept Diana from the horse as the police believed, he went that far without her. Josh said he found Vagabond in the woods tied to a tree near where the rope hung. He'd been right to wonder about that rope. None of it made sense. I wished Vagabond could talk and considered asking Mary Anne to have a person-to-horse conversation with him.

As much as the peaceful spot soothed me it was time to move on. I had a job to do. I was making my way back to the house when I heard a ruckus and saw the deputies and FBI agents jump into their car and race away. I wondered if there was news on Mrs. Quigley and hurried toward the house.

What slowed my arrival was an area near the front door that contained several lush flowerbeds. I'd never seen such a variety of flowers and assumed it was Josh's work. He may have been a good horse handler, but he had a genius for growing things. Except for a few pieces of paper that had blown in, the displays were perfect. I couldn't help myself. I picked up the scraps and shoved them in my jacket pocket to restore the scene and appease my sense of order. I also made a mental note to compliment the gardener next time we talked. Josh was a man who had a way with horses and gardens. Those didn't strike me as characteristics of your typical kidnapper, but maybe typical wasn't a word that could be applied to a kidnapper.

The housekeeper that Josh mentioned, Mrs. Allen, was next on my list for an interview. She managed the household and cooked for the couple, and had been with them since they moved in after their wedding ten years earlier. According to Mr. Quigley, Mrs. Allen told the police that she had helped Mrs. Quigley lay out clothes for after the ride. Diana knew she wouldn't have much time when she returned and wanted them ready to slip on after her shower.

Mrs. Allen also told them that as she stood at the sink looking out the Quigley's kitchen window she saw thirty-three-year-old Diana Quigley mounting her horse by the barn. She returned to the breakfast dishes and checked the clock. It was nine.

Her testimony helped investigators narrow the time of the kidnapping to between nine and noon. It was just before twelve when Mrs. Allen realized she had not heard Diana return, and that she was late for her meeting. When she didn't find her in the house, she told Josh to look around the estate. His search took him to the woods where he found Vagabond and the rope but no sign of Diana. Mrs. Allen called David Quigley at his office. He told her to contact the police and that he was on his way. Her call brought the sheriff's department who notified the FBI. It was over 48-hours later before I arrived on the scene, and shortly after that an event in Chicago dramatically reduced the number of investigators.

I learned the reason for their hasty retreat from Mrs. Allen. She'd heard on the radio that all hell had broken loose in the city because of the Democratic Convention. That wasn't the term she used to describe it, but it was how my brain deciphered her description.

Minor altercations between demonstrators and police began when the convention started on Sunday. It came to a head when sweltering August temperatures pushed angry citizens and equally irate police officers and National Guardsmen to their limit. The FBI agents headed to the city and local deputies returned to police their community as protests in surrounding suburbs were escalating.

My stomach did a quick flip-flop at the news. It meant that Mr. Quigley's crack investigative team now consisted of a sheriff who would rather be busting heads of protestors than working with a female PI, a deputy who felt the same way, and a rookie PI. I put those thoughts out of my mind. I had a job to find Mrs. Quigley and that was what I planned to do.

Mrs. Allen told me, with a slight unidentifiable accent, that everyone liked Diana Quigley. Although not overly social, she belonged to a few clubs and sat on a small number of boards with other friends and neighbors. "Did you talk to Mrs. Quigley often?" My cousin Ginny worked for a well-to-do family in the city and they didn't have much contact with the people on the household staff. That apparently wasn't true of Diana Quigley.

"Oh yes. Miss Diana is very kind. She and Mr. Quigley do not go to many social events, but I see her do many things for people and volunteer for charity events."

"Have you ever seen guests that you didn't know, Mrs. Allen? Strangers? Men showing up during the day or anything like that?" The housekeeper took a minute to digest my words and then responded with one of those looks my fifth-grade teacher, Mrs. Schubert, used to give when I'd said something she perceived as sass or stupidity. A look that said, "Your parents must be so disappointed." I tried to placate the housekeeper. "I have to ask these questions so I can find her, Mrs. Allen. I don't mean any offense. Okay?" After another short and slightly less disagreeable look, she assured me that Mrs. Quigley did not have strange male visitors. She also repeated what Josh had said about Mrs. Quigley being a good boss and a good person. At first glance, Diana appeared not to have any enemies. It didn't take long to discover that in Lake Oak, like everywhere else on the planet, first glances can be deceiving.

Chapter 3

When Mrs. Allen and I finished our rather stilted conversation, I went to the living room to converse with David Quigley. He didn't invite me to sit, and judging by the path he was wearing in the deep blue background of a floral Persian carpet, that was because he couldn't sit himself. When I met him in my office, I figured he was an even-tempered, friendly guy. I still thought that was true, or would be, if someone hadn't abducted his wife.

He was right around six feet tall with dark gray eyes and uncombed blond hair that hung slightly over his collar. The length might have been intentional because men had been growing their hair longer in the last few years, but I guessed the uncombed part had more to do with his missing wife. He asked me what I planned to do next and I told him I wanted to meet Kathleen McCarthy, the young woman who assisted Mrs. Allen with the housework. I also told him that when we finished, I wanted to visit the furniture plant. He couldn't see the point, so I explained that it was not unheard of for an irate employee to seek revenge on his boss. He agreed to take me, but just as when he first came to my office and wasn't pleased about hiring a female PI, I had the feeling he was too exhausted to do anything else.

"I'll get Kathleen."

"Before you do that, do you have a current picture of Diana?" He led me to an oil painting over the stone fireplace that filled half of one wall. It was a portrait of Diana and David Quigley. He said they'd had it done the previous year.

If the artist had painted an accurate likeness of the missing woman, Diana's beauty could stop a parade. Reddish-brown curls spilled down both sides of a long, thin face and her brown eyes sparkled over a relaxed smile. I knew from information Mr. Quigley provided that she was six years older than my twenty-seven years. I'd have guessed her younger.

She stood next to Dave, a man with his own share of good looks, with her arm wrapped in his. They both appeared happy with life and each other. Diana was as long and thin as a willow, and judging by her well-proportioned limbs, might have been as agile. While I studied the portrait, Quigley re-entered with Kathleen McCarthy. After a brief introduction, he left us alone.

"Kathleen, I'm a private investigator working for Mr. Quigley. It's nice to meet you." She gave me a quick nod without raising her eyes. I could see she was scared.

She didn't wear a maid's uniform, just pants, a plain blue cotton shirt, and white Keds on her size five feet. Her hair was the same color brown as mine, but while mine stopped at my shoulders, hers hung in a long braid down her back.

"Have you seen any strangers visiting Mrs. Quigley during the day?" I kept my voice quiet and what I hoped was soothing, but instead of calming down, she became more agitated. It took me a minute to guess the cause of her distress. "Did the police interview you?" I asked.

"Oh, yes ma'am. I thought they were going to throw me in jail the way they talked. I like working for Mr. and Mrs. Quigley and can't think why anyone would kidnap Miss Diana." As her fear grew, her words came faster and her brogue thicker.

"I know you're not involved, Kathleen. I'm sure the police know that too. They just come across a little heavy-handed." I didn't mention their arrogance and lack of manners. Instead, I reached in my purse and pulled out a business card. "Will you call me if you think of anything that might help us find Mrs. Quigley?"

"Yes, ma'am. I will." Her hand trembled as she took the card from my fingers. She never did relax. At least not until I told her she could go.

As Kathleen left, Mr. Quigley returned. "Any luck?"

"Nothing yet, but people that work here think a great deal of you and your wife. They've all promised to let me know if they remember anything that might help. Why don't we head over to Q & S Design?"

We drove in silence and I wondered if Kathleen knew things she wasn't saying. I wondered, too, if I would run into the same situation with workers at the plant. If they knew of any problems, would they tell me? Besides a sense of loyalty to their boss, workers like Kathleen and the employees at the plant had a paycheck to consider.

We entered a gateway into a small industrial area. Across the top of the gate was a sign with the Q & S logo and the words Quigley and Sumner Design. I could see two buildings, one large and flat, and a smaller two-story brick building. After parking by the brick building, I followed Mr. Quigley to the flat metal-sided building, which turned out to be where they manufactured furniture. It was huge and appeared to stretch the length and width of a football field. The size surprised me, and once inside, so did the noise. It was as loud as the fourth quarter of a Bears-Packers game. I noticed a number of distinct smells too. Some were strong and unfamiliar, but one recognizable odor came from stacks of cut wood that filled a large section of the plant. I wanted to wander around, but noise from the machines would have prevented conversation. I shouted that thought into Mr. Quigley's ear.

"You're right, Miss Draper. You won't be able to talk out here." He pointed to a door and took us into an area where the noise decreased so drastically, I guessed it was soundproofed. I could hear myself think even with the residual buzzing in my ears.

The room was large and windowless. It had around twenty tables and four times as many chairs with workers reading papers or eating. It was after three, but I knew from my own experience in a factory that some places staggered breaks and meal schedules to avoid stopping production.

Mr. Quigley told me he'd send a few people in and that I should come to the office when I'd finished, the brick building where he parked. I didn't like that he was selecting the people I could talk to, but he didn't give me much choice.

Martin Schmidt was first to join me. He supervised the cutting of raw wood and spoke with obvious pride about his job and crew. When he finished explaining the steps involved in turning raw wood into furniture I asked his opinion of his bosses. "How do you like working for Mr. Quigley and Mr. Sumner?"

"Good men. They are both good men." His deep voice had a strong German accent so it sounded more like, "Day are boat goot men." By the size of him, I guessed his accent wasn't the only strong thing about him.

"Do you know Diana Quigley?"

"*Nein.* I see her, of course, but she does not come to the factory often. It may be a little too noisy, I think." Although the comment was lighthearted and probably meant as a joke, his next remark took a serious tone. "She is a fine lady. You will find her I hope."

"I'll do my best, Mr. Schmidt. Do you know if anyone around the plant dislikes Mr. Quigley, or if he has enemies?"

He stood quietly for a minute, apparently thinking about my question. Then, in a single unhurried motion, he raised and dropped his giant hands, arms, and shoulders. "No, I don't know if he has enemies, Miss Draper. Everyone likes working for Mr. Quigley."

Over the next thirty minutes or so I talked to three other supervisors and they agreed that Mr. Quigley and Mr. Sumner were good to work for and that Mrs. Quigley was a fine lady. The only interesting comment came from a worker eating lunch that I had a chance to talk to after the last supervisor left. He mentioned that there had been several accidents around the plant, but seemed to regret the admission as soon as he said it and wouldn't say more. I had been right that no one would discuss their bosses or the company in anything but a flattering way.

I didn't blame them. Many of the workers were immigrants or first generation Americans whose parents were immigrants. They didn't welcome conversations with anyone who asked questions. That included private investigators, even one as sweet as me. I left the factory and made the short walk to the office building to find Mr. Quigley.

The difference in the environments of the two structures couldn't have been greater. Inside the brick building I heard little other than clicking typewriters and ringing phones. Even those sounds seemed hushed in the more sedate environment.

Lush carpet covered every inch of the place and my nose sniffed only subtle aromas of cologne, perfume, cigarette smoke, and brewing coffee. That last smell pushed a button that notified my brain of a caffeine deficit.

I scanned the area for a coffee pot but saw only finely crafted tables and chairs, which I assumed were finished products from the factory. The pieces took my breath away and gave me an even greater respect for the folks in the other building. It took a great deal of skill to coax raw wood into the highly polished works of functional art that filled the lobby. I guessed that whoever was in charge of such things at Q & S Design was smart enough not to put a potentially dangerous coffee pot in a place where anyone could walk in and spill.

I squelched my coffee urge and noticed a woman behind a black walnut desk that enclosed her in a graceful semi-circle. Unlike my battered and messy desk at the office, neither pen nor paperclip appeared out of place. The woman behind the furniture looked pretty well made herself. She had a mound of blonde hair piled on her head, and though her suit had a conservative cut, the bright red color shouted, "Look at me!"

I watched her type with long fingernails painted to match the suit and wondered how she managed without hitting two or three keys at the same time. My curiosity won out and I leaned over to watch her confident and quick fingers move.

She sensed my presence and raised her head, a little startled to find someone hanging over her desk. I took a step back as she spoke. "Can I help you?"

"Please tell Mr. Quigley that I'm finished at the factory. I'm Mattie Draper, a private investigator working on his wife's kidnapping."

Her eyes didn't flood with confidence as they studied me, but she did want to discuss the kidnapping. "Oh, isn't it terrible? Who would kidnap poor Mrs. Quigley? She's such a sweet woman."

"That's what I hope to find out. Did you know her?"

"We weren't close friends, of course, but I knew her. She was quiet but friendly, sometimes almost shy. I found that surprising considering her modeling career and involvement in various organizations."

The modeling career was news to me. I checked the nameplate on the desk. Rachel Jankowski was located at the very center of the office building. Her physical location and her occupation could make her a valuable resource. "Rachel," I reached in my purse for a card. "I'd like to talk to you again. Can we meet for coffee? You may have seen something important to the case and not realized it, and I can fill you in on what I've learned so far." I added the last part because one thing I remembered from being a secretary was the value of good gossip. Rachel looked interested.

"Sure, just let me know when and where, Mattie. I'll tell Mr. Quigley you're here." She picked up a phone and before she'd returned it to the base Mr. Quigley had me by the elbow and was ushering me through a doorway. I waved my fingers at Rachel as he whisked me from the reception area.

"Jeff said he'd see you as soon as you came in. Are you ready?" Before I could answer, he led me to one of only two doors in the corridor. We stood at the doorway and faced a person I assumed was the S of Q & S Design. From the look on Mr. Sumner's face, I wouldn't have been surprised if he planned to interview me instead of the other way around.

"I'll leave you two alone," Dave said. "My office is across the hall when you're finished, Miss Draper." Mr. Quigley hurried out and I turned to the man seated behind an expansive desk.

Jeffrey Sumner was in his early to mid sixties and large, not fat, but broad. If he came from behind the desk, he'd no doubt fill the doorway. Unlike Mr. Quigley's hair, he kept his gray strands trimmed and combed with care to camouflage their retreat. His eyes were a light blue, or maybe bluish-green. I couldn't tell from where I stood. I could tell that his suit would have cost two or three months of my salary as a secretary and maybe even more than what I'd made so far as a detective.

His furniture was the same high quality black oak I'd seen in Rachel's area. The massive desk boasted red oak inlay panels on the front and solid brass hardware. That stuff would look silly in Frankie's and my offices, and I doubted it would fit, but it might be fun to find out.

"Thanks for seeing me, Mr. Sumner."

"No problem. Do you think she's dead?"

Chapter 4

Mr. Sumner's question stopped me cold, but I regrouped as I sat in the nearest of two chairs in front of his desk. "No, she's alive. They want the money. I doubt they'd kill her before they were sure they had it. Do you think she's dead?"

"No, I agree with you, Miss Draper. If the reason they took Diana was money, they'll keep her alive until they're paid."

He surprised me again, implying that if she wasn't dead yet, she would be when they had the money. Although I agreed, he didn't appear overly bothered by that conclusion. Of course, you can't know a person's mind after five minutes. Under his chilly personality, he could have been a warm and caring guy—or a kidnapper and a murderer. "Can you think of anyone here at Q & S who might want to do this to Mr. or Mrs. Quigley?"

His hands were folded and rested on the desk giving him a serene look, not that of a kidnapping murderer. "No, I'm at a loss," he said, and the large hands lifted and spread to reflect his bewilderment. "Dave and I have been partners for seven years and I've never seen him do anything unprofessional or unkind to anyone. He's a good man."

My inquiries to that point had uncovered nothing but good people. Having had a little experience with human nature, I doubted that was as true as everyone wanted me to believe. "What did you mean when you said 'if' they took her for money, Mr. Sumner? Would there be another reason to kidnap Mrs. Quigley?"

The corners of his mouth curled in a half-smile, another strange response. "You don't miss much, do you, Miss Draper? That's good to know."

Then I understood. His smile was because I'd surprised him by both remembering what he said and questioning its significance. Although relieved, I bristled that he was so damned amazed to discover I had a brain tucked between my ears. "Thanks. So, you think there could be another reason for Diana Quigley's kidnapping?"

"I suppose if a person were angry with Diana or Dave, they might kidnap her for revenge."

"Do you know anyone who had a motive for revenge?"

"It's a tough world, Miss Draper. If you have a successful life, others want it. If you are doing well, people desiring to do as well or better might mistakenly believe that their success can only happen by your failure. Mrs. Quigley made a fortune as an international model before she retired eight years ago. In fact, she's worth more than Dave is at the moment, and he isn't impoverished. Perhaps someone who isn't doing quite so well wants to change that. Would you care for a cup of coffee?"

I looked up from my notes and muffled the "Oh brother, would I" that I suspect would have sounded pitiful. "Sure Mr. Sumner. Coffee would be nice." He might have needed caffeine as much as I did, because he immediately clicked the intercom, requested two coffees, and clicked it off again.

The remark about Diana's modeling career and the thought of a cup of coffee nearly sidetracked me. I ran my finger down my notes and found the next question I had for Jeffery Sumner. "I heard that this is a tough time financially for Q & S Design. Is there any truth to that?"

This time he didn't smile. "Where did you hear that?" His eyes locked on mine for a moment and then he quickly waved his hand as if to brush aside his brusque response. The sage persona returned. "Miss Draper, in our business the competition will start rumors that they hope have a negative impact. We are as solid as ever and growing. Dave and I may disagree on a few things, but we are good business partners and our company is quite competitive."

The door opened and Rachel carried in two coffees. She handed one to me, and put the other on a coaster by Mr. Sumner's right hand. I didn't see a coaster in front of me and thought I'd have to hold the cup, but the veteran receptionist spotted my problem, grabbed a coaster from a credenza near the door, and smiled as she set it on the desk in front of me.

When she shut the door, I took a much-needed swallow before setting the cup down to return to my notebook. I'd have to shoot myself if I spilled coffee on his desk. "Mr. Quigley told me that your son Joseph is also employed at Q & S."

My statement caught him mid gulp and he lowered his cup to answer. "Yes. He is."

"Is he around? I'd like to ask him a few questions."

"I'll have him join us." Jeffrey Sumner didn't wait for my reply. He picked up the phone and had a brief conversation. When he returned it to the cradle he told me that Joseph would be down in a few minutes.

Did the senior Sumner want me to talk to Junior in his company? I considered that possibility as I enjoyed a cup of java that was far better than I had ever made as a secretary. It amazed me that bosses figured every secretary knew how to make good coffee. It was a misconception I corrected for most of my ex-employers.

While I emptied the cup, I looked around the office and noticed a painting of two horses. "Are they yours?" I pointed with my cup.

"They were. The mare passed on four years ago. One of the finest horses I've had the pleasure to ride."

I recognized the other horse. "That's Vagabond, Mrs. Quigley's horse." I put the cup on the desk and stood for a closer look. "She was riding him when she disappeared."

"So, you've met Vagabond. He's a handsome horse. Yes, Diana bought him after Dolly, his mother, died. Diana's good with him. He was a handful before Dolly's death and that didn't settle him any. Diana was the only one who could really handle him, except for Josh Spencer, of course. He has Diana's touch."

I took one more look at the painting, and noticed that Vagabond got his good looks from his mother. Josh had said that not too many people could work with Vagabond. Someone tied that horse to a tree, or Josh lied about finding him tied. I couldn't think of a single reason for Josh to lie about that, whether he kidnapped her or not.

The office door opened as I returned to my chair and a younger Mr. Sumner entered. Their features were the same, but the gray hair Jeffery now wore was sandy blond and quite a bit thicker on Joseph. The features he shared with his dad were sharp. On Jeffrey's aging face they had softened. I was close enough to see that young Mr. Sumner had light blue eyes.

"You must be Miss Draper. I'm Joseph Sumner. It's nice to meet you. Please call me Joe."

When I stood to shake his hand I saw that Joe had a slighter build than Jeffery. He must have taken after his mother in that area. "Call me Mattie." Jeffrey hadn't offered to shake my hand and Joe did the fingertip grip that some men, and even some women, considered the feminine form of a handshake.

"What can I do for you, Mattie?" The chair next to me was empty, but Joe leaned against the wall next to the horse painting and folded his arms.

"Since you know who I am, then you know why I'm here. Can you think of any reason for a person to kidnap Mrs. Quigley?"

He raised his shoulders slightly. "I'd guess for the ransom. He may not even know Diana Quigley, but he'd know this company is an extremely successful furniture manufacturer. And if he reads the trade publications, he knows we're a top rated business in the state."

I wondered if kidnappers read trade publications but kept my thoughts to myself. "Do you think it could be a Q & S employee?"

Joe shrugged again. Neither Sumner appeared overly alarmed about the abduction. He uncrossed his arms and put his hands behind his back, tapping what I assumed was the gold wedding band I noticed on his finger against the wood paneling. "It's possible I suppose, but I couldn't name one employee that has a grudge against Dave or my dad. They're good men."

"Yes, I've heard that. When did either of you last see Diana Quigley?"

They exchanged glances and Joe answered. "We went to a party at their house the evening before her kidnapping."

That was another new revelation. "Was there a special event, or was it just a social gathering?"

Jeffrey fielded that one. "We were there to celebrate Dave's thirty-fifth birthday. I rather doubt it will be one he'll forget." His response was grim, and the first with any real feeling.

"Did you talk to Diana?"

"We chatted about horses," Jeffrey told me. "I like to keep up on Vagabond, and I'm considering buying a horse or two when I retire. Diana keeps current on equine news and events in the area."

When I turned to Joe, he was staring off into space. It took him a minute to realize I was waiting for a response. "Diana and I aren't close. I drank too much at a party once and flirted with her. She avoids me, but she and my wife, Sandra, are still friends."

I was surprised that he'd share that information with a complete stranger when he could have just said no. "Thank you, gentleman." I stood, as did Mr. Sumner senior. "I've taken enough of your time." At their matching uninformative smiles, I showed myself out.

Before I went to David Quigley's office, I paid a visit to Rachel. "Can you meet me for breakfast tomorrow?"

"Sure. Do you know the pancake place on the edge of town? They have the best coffee. It has to be early, though. I clock in at nine."

My idea of early is five a.m., but I didn't see any reason to mention that. "Sure, I can do that. What do you say we meet at seven-thirty?" I hoped Rachel's prime location at the office, and her likely interest in gossip, would bring me a lead. I needed it. I left to ask Mr. Quigley for a ride to my car.

My knowledge of furniture manufacturing was slim, but I'd worked in a variety of industries and found it strange that no one ever lost his or her temper, or complained about anyone or anything at Q & S. As it turned out, murmurs of discontent did eventually arise, just not from where I'd expected them.

Mr. Quigley didn't say much as we rode to the house. He asked if I learned anything, and after I told him I needed to go over my notes, the rest of the trip was quiet. When we arrived at the estate, he went straight inside without another word. I knew he had Diana on his mind, but I didn't know if it was because he missed her or because he kidnapped her.

My faithful '56 Chevy chariot awaited, but I decided to go through my notes before driving home. As I flipped the pages, I realized that everyone at Q & S had answered my questions, but no one told me anything except that the Quigleys had no enemies, and that Vagabond was a handsome horse but hard to handle.

I pegged Joseph Sumner as a guy who regarded himself as better than us working stiffs. The kid was born into money and probably had his job handed to him by daddy. I doubted that he put a great deal of energy into his work, whatever it was. I wanted to remember to ask Mr. Quigley what Joe did at the company.

When David Quigley left my office that first day, I phoned my friend Lynette who worked in the business section of the Chicago Tribune. She told me that they'd received an anonymous letter saying that Q & S was having financial problems. The paper never printed anonymous tips, but that didn't mean rumors didn't spread in a hurry. The tip said that Mr. Quigley and Mr. Sumner were negotiating a new contract and had invested personal funds into the company to make the sale. If everything went well they'd make a bundle, but if not, they'd be teetering on bankruptcy—in both the business and their personal finances. The writer said he knew that the company wouldn't fill the contract and would go under. I had a hard time imagining that the furniture business was cutthroat, but that appeared to be true.

Jeffery Sumner told me the company was in great shape and that competitors often spread rumors. Since the tip came anonymously, that might have been what happened. Lynette promised to keep me posted if she heard anything more.

I put the key in the ignition, but before turning it saw Mr. Quigley storm from the house and head to the barn. Seconds later I heard him yelling at either Josh or Vagabond. I doubted it was Vagabond and hurried over, arriving in time to nearly crash into Quigley making a fiery exit. As he stomped back to the house I went inside and found Josh staring at the space his boss had just vacated.

"What was that about?" I said.

"Nothing really. He came in and told me that Diana would be back soon and that Vagabond had better be in good shape. Maybe it's his way of coping."

"You're right, Josh. Don't take it personally. He's scared is all."

"Thanks."

"Josh, are you and Diana the only people that handle Vagabond?"

"Far as I know. Mrs. Quigley said that Mr. Sumner worked with him some when Dolly was still alive. After her death, Vagabond became too much of a handful, and until he retires, Mr. Sumner doesn't have the time he needs to develop their relationship."

"Who do you think tied Vagabond to the tree?"

"I hadn't given it much thought. Maybe Mrs. Quigley dismounted when she saw the rope. She could have tied Vagabond, and then while she was checking on the rope someone grabbed her."

"That's a possibility. Thanks, Josh. I'll see you tomorrow."

"I hope you can find her soon, for everyone's sake."

"That's my plan."

Moments later, my Chevy careened down the long driveway and out to the street. I checked my watch and remembered I had a date to meet Frankie at Benny's Tap for a beer. I looked forward to discussing my day with him, but as much as I wanted his feedback, I didn't want him to think I was asking for help. He would anyway.

Chapter 5

I found Frankie bellied up to the bar nursing a cold draft. He said he'd saved me a stool, but a quick glance around the empty place told me he hadn't had to chase anyone away. I thanked him just the same.

Benny's Tap had been in the neighborhood since prohibition ended in the 30s. It was there earlier, but not so you'd notice. His dad, Benny senior, ran it before him. I always wondered if Benny was the junior bar owner's real name or if he just used it to make life easier for him and his patrons, and to save on the price of a new sign.

The windows hadn't seen a soapy sponge since Senior stood behind the bar, and the odor of stale smoke and alcohol added little in the way of ambiance, but Frankie and I liked the joint. It was small and never too crazy, and most of the songs on the jukebox were from the 50s. That suited us fine.

"How's the case going, Mattie?"

"Give me a draft, Benny," I told the bartender and sucked the salt off a pretzel stick before answering Frankie. "Still a mystery. I'm a little concerned that there's only a skeleton crew from the Lake Oak Sheriff's Department and me working on this thing. With the excitement going on around town, other agencies and departments aren't going to volunteer to assist in a suburban kidnapping, no matter how exclusive the suburb might be."

"You're probably right, Mattie. I checked out Grant Park earlier. What a mess! Some guys called Yippies are making headlines. They brought a live pig to run for president. Who'd ever want to call themselves a Yippie? I'm not sure this mess is entirely their fault, though. From what I saw, the Mayor brought in enough uniforms to defend a small nation and not all of them are making the best decisions." Frankie shook his head slowly at whatever troubled him and came back to the kidnapping case. "I wondered if this riot might make the kidnapper try for the money again soon. They know there won't be many cops available to look for Mrs. Quigley."

Frankie stood six four and weighed a little under two hundred pounds. He'd served as a Marine and still wore the bristled shaved head look. I wasn't completely sure what color hair he had, but it was dark, or at least his eyebrows were dark. By looking at him, you wouldn't think he'd be the brightest bulb in the bunch, but he fooled people. He could see things cops and other PIs never saw. That's why his agency kept him busy—he knew his stuff.

People often peg him as macho, maybe even a misogynist, but he's had more faith in my skills as a detective than my female family and friends. Don't get me wrong, he still has a few old-fashioned ideas, but he listens and tries to learn. I see that as a mark of intelligence. "It said in the paper that Yippie stands for Youth International Party," I told him. "They used to be part of the SDS. You remember them, Frankie, Students for a Democratic Society. I didn't read what the Yippies believed politically, but if they want to nominate a pig for president, I'm guessing they disagree with the folks in charge over there. Listen, I appreciate your meeting with me to talk about the case."

"Come on, Mattie. You know better than that. Say the word and I'm here for you. So tell me where things stand."

"Dave and Diana Quigley had a party the night before Diana's abduction. It was Dave's thirty-fifth birthday and the guests were friends, neighbors, and family. I asked Mr. Quigley to make a list of everyone who came and he promised he'd do it as soon as he could. I hope he doesn't forget. The guy's having a hard time concentrating. As far as his business, other than the letter I learned about from Lynette, I haven't uncovered anything negative concerning Q & S Design. The company looks solid. Of course, it's hard to tell what's real by what they let you see. I doubt they would have taken me there if I'd be able to spot a problem."

He took a draw on his beer. "You think the kidnapper is a family member, or associated with the family?"

"My gut says yes. They're not the Rockefeller or Kennedy clan. Even if Diana Quigley does have her own money, she hasn't been in the news since she retired as a model eight years ago. I'd be surprised if a stranger kidnapped her." I picked up another pretzel stick, stirred the foam on my beer, and sucked it off along with the salt, ignoring the strange look Frankie gave me. "What bothers me most is that everyone involved, at both his home and business, likes everyone else. No, that's not true. Diana Quigley doesn't like Joseph Sumner because he flirted with her."

"Need I tell you again how weird you women are? You get mad at a guy if he does flirt and you get mad at a guy if he don't. Go figure."

"Joe Sumner and Diana Quigley are both married, Frankie, and Joe's wife, Sandra, is Diana's friend. That's tacky and in bad taste." He agreed, or at least he acted as if he agreed. He might have wanted to end the conversation.

Neither one of us expected to change our opponent's mind. "Anyway, every person I talked to told me that everyone else was good people. I know the workers at the plant won't risk saying anything. They don't know me from Eve and want to keep their jobs. One guy did mention there had been accidents, but when I asked for more information, he clammed up. I'll have to keep digging into that."

"That's your job, kiddo. Dig, dig, and dig. What say we go dig into a couple of steaks? I'm buying. I collected my fee for the Banyan case."

That perked me up. "That's just how I like my steaks, Frankie, medium rare and paid for."

Frankie felt extravagant after dinner and offered to take me to a movie. We went to the Uptown, a theater that had been around since the mid-1920s. One of the largest in the country with over forty-three hundred seats, and although it's fairly plain these days, it once had marble staircases, brass chandeliers, sconces, paintings, and carvings. Unfortunately change happens to the best of us, and the grand Uptown Theatre was no exception. The popularity of radio and growth of television brought an end to stage shows in the 40s but the theater stayed in business showing movies. In the early part of this decade, they sold the ten thousand-pipe Wurlitzer organ and auctioned off most of the paintings, sculptures, and even pieces of the theater. The once cared for showplace now had sticky floors and worn seats. I hope it survives.

The movie they were showing was about a space station run by a computer named Hal. The people who put him together must have been disappointed in Hal because he took over the station and tried to kill everyone. They called it *2001: A Space Odyssey,* but Frankie decided "a space oddity" was more like it. Since I didn't understand the ending, I couldn't argue. Frankie and I both wondered if that was what life would be like in thirty-some years—computers running everything. It was hard to imagine, but I'd heard that the computers the government used could do complicated mathematical calculations in seconds. Of course, the machines were the size of a two-story bungalow and stopped working if the vacuum tubes overheated or burned out.

I didn't understand the movie, but I liked it and its strange ending. It made me think, and I liked to challenge my brain as often as I could. I'm a big fan of the television show *Star Trek.* I could see traveling around the universe and landing on planets in another galaxy. Frankie prefers *Gunsmoke,* but he loves to shout, "Beam me up, Mattie" into the intercom when he buzzes my apartment from the front door.

I suspected it was going to take a few more challenging movies with spaceships to help me solve the Quigley case. Maybe even a chat with Mr. Spock.

When Frankie dropped me off at my car, I realized I still had energy for the drive home, but when I arrived at the front door of my apartment building, the long day caught up with me and I wished we had an elevator. I don't usually mind living in a third floor walk-up, but some days it felt like there were more stairs going up than when I'd trod down in the morning. This was one of those days. Since I almost fell asleep in the theater, I was sure the climb would do me in, but it didn't. That was mostly because the minute I walked in the door, Sebastian led me to the kitchen. His nonstop whines made it clear he wasn't pleased with my tardiness.

Cats are strange creatures, and my relationship with Sebastian is one of wariness and devotion. I think that's true for him as well. I love the little dickens, but I know better than to trust him farther than I can throw him. If you've ever tried to pick up a cat that didn't want that to happen, you know that isn't far. Sebastian treats me with a kind of loyal detachment. He allows me to pet him on occasion, and once in a while, when he doesn't think I'm listening, he'll purr.

Following a brief game of Sebastian rubbing against the can opener while I tried to open his dinner, we managed to put the food in his favorite dish and the dish on the floor. I've often wondered what my downstairs neighbor thought was going on when the fourteen pound tabby hit the floor from the top of a cabinet or the fridge. Sebastian, much like his human, was not dainty.

I left the feline to his dinner and stood in the parlor fending off a barrage of thoughts about the Quigley case. My mind wouldn't slow down, and although it didn't have much in the way of facts, it spun like a Mixmaster on high speed.

I pulled off my blazer to hang in the closet and studied the stains I'd collected over the past couple of days. I couldn't remember when it had its last cleaning and rather than take a whiff, I tossed it in a pile for the dry cleaners. Sebastian arrived as I kicked off my shoes and did a back flop on the couch. I swear I heard him snicker as I wiggled out of my panty hose.

It's not likely I'd be mistaken for a fashion conscious PI. My shoes all have low heels and are as comfortable as they can be without being slippers, but even so, wearing them all day could leave my feet numb. I wear skirts and jackets, but I gave up dresses when I started my new career. I've been considering buying a pantsuit or two. Everyone's wearing them, and though fashion is a low priority, they'd make my job a little easier. I decided that if I solved the Quigley case, I'd consider a little wardrobe expansion. If I solved the case.

It was time to turn down the speed on the Mixmaster and put the facts in order. Since I didn't know where to start, I threw all the names of the people I'd talked to into a mental hat and picked one. I drew Jeffrey Sumner. He had said that he and David disagreed on things. What were those things? Was Jeffrey telling the truth about the financial condition of the business? Why would he lie? Maybe to protect the company. That wouldn't make him guilty of kidnapping Diana Quigley, though. What if there was a different reason? If the rumors were true, maybe David Quigley was cash poor. If Sumner wanted to take over, he could offer to loan Quigley the hundred grand to pay the kidnapper. It took me less than a minute to see why that theory didn't hold water. If the rumors were true, they'd both made investments. Sumner couldn't come up with a hundred grand either. I threw Jeffrey back into the hat.

Next, we had Joseph Sumner. Could Joe dislike Diana Quigley enough to want to hurt her? Maybe Diana hurt his ego by rejecting his proposition and he wanted revenge. That didn't make sense either. He wouldn't need to kidnap her. There were too many ways to get revenge less complicated than kidnapping. Besides, he'd said she was mad at him, not the other way around. Of course, just because Joe told me that she was mad at him, that didn't mean that he wasn't mad at her. Frankie taught me that Rule Number One of private investigating work was that no matter how truthful an explanation sounded, that didn't make it true.

The sloshing sound in my skull helped me decide it was time to turn in. That and Sebastian staring at me from the coffee table. Once we were both comfortable, Sebastian on his pillow and me on mine, another thought struck, a very depressing thought. What if Jeffrey Sumner had it right on the money and Diana was dead?

*

As I drove to meet Rachel for breakfast the next morning, I wondered why I felt such an instant connection with her. Then it hit me. She reminded me of my youngest sister, Susanne. Rachel and Susanne didn't look much alike, but they both had ready smiles and laid-back attitudes that made people around them feel better just by their presence.

Susanne, the baby of us four kids, was now twenty. She and her hubby had two little ones of their own, twins, a boy and a girl. They say that you're not supposed to have a favorite sibling, so I never told my brother Bill or my sister Mary Anne that Susanne was mine. It might have been because I was seven when she came along. I was amazed at the tiny person who smiled every time she saw me. At first, I thought she had a defect because no one had ever acted that glad to see me. I didn't need to flatter myself. She liked almost everyone she met.

Susanne had the same brown hair and green eyes as the rest of us, but she was never as big. Bill, two years younger than me, grew to be six foot, the same height as my dad. Bill was the unusual one of us kids. He didn't enjoy physical or social activities. He liked his books. He read constantly and believed that the growing popularity of television would destroy our culture. I had noticed more shows these days that made me think he was right.

Mary Anne trailed me by four years, but as we grew, we remained close, in our relationship and physical attributes. At five ten, we both had good builds and neither of us picked up much weight over the years. Susanne took her size from our mom; when she hit five two, she stopped growing.

She was still petite, but those who knew her were careful not to let her small stature fool them. She had our father's temperament, though she never knew him. He died in an accident at the factory where he worked when she was three months old. Susanne kept us smiling during that terrible time after his death. She kept him alive for us, and continued to do that even after she'd married and had her own kids. Mom never said so, but Susanne might have been her favorite, too.

I looked forward to my meeting with Rachel because she had that same easygoing manner as my squirt sister. You knew she could handle things without having to say a word. Susanne was also very observant and aware of what went on around her. I hoped that was something else that she and Rachel shared.

Chapter 6

My eyesight is good, both far away and up close, but even if it were less than 20/20, I wouldn't have had any trouble spotting Rachel when I entered the restaurant. She sat in a booth near the front and wore another attractive suit. This one, an aqua skirt and jacket, was as impressive as the red outfit. With her elbows propped on the table, her hands held a cup of coffee at mouth level and she studied the newspaper below. She must have sensed my approach because she raised her head. "Morning, Rachel. Nice outfit."

"Thanks. Q & S doesn't tell us what to wear, but there is an unspoken understanding. They pay us well enough to afford to dress better, so it isn't a problem. It must be nice to work in comfortable clothes." She tipped her head in my direction.

Instinct told me Rachel wasn't a nasty person and hadn't meant it as an insult, but I hoped my face wasn't red. I didn't plan to tell her I was wearing my best clothes. I felt embarrassed enough about how shabby I looked next to her. That settled it; when I finished the Quigley case, I'd work on my wardrobe. Maybe I could pick up a little fashion advice from Rachel.

The waitress gave me a cup of coffee and left relieved because I'd told her it was all I wanted. She'd been there for a few hours, and judging by the size of the breakfast crowd, she was beat. Waiting tables was one job I'd never tried. After picturing myself working at the local diner—forgetting who ordered what, spilling food and drinks, watching the boss deduct broken cups and dishes from my pay, and dodging the pats and squeezes of neighborhood degenerates—I decided it would be an unpleasant disaster for everyone involved.

I tasted the coffee and put another check on the "Why I like Rachel" list in my head. She had been right. It was great coffee and it cleared my cluttered cranium enough so I could lower the cup and study the star receptionist across the table. I hadn't realized when I saw her at her desk or in the senior Sumner's office that she was a small person, another similarity to Susanne. The beehive hairdo gave her an illusion of height, but she had small bones. She also had a smile that made her as approachable as Susanne. "Rachel, do people from the office or plant go to parties at Dave and Diana Quigley's home?"

She pondered the question as she set her cup on the saucer. I noticed her nail polish matched the lipstick mark on her cup and guessed it was intentional. I might learn a few fashion tips without even asking.

"No. They pay us well, but they don't socialize much with the help. They don't socialize that much period. Are you referring to Dave's birthday party?" She continued at my nod. "A friend of mine in accounting overheard Sumner say that it was as boring as the others he'd been to at their house. The younger Sumner I mean. Joseph. He and his wife, Sandra, like to think of themselves as jet-setters."

I made a quick mental note to learn a little more about 'jet-setters.' "Rachel, Mr. Quigley promised to give me a list of the people who were there that night. He hasn't yet, but when he does, if I have questions, can you help?"

"Sure, but I can give you the list. It's generally the same people who attend their parties."

She ticked the names off on her fingers as she said them. "Wait," I touched her wrist. "Could you write them down?"

I was handing her my notebook and pen when I noticed a number of teeth marks on the barrel of the pen. I dropped it in my purse and while I was digging around for one I hadn't chewed, Rachel produced a pen of her own. "I prefer writing with this," she said.

A good secretary was also a diplomat. Rachel had noticed the reason for my embarrassment and saved me further humiliation by retrieving a writing instrument from her purse without comment. She quickly came up with a list of names, capped the pen, and returned it to her bag. "There. Let me tell you who they are." She turned the list toward me, pointing at the first pair of names.

"Jeanine and Gregory Sandburg are Diana's parents. Renee Sandburg is Diana's sister. She moved in with her parents after her divorce, and the happy little family home is a few miles from Diana and Dave. Mr. and Mrs. Sandburg are the reason workers from the factory and office don't attend their parties. Dave and Diana don't care, but her parents are snobs—old money with old-fashioned ideas about people staying in their place. If you have to talk to them, I suggest you leave that pen in your purse." Her smile said she was kidding, but buying a new pen remained on my list of things to do.

"Renee is two years older than Diana and I've heard that she drinks quite a bit since her marriage ended. She and Diana had been close, but I can't tell you what their relationship is like these days." Her long nail moved to the next pair of names.

"Arthur and Arlene Quigley are Dave's parents and they live south of Chicago, in Kankakee. They're a working class family and rumor has it that Diana's parents were not pleased to have them as in-laws. Diana disappointed them when she went into modeling, and blew them away when she married Dave. I don't know if the Sandburgs have recovered yet or not. Ten years is a long time to hold a grudge, but as I said, they're old school and grudges may be a way of life. Dave built his company from scratch and made his money by working hard. Gregory Sandburg's family was among the original elite in Chicago during the 1800s."

I was stunned at the amount of information Rachel had on the various relatives. And she wasn't finished.

"Robert Quigley is Dave's brother and he's two years younger. He inherited a great deal of money and an extraordinary house when his wife died a few years ago. I didn't know her at all, but I heard a rumor that she suffered from depression. I can't confirm that. You'd have to ask Robert. I also heard that he's gone through quite a bit of her money gambling and making bad investments. You might find it hard to believe that he's Mr. Q's brother. You'll know what I mean when you talk to him. If he's been drinking, he'll probably be fairly obnoxious."

Rachel suspended her monologue to watch the waitress refill our coffee cups. After a quick sip of the fresh brew she continued. "Jeffery—the elder Sumner—lost his wife twelve years ago and never remarried. He's been seen escorting women to dinner and the theater, but there haven't been rumors of a romance or anything. I think he enjoys the occasional company. Joseph and his wife Sandra live in a large estate next to Dave and Diana. Sandra is Diana's friend, but they're very different people. You'll see that, too. Joseph joined the firm last year. The talk around the office is that his dad wouldn't give him his share of the business when he retired unless he did."

"Is that everyone?"

"That's the usual crowd. Occasionally someone different drops in, but not often. Dave and Diana Quigley don't have huge parties and they really don't have many. As I mentioned, as sweet as Diana is, she isn't a social person. Maybe when she left modeling she was tired of parties and things. The other people at the house are Mrs. Allen and Kathleen. If there's a dinner or special event that's more than they can handle, Josh helps."

"How do you know all this?"

The straight-faced receptionist placed the tips of both index fingers on her temples, closed her eyes, and whispered, "I am the channel for Madam Rakia. She sees all and knows all." For a full five seconds I stared, wondering if Madam Rakia was nuts. Then, she opened her eyes, picked up her coffee, and grinned. "I had you for a minute, didn't I?"

"Yep. You did. So Madam Rakia, how do you know all this?"

Rachel sipped her coffee and took another few seconds to enjoy her joke. "I'm the one who does the invitations and the RSVPs come to me. Then I work with Mrs. Allen to make sure she has everything she needs as far as caterers if they're necessary, and I order the booze. Mrs. Allen isn't a drinker and doesn't like to deal with buying the liquor."

"Do you handle things for the Sumners, too?"

"I do. Jeffrey doesn't have parties, but even though Joe hasn't been with the firm that long, I've helped with at least a half dozen for them in the last year. They have a maid, but she can't take care of everything and they hire extra people to serve and tend bar. Joe and Sandra also have a much larger and younger group and they have more contemporary views. Jeffrey isn't invited, and I rather doubt he'd attend even if he were, and if Dave and Diana go, it is usually only for a short time. The Sumner parties are catered, so I take care of that and the invitations, and, of course, Sandra reviews everything."

"Let's leave the party goers for now. Have you heard rumors of any annoyed employees at the plant?"

"No, not recently. Did you talk to Mr. Schmidt?"

"Yah," I said firmly with what I thought was a German accent, but her blank stare told me either my accent or my sense of humor needed work. I went on. "He told me he liked working for the company and he liked his employers. It seems no one at the plant is going to tell me if they're unhappy."

"I'm sure you're right, but I haven't heard of any major problems in a while. I can keep my ears open."

"That might be a good idea. When you say 'in a while' do you mean in the last few years?"

"There was an incident about three years ago. We had a guy working in gluing that, well, came unglued." She covered her mouth to hide a smile but immediately looked regretful. "I'm sorry. It was a very sad case and not at all funny." The incident might not have been funny, but her comment amused me. Rachel went on. "He'd been with the company for five years and met his wife there. One day he came in acting crazy, throwing things around and screaming that Q & S killed his baby. His wife had been on sick leave because of complications with her pregnancy. She ended up losing the child. At the time, no one knew what happened, but later we learned that the chemicals in the glues could have been responsible. The police had to restrain him and take him away. I haven't heard anything since. Give me a minute to think of his name." I waited quietly, knowing she'd remember. "Oh, yes, it was Chet, um, Chet Dowling."

"Do you have his current contact information?" I asked.

"No, I don't have anything current on him, and the old files will be in storage. You might want to ask Dave if he knows."

As I wrote Chet Dowling in my notebook I wondered how I could contact him. I wasn't sure I could convince David Quigley it was important enough to go rummaging through the old files, and even if he did, there was no guarantee Dowling was at the same address. It occurred to me that Frankie might know how to track him down. I hated to keep asking him for favors and knew he'd do it for nothing, but I'm not okay with that. I want to pay him something, even if it's only dinner.

I filed that thought and looked from my notes to Rachel's calm, smiling face. In my mind, one of the benefits of a PI license is that it allows me to stick my nose in other people's business. I noticed the absence of a wedding ring on Rachel's left hand. "You're not married?" The way she reached for the blank spot on her ring finger told me she had been for at least a few years. The deep sigh before she spoke told me things hadn't been that great.

"Five years, until I found out the bum cheated on me, and had been cheating for a while. I'd just turned eighteen when I married him. Of course, my mom told me not to, but you know how that goes. The divorce turned out to be the best thing that could have happened. After I threw him out, I joined Q & S Design and began supporting myself. Then I went back to school. I take one class a semester at the community college, so it's slow going. That's okay, though. I haven't decided what I want to be when I grow up." I enjoyed her grin and her easygoing attitude. "What about you, Mattie? Did there used to be a ring, or do you take it off when you're working?" She pointed at the hand I had wrapped around my coffee cup.

"No ring yet. I've been going out with a great guy. He's another PI, but neither of us is in a hurry for wedding bells." At least I didn't think either one of us was in a hurry.

"Good. Take your time. You have a great career and you'd better make sure he doesn't expect you to give it up after the wedding."

"I doubt that thought would enter Frankie's mind. He's the one who convinced me to give investigating a try."

She gave me a pleased nod, but her approval turned to surprise when she checked her watch. "Oh brother, I have to take off. A couple bucks should cover my share." She pulled a few bills from her wallet and waved them. "Would you mind paying?"

"Put your money away. This is on me. I'll see you at the office soon, Rachel, and thanks for your help." When she walked away, I opened my wallet with a prayer on my lips that I wouldn't be washing dishes. I found a five-dollar bill and a buck's worth of change. We had two coffees and Rachel had a sweet roll. I could cover it, but I needed to come up with another plan to pay Frankie for his help.

Chapter 7

I saw David Quigley's car in the drive when I arrived at the estate, and when Mrs. Allen answered my knock and waved me in, she pointed to the dining room where he sat with his elbows on the table supporting his head in his hands. He almost convinced me he'd been reading the paper, but his eyes were red rimmed with good-sized bags. He didn't look like he wanted company, but that didn't stop me. "Good morning, Mr. Quigley. I take it you're not getting much sleep." The observation, although accurate didn't require a trained detective. He looked awful.

"How the hell can I sleep?" He banged his fist on the open paper, but seconds later covered his eyes with the offending hand. "I'm sorry, Miss Draper, I'm not.... Please call me Dave."

I eased the chair out an inch at a time so if he preferred I left he could tell me. He didn't. "Call me Mattie. Are you up to answering a few questions?" He gave what might have been a nod and I opened my notebook. "Jeffrey Sumner said you and he disagree about certain parts of the business. Are they serious differences?"

"Jeff said that?"

"Yes. He did."

"I suppose he's referring to Joe's ideas for modernizing. Joe wants to develop a line of cheap, particleboard furniture. I'd be embarrassed to have my name on that junk. It would be profitable, but garbage."

"What does Joe Sumner do at the firm? I don't remember him mentioning."

"He's Vice President of Marketing, and before you say it, you're right, that has nothing to do with manufacturing, and it will not give him the experience he needs to take Jeff's place." I would probably not have said anything close to that, but I didn't interrupt and Dave continued. "Joe has big dreams when his dad retires. He's told me more than once that when that happened there would be changes. Of course, there may be, but he won't talk me into selling a line of junk furniture. I'll buy him out before I'll let that happen."

"Would you be able to do that?"

"I might, if I don't spend a large amount of money in the meantime."

"Like $100,000?"

"What are you getting at?" This time, his brusque reply came without an apology.

I didn't want to sail that particular ship any closer to shore, so I changed course. "Nothing, just fishing. Dave, I understand that Diana has quite a bit of her own money from her modeling career. If you and she have been together for ten years and she's been retired for eight, she still modeled while you were married. Did you have special contracts drawn up to keep your money separate?"

"We did. I didn't want her to be at risk if anything happened to my business. She has a fortune in various funds and investments. On top of being beautiful, she's an astute business woman."

"Would you inherit those investments if she died?" Since they didn't have kids, the chances were good that he'd be the sole heir.

"Yes, the police have that information." He ran his hand through his hair. "If either of us dies, everything goes to the other. That's the reason the sheriff has questioned me so often, and why I'm his number one suspect. He was here this morning."

"Gee, I'm sorry I missed him." Dave neither heard nor cared about the sarcasm in my voice.

Since the information concerning their financial arrangements incriminated him, Dave had no reason to lie. He was right that the inheritance gave him a prominent spot on the suspect list. I could see why the sheriff would treat him as such, but hoped he was checking on other possibilities. "Do you remember a problem you had at the plant with an employee named Chet Dowling?"

As hard as it was to imagine Dave looking even grimmer, he did. His face darkened and his shoulders dropped. "That poor family. We didn't know. They'd recently published studies showing that certain toxins affected pregnant women and their babies, but it was too late for Linda Dowling. She went into labor two months early and the baby was born dead."

"Was that when Chet Dowling tore up the plant?"

"Right after the baby died, Chet found information about the chemicals in our epoxy and that they were likely responsible for what happened. I knew money would never make up for their loss, but I gave them $10,000. My lawyers said because no one knew the epoxies were deadly, the Dowlings would never win a lawsuit, even if they were considering one, but I had to do something. I felt responsible for their child's death. I mean, I didn't know what the glue could do, but they lost their baby because of it." Dave dropped his hands to his lap and shook his head. "Diana and I wanted children, but we found out she had a problem and couldn't have them. Our years of trying to have our own family made what happen to the Dowlings that much more painful. Diana felt even worse than me."

David Quigley was either a good man or a good liar because I came close to having to find a tissue. "Where are Chet and his wife now?"

"The last I heard he was working at a factory in the city. They sent a request for a reference and I responded immediately. He was a good worker."

"Do you have a current address for Chet?"

"The letter the company sent had Chet's contact information at the time. I don't know if it's still good, but I'll get it for you."

"That would be helpful. Thanks, Dave. Do you keep pregnant women out of that area of the plant now?"

"We have a new setup with a separate room and state of the art ventilation. You saw the room when we visited the plant. Everyone wears respirators and pregnant women can't enter. It's a little late for Chet and Linda, but at least it won't happen again." I remembered that we stood outside a room where everyone wore facemasks. Dave continued. "The problem is they discover new dangers daily. We do our best to stay on top of the requirements. Hell, we go beyond federal guidelines to make sure everyone is safe, but how can we know for sure?"

"That would be difficult," I said, doubting it was very consoling. "Okay, so you'll get me an address for Chet and I'll see what I can find out. Maybe his wife tried to have another baby and had problems. He might have come after your family for revenge."

I left Dave and went to find Mrs. Allen, but when I reached the hall, the phone rang. It rang a few more times, and when no one answered, I picked it up. "Hello."

"Who is this?" A voice asked the question I had been about to ask.

"Mattie Draper. Who do you want?"

"I wanted David Quigley, but I guess I can talk to the maid. You can call me, Mr. Kidnapper."

The voice was muffled and difficult to hear and the "call me Mr. Kidnapper" remark sped up my heart a beat or two, but at the same time, it gave me hope. Frankie once said that when a criminal thinks he has you fooled, he'll get cocky, and you could bet he'd make a mistake. "What do you want?" I asked.

"Tell your boss I'll give him one more chance to do this right, but I swear, if the cops show up again or he tries anything stupid, Diana Quigley is dead."

"He'll want to talk to her."

"He can talk to her. I'll tell him the details when I call again. It won't be for another few days. I have a busy schedule. No cops. Make sure he understands." The connection ended.

Even with his voice disguised, I could hear the caller's delight at having Dave on the ropes. I decided my visit to Mrs. Allen could wait. I needed to inform Dave about the call. He'd told me when I first arrived that he'd had the sheriff remove the listening device, and I understood, but it was too bad, because having a recording of that call might have helped. On my way back to the dining room, an enthusiastic visitor banged on the front door. Since I was right there, I opened it, feeling more like the maid the caller mistook me for than a private investigator.

"Who are you?" A dark-haired woman asked as she marched into the entryway.

I wasn't likely to forget who I was because people kept asking. "I'm Mattie Draper, a private investigator working for Mr. Quigley. Who are you?"

"I don't see why I should tell you, but I'm Sandra Sumner. Has there been any word on Diana? Where's Dave?" I pointed to the dining room and she left without waiting for an answer to her first question. Dave would fill her in on the details, but I wanted to chat with Mrs. Sumner. I stuck my head in the dining room and saw her sit at the table where she helped herself to a cup of coffee and lit a cigarette.

"I'd like a few words with you before you leave, Mrs. Sumner." Without turning around, she fluttered the hand holding a thin brown cigarette behind her head. I assumed she'd agreed. Rachel told me that Sandra was Diana's friend. She also told me that I'd see how different they were. I didn't know Diana Quigley, but by how well people spoke of her, I would wager she wasn't rude and condescending.

I guessed Sandra to be a good six inches shorter than Diana, and though she dressed well and wore her seriously black hair in a fashionable style, she was not as attractive. Considering Diana's amazing looks, few people were. Sandra and Diana hadn't met on the runway, but I noticed as she brushed by without making eye contact that her clothes were expensive. I'm not one to judge on appearances, but I doubted I'd be adding Sandra Sumner to my list of close friends, and I was fairly sure she wouldn't be adding me to hers.

"How are you Dave?" she asked, her voice bordered on impatient. "Have you heard from the kidnappers?"

"No, I haven't, Sandra. Weren't you going out of town for a few weeks?"

"I called Joe from New York as soon as I arrived on Monday and he told me what happened to Diana. I flew home as soon as I could. Is there anything I can do?"

I wasn't sure if I should say anything about the call in front of his guest, but decided he needed to know. "He called, Dave."

When the words hit, he bolted to his feet. "What did he say?"

"That he'll call in a few days and give you instructions. He said to make sure the cops don't show up this time."

"Why is he waiting? I'll give him whatever he wants right now."

"He's making you sweat. The good news is he said you could talk to her before the payoff. Diana is alive." As hard as his head fell, the guy might have bruised his chest. His pain looked pretty convincing to this detective.

Sandra took his hand and asked what she could do to help. "Please give Mattie whatever information you can," Dave said, and with obvious relief pulled his hand away and headed toward the door. "I'm going to the office for a while. I have to do something. I can't sit here." Sandra sent a sidelong contempt-filled glance my way as he left.

I joined her at the table, noting her lack of delight at my presence. "I met your husband. He said that you and Diana are friends. Did you know about her plans to be at the museum for the arrival of some new paintings?"

She used her cigarette to push ashes around in the glass ashtray while deciding whether to talk to me. "Diana and I belong to a number of organizations. I don't recall discussing her schedule. Maybe Mrs. Allen can tell you, or at least she can show you Diana's calendar."

"That's a good idea. Thank you. I'll be sure to ask her. How has Diana and Dave's relationship been? Has Diana mentioned any problems?"

That question earned me a nasty look and a full body exam by a pair of disdainful dark brown eyes. "That is hardly your business, Miss Draper."

"Two days ago it wouldn't have been my business, Mrs. Sumner, but today I'm trying to find Diana Quigley. Anything remotely connected to her life or the people in it is my business. To your knowledge, have they been having problems?"

She reviewed me again. It amazes me how much of a person's thoughts you can see in a negligible look. She confirmed her assessment of my low-class status. I wasn't offended. I suspected, like her husband, she considered most people beneath her. It doesn't matter much if I like a person, or if they like me. My job is to find answers. Even if it meant finding them with my teeth clenched.

"They've had problems, but I'm sure it's nothing they can't solve. They've been married for ten years and have survived a great many tests, as couples do." She looked at my bare left hand and didn't hide her smirk.

"What tests? Do you mean Diana's finding out that she couldn't have kids? That would be tough on any couple wanting a family."

It surprised me how wide and quickly she opened her eyes with the amount of eyeliner she wore. The fact that I was aware of such an intimate problem shocked her, but it also loosened her jaw. Maybe she didn't want to be the one to tell me Diana couldn't get pregnant and my knowing came as a relief. "Yes, that situation had a major impact on both of them."

"How long have you and Diana been friends?"

"Since Joe and I moved next door six years ago."

"Sandra, do you think Dave could have done something to Diana?"

She hesitated for the briefest instant and then snapped a reply. "He's paying you to find Diana. Isn't that reason enough to think he didn't do it?" It wasn't actually a question. She'd run out of patience and with one more spiteful look told me so. "Do you seriously think you can find Diana, Miss Draper? There aren't a great many female detectives, and I assume there's good reason for that."

"In my opinion, there are fewer female detectives because too many folks still believe that men are smarter than women. I can tell by looking at you, Mrs. Sumner, that you don't believe that."

Oddly enough, the statement made her uncomfortable. She took a final drag on her cigarette, smashed it in the ashtray, and glanced at her watch as she stood. Our discussion was over. "I have an appointment in an hour. Please call if there's anything I can do to help." She hurried out.

What appointment could she have since she returned home from her trip unexpectedly? I suppose it was possible she had an emergency session at the beauty parlor. Something about Mrs. Sandra Sumner didn't ring quite true. It could have been that she was a pretentious snob and nothing about her was true. Whatever the answer to that mystery, I would need to talk to her again. I wasn't sure if she could help, and I wasn't looking forward to another chat, but I wanted to know as much as I could about everyone involved with the Quigley clan.

Chapter 8

After Sandra's hurried exit I went to the kitchen to talk to Mrs. Allen, but she wasn't there. Rather than search for her, I went to Dave and Diana's bedroom to look around. Dave gave me the go ahead even though I told him I didn't know what I hoped to find. Leads can come from places where you least expect them. Or they might not come at all.

The room was large. Actually, it was two rooms. The bigger space had a bed, two nightstands, and two dressers, and opened to a smaller room with two stuffed chairs facing French doors. Through those doors was a postcard-worthy view of the woods.

It was amusing how easily I could tell which side of the room was Dave's and which was Diana's. A tall six-drawer dresser with nothing on top but a pair of gold cuff links, a comb, and a few coins, obviously belonged to Dave, while across the room, a long dresser opened in the center with a rectangular mirror and the surface barely visible beneath jewelry boxes and numerous jars and bottles, was clearly Diana's domain. A matching bench sat in front of the mirror. I took a seat and scanned the impressive setting.

The bedroom furniture wasn't as imposing as what I'd seen at Q & S Design, but it equaled it in beauty. Instead of dark stained wood, it was blond, lighter in both color and design. Soft curves and sweeping lines suggested Diana had selected the furnishings.

I turned to the mirror and surveyed the products cluttering her dresser. I had no clue what purpose some of them served but guessed they were, like the products I did recognize, beauty aids and makeup. Diana would have used many such items during her years as a model. In the painting I saw, she didn't appear to wear a lot of makeup, but Mary Anne once told me that some women go through great pains to look like they aren't wearing makeup. I made the decision long ago to cut out the middleman, a decision based on finances rather than fashion sense.

When no clues jumped out, I went to the closet. The couple shared a large walk-in nearly the size of my bedroom. Dave's suits hung in an orderly row, along with his shirts and a few pairs of casual slacks. His shoes lined the floor beneath them. There was six pair, four black, two brown and a pair of white sneakers. I guessed by what I'd seen in the short time I'd known him that Dave didn't have much more fashion sense than his investigator. Diana no doubt helped him with much of his wardrobe, although he didn't strike me as a person who even Diana could talk into wearing anything outrageous. A rack on the side wall held ties and belts—also black and brown and as neatly arranged as his suits.

On Diana's side hung dresses, blouses, and skirts in a variety of colors and fabrics. There were also one or two pantsuits and an assortment of sweaters and scarves. On the floor were three times as many pairs of shoes than on Dave's side. At the end of the back row, I noticed a pair of expensive, handmade Italian leather riding boots. At least that's what I saw printed inside. It didn't say "expensive," just "handmade in Italy." I wondered if she had more than one pair of boots or if she didn't always wear them to ride.

I scanned the rest of her wardrobe and checked the top shelf where I found hats. They were almost all Diana's, but a shiny top hat on the end undoubtedly belonged to Dave. I grinned picturing it on Frankie's shaved head.

Nothing else inspired my detecting brain cells so I grabbed the boots and went downstairs. "Mrs. Allen," I called as I walked into the kitchen and found the previously missing housekeeper. "Does Diana have more than one pair of riding boots?"

She touched the pair I held and looked bewildered by both their presence and the question. "No. I am sure that is her only pair. She must have decided to wear shoes." After a brief pause, she added, "That's odd."

"I need to talk to Josh. Is he here?"

"I just left him in the back garden."

I went out through the kitchen door and found Josh on his knees in front of one of the flowerbeds. "Josh, did you notice what Diana had on her feet when she mounted Vagabond?"

He stood and pulled off his heavy canvas gloves. "What she had on her feet? No, I didn't notice. I assumed she wore her boots. She always did." He pointed at the pair in my hand. "Are those hers?"

"Yes. I found them in her closet. She must have worn shoes to ride. She's never done that?"

"I don't think so." He answered while still searching his brain. Then he shook his head. "I can't be sure, but I thought she always wore those. I told her once I thought they were nice boots and she said the only thing she minded was how difficult it was to put them on and take them off, especially if she was in a hurry. I suppose because she had that appointment at the art museum she might have decided to ride without them."

The boots were long and had no zipper to make it easier to slip them on. I could see why she'd complain about that.

"But you don't ever remember seeing her ride in regular shoes?"

"Mattie, if you weren't holding them in front of me, I would've said she *always* wore her boots, but I honestly can't remember what she had on Monday. What does it mean?"

"I'm not sure." That was the truth, but I did know that if Diana acted differently that morning, she might have had plans that she didn't want Josh or anyone else to know. I hoped those plans didn't include setting up a fake kidnapping.

*

The phone was ringing when I walked into my apartment. I decided to sit on the couch to answer so I could take off my shoes as I reported my activities to the caller who I was guessing was Frankie. Sebastian had other ideas. He seemed to think his dinner was more important than a call, no matter who it was. I picked up the phone, but the cat's complaints were so loud that Frankie heard him on the other end and told me I'd better feed my poor, starving, but chubby kitty.

I was anxious to tell Frankie about my day and stretched the phone cord as far as it would go to reach the kitchen. After a brief round of the can opener game, complicated by having one shoulder raised to hold the phone against my ear, I accomplished my goal. His majesty dined and I returned to the parlor to fill Frankie in on everything I'd learned. I also asked him if he could find out where Chet Dowling lived because I wasn't sure if Dave would remember to check his files. Frankie had a job, but he promised to see what he could find as soon as he finished.

When we ended the call, I discovered that I was too antsy to sit and considered going back to the Quigley estate.

That was until I heard a loud roar. It wasn't Sebastian. It was my stomach. Before I did anything, I had to eat.

The large feline stood at my side in front of the wasteland that is my refrigerator. I'd been ignoring the appliance even more than usual of late. Sebastian noticed that too and left me staring at the empty shelves and glaring light bulb. I pulled a drawer open and found a partial loaf of bread and a few surviving slices of bologna. The scant discovery would have to serve as dinner.

While the bologna sizzled and crackled in a frying pan, I made a pot of coffee and smeared mustard on two slices of bread. I never quite understood how anything as cheap and of as questionable nutritional value as bologna could smell so good when you fry it. Sebastian returned to sniff a piece of bologna on my finger. He too found the fragrance enticing, but eating it was a different matter. He departed, this time with his nose in the air.

After my dad died and mom went to work, we kids found many creative recipes, but bologna, fried or not, was the mainstay. With my tummy appeased by the nostalgic treat, and caffeine coursing through my veins, I decided to return to the scene of the crime. I tried not to think about the amount of gas I'd used to drive home for a bologna sandwich. When I found a satisfied Sebastian sleeping on the sofa and said goodbye, I knew there had been a much better reason for the trip.

My car, which I'd parallel parked in front of the apartment building, now sat between two vehicles that hadn't been there earlier. The car in front was two inches from my bumper, and the one in back, less than an inch. It took several minutes of nudging the Chevy forward and back, cutting the wheels, and stomping on a clutch that sometimes took both feet to engage, to pull from the space.

That wasn't uncommon in my neighborhood, and except for briefly wondering if I should buy one of those little German cars they called a "Beetle," I didn't think about our crowded streets again until I turned into the Quigley driveway, where there was enough parking for my entire neighborhood, including space for a CTA bus stop. I wondered if Frankie had ever considered living in the suburbs.

Thirty miles is not a great distance relative to the size of our blue-green planet, but entering the Quigley drive reminded me that even on the same planet, many of us lived in different worlds. At dusk, which it was by the time I returned, small lights were on around the gardens and on the front of the house, giving the place an even more majestic feel.

I found an unobtrusive place to park and, as I climbed from the car, saw Mrs. Allen walking toward her three-year-old Ford Fairlane. "Are you finally going home, Mrs. Allen?" She was either kind or tired enough to not comment on my brilliant deductive reasoning.

"Yes, Miss Draper. I listened for the phone like you asked, but the only one to call is Mrs. Sumner from next door. She has called quite a few times because of her concern for Mrs. Quigley."

"Mrs. Allen, have you noticed problems between Mr. and Mrs. Quigley?" She looked everywhere but at me and I could see she didn't want to say anything. "You can tell me. I promise I won't breathe a word to anyone."

"Well, if you promise." Frankie would have been all over the woman for being so trusting. "Mrs. Quigley has wanted the mister to spend more time with her. He works many hours and she feels alone in this big house." She waved at the structure. "She tries to keep busy with her board meetings and things, but she is lonely and needs time with her husband."

I remembered another question for Mrs. Allen and clapped my hands in excitement, an action that nearly caused her to jump out of her shoes. When she threw her hand over her heart, I hoped it was strong. "I'm sorry, Mrs. Allen. I thought of something I wanted to ask. Was the art museum the only appointment Mrs. Quigley had planned for Monday?"

"Yes, just the art museum," said Mrs. Allen, calming down a bit. "I can check her calendar to see if there was something she did not mention if you like."

"Not tonight. You go home and rest. I know you've been on your feet all day. I'll be back in the morning and we can look for it then. You've been putting in long days since this happened."

"I want to help."

"I know you do. You're a good person." Was it possible that excessive exposure to the "good person" phrase had created a glitch in my brain forcing me to repeat it? I hoped it was temporary and made a point to limit my use. "Go home. I'll see you in the morning."

I watched her climb into the Fairlane, which started immediately, and gave her a wave. My twelve-year-old Chevy, even with its temperamental clutch, was another reliable car. What it lacked in glamour and charm, it made up for in dependability. When Mrs. Allen's taillights were out of sight, I went back to said Chevy and grabbed my large flashlight from the glove box. I wanted to take another look at the woods where the abduction took place.

Dave mentioned that the sheriff thought Vagabond broke into a trot before Diana hit the rope. I aimed my flashlight at the trail. There were hoof prints all over, and although some were deeper indicating the horse picked up speed, how did he know when that happened? It hadn't rained in a week, and Diana rode every day. I couldn't tell where she hit the ground and since I had no idea where the rope was, I couldn't guess. Then it hit me—since Josh found the rope, he could show me. I made a mental note to bring the gardener out the following day.

It troubled me that Vagabond continued to the clearing. If he and Diana were the pals Josh said they were, I would have guessed he'd have stopped when she fell. He didn't. I was sure he went to the clearing because of the fresh manure I'd found there.

Frankie was impressed when I told him how I determined where Vagabond had gone by inspecting the droppings. I explained to the intrigued PI that after a few days, most dung looks pretty much the same, but the ones I found in the clearing were intact. They shouldn't have been, but because investigators filled the area shortly after Diana disappeared, birds couldn't get near them to dig out insects and grubs. They remained relatively undisturbed. Okay, that might not convince a jury, but it made sense to Frankie and me.

As brilliant as that bit of detective work was, searching the woods at night with a flashlight was not a smart move. I couldn't see much of anything. Unfortunately, I was too wound up to go home, and I didn't want to face David Quigley without a plan. I continued moving the beam across the clearing and noticed an area of torn up grass that might have been created by the hooves of an excited horse. Had Vagabond struggled with the kidnapper in the clearing? But why would someone wrestle with a horse only to tie him to a tree? Why bother with Vagabond at all once he had Diana?

Maybe Diana was still on the horse's back when they got to the clearing and the kidnapper was waiting for her there. That didn't make sense either. They rode every morning, but Josh said the time and length depended on what meetings and things she had that day. Her kidnapper would have had to have known her plans or had access to her schedule. The two people with the greatest opportunity to abduct her were Josh Spencer and David Quigley, assuming it was a man. Since Diana was almost six feet tall, it probably was a man, or a woman with more than average strength. I liked to think I fit in that category, but I hadn't kidnapped Diana Quigley.

What would Josh gain by kidnapping Mrs. Quigley? A ransom of $100,000 made for a good motive. If she died, Dave would collect her life insurance—another $100,000 prize and her fortune of almost $500,000. Mrs. Diana Quigley was worth quite a bit of money dead.

My brain felt thicker than the nearby woods and flashes of wisdom had no more luck penetrating my skull than my flashlight beam had piercing the surroundings. I turned, and as I started back to the house, heard a twig snap. I stayed stock still listening but heard no other sounds and decided that it must have been the local critter population running out of patience with my intrusion. "Okay, kids. I'll leave you alone."

As I stepped from the clearing back into the woods the flashlight beam caught something on the ground that shimmered briefly. It didn't register at first and I walked passed it. When my brain understood, I stopped and took a slow backward step, pointing the light where I thought it had been to try and catch it. Nothing sparkled. I took another half step back and heard a noise. "Josh, is that you?"

When you grow up in a city like Chicago you develop a little street sense. You almost have to. It is not that you are always in danger, but it doesn't hurt to be ready for the unexpected. It becomes instinctive, and I count on that instinct to kick in when there really is danger. I do carry a gun under my jacket, and if I feel the situation warrants it, I'll pull it from the holster, but I felt fairly safe in the woods of a northern suburb and maybe a little over confident. I patted the holster for comfort and returned my focus to finding the shiny object.

Inching forward, I moved the light across small sections of grass and bent to slant the beam and catch as much surface as possible. To my relief, something sparkled and I held the light steady as I leaned down to retrieve what turned out to be a beautiful silver earring. It was the kind you clipped on— the same as mine—but worth a whole lot more than the ones adorning my lobes. The handcrafted silver had a crescent moon and a star design. It was loaded with what I guessed were real diamonds. Diana might have struggled with her kidnapper as he dragged her away, because if the rope swept her off the horse, the earring was a good distance from where she fell.

I held the earring in my palm and examined it closely. It was surprising light considering all the gems it contained. Without thinking, I tossed the costly piece of jewelry a few inches in the air and nearly dropped it as it fell back into my hand. Yes, that was a dumb thing to do in the dark. One more look at the earring and I slipped it in my pocket ready to call it a night.

As I stepped into the woods, I felt those tiny soft hairs on the back of my neck stand up and reached for my weapon. Someone was behind me, but before I could grip the gun's handle, what I could only assume was a branch from one of the largest trees in the Lake Oak area landed on the back of my head.

Chapter 9

At first I thought someone was beating a drum, one large enough to vibrate my bones. My second thought was that I was lying face down on my bed on top of various objects that Sebastian had hidden under the sheet and someone was running a jackhammer on the street below. I moved my hand to investigate further and instead of my comfy mattress or Sebastian, I felt stiff grass and hard ground. I wasn't in my bed. "Oh, geez. What the hell happened?"

"Mattie. What happened?" Someone knelt at my side and repeated the question I'd heard in my head. Or maybe I'd said it out loud. I wasn't sure.

"It's me, Josh." He aimed a flashlight at his face and his fuzzy and rather eerie looking features came into focus. "Are you all right? What happened?" His concern sounded real.

"I was just asking myself the same thing. If you don't see a tree lying nearby, someone slugged me. Help me stand, will you, Josh? And keep a grip until we're sure I'm steady. That might take a minute if things are spinning as much up there as they are down here."

"Maybe you should keep still and I'll go call for an ambulance."

"Help me up. If I fall, we'll consider our options." I turned on my back and sat up. My brain wasn't working well enough to figure out how to climb to my knees in a lady like manner, so I maneuvered various body parts with as much dignity as I could muster and gave it a shot. If I planned to stay in the investigating business, I needed to either buy pants or avoid ending up on the ground.

Josh held his hand out and helped me to my feet. "I'm okay," I said.

That was true except for the pain in my head and the hole in my new pantyhose. I didn't know which one ticked me off more. I touched a tender spot on the back of my head and immediately removed my fingers from the sensitive lump. I checked for my gun. It was there. Then I remembered the earring and reached in my pocket. It was empty. "Damn it. Josh, where's my flashlight?" He picked it up from where it had fallen a few feet away. The beam was a little weaker, but still on. I grabbed it from his fingers, shining it around the area where I fell. I wasn't surprised not to find it. Whoever smacked me, took the earring. After a short bout of self-reproach, I decided that when I could think again, I'd make a sketch. The expensive earring would be easy enough to remember.

Josh's presence prompted me to brush the dirt and leaves from my clothes and person. Unfortunately, I was still a bit shaky and didn't want to end up on the ground. I gave up the cleaning attempt. Everything would fall off soon enough. A quick look at my jacket told me I couldn't put off a trip to the dry cleaners much longer. "What were you doing out here, Josh?"

"I was in the barn cleaning tack earlier and saw you go into the woods, but never saw you come back. I figured I could have missed you but your car was still in the drive and when I checked with Mr. Quigley, he said he's been back for a half an hour and hadn't seen you. I decided to come looking."

Another good guy or another liar? The pounding in my head prevented answers, so I put my brain in neutral. "Why don't you walk me to my car?" As he held my elbow and led the way, I wondered if he was a good dancer. He sure looked good on my arm—black hair with deep waves and blue eyes that I'd noticed earlier changed shades at a whim. "What did you do before you came to work here, Josh?"

"Different stuff in different places. These days I couldn't work inside at a desk all day. Outside work is easier on a person. That is, of course, unless someone outside wants to knock a person on the head."

I appreciated his attempt at humor and told him I knew what he meant. I was about to ask another question, but as we approached the driveway, we heard Dave yelling.

"I don't believe it! I don't believe it!" He kicked an obviously flat tire on his car, and I could see from where we were that at least two others were flat.

"What's going on?" I yelled.

"There's a fire at the plant and my tires are flat." He circled the car until he kicked every deflated tire at least once.

"Come on, I'll take you," I said.

"Are you sure you're okay, Mattie?" Josh asked.

I'd forgotten he was there and turned to answer. "I'm fine. It's my ego that's bruised the most. Thanks. You'd better call a repair truck to tow Dave's car in and have them replace the tires.

"Sure," Josh said, and Dave, who'd overheard, handed him the keys.

"Make sure you have them throw the old tires in the trunk so we can look at them," I said. I wasn't sure if we could tell much from slashed tires, but I'd be sure to ask Frankie.

We climbed into my car and were at the plant in five minutes. I wanted to ask Dave if he had any idea who might have slashed the tires, but he looked bad. I figured we could solve that one later. As we neared the plant entrance I smelled smoke, and although we couldn't see anything burning in the front of the large manufacturing structure, as we came around the building, we saw firemen dousing flames in a relatively small section at the back. They appeared to have it under control. As I stood watching the flames surrender to the stream of water, I felt sure there was a connection between the fire and the kidnapping. Someone wanted to destroy David Quigley.

"Is there anyone in the building, Dave?" I asked.

"There shouldn't be. We don't run a night shift."

Dave may have been going to say more, but another voice interrupted. "Dave, what happened?" Joseph Sumner grabbed Dave's arm. "What's going on?"

Without answering, Dave turned from Joe back to the smoldering building. I could see the stress pushing him closer to the edge. His eyes had taken on a haunted look. Mr. Quigley was running out of steam. "Dave, let me take you home." I put my hand on his arm. "There's nothing you can do here and the police and arson squad won't be able to tell you anything until tomorrow." He walked to my car without saying a word. I turned to Joe. "What are you doing here?"

"I came back to pick up my golf clubs. I'd left them in my office. When I was leaving I heard a commotion and saw the fire truck so I came around back."

"Did you call it in?"

"No, I just got here."

I couldn't remember a car driving in after us, but once I saw the blaze, I wasn't paying attention to much else. "See what you can find out, Joe. They'll talk to you before they will me. And you'd better call your dad and make sure he knows what's going on." I hoped Dave remembered to get Dowling's address, because I needed to talk to him. Those fire hoses pointed right at the gluing room.

Mr. Quigley stayed quiet as I drove to the estate. I hated to ask him if he got the information on Chet Dowling, but I had to in case Frankie couldn't manage it. He didn't say anything when I asked, just reached into his pocket and laid a piece of paper on the seat between us. Talk about a lousy night.

I hurried home in a foul mood of my own, feeling a slight throb in my head and a sense of frustration. As soon as I locked the apartment door, Sebastian wound his body in circles around my feet and the phone rang. It was Frankie. I found comfort in knowing I could count on the males in my life to show up when I needed them. "Hey, Mattie, I heard there was a fire at Q & S. Are you all right?"

"I'm all right, Frankie, but this thing is a mess." I didn't ask if he had a minute to talk before dumping my frustrating evening into his attentive ear. At least I thought he was attentive. I stopped to make sure he was on the line. "Are you there?"

"I am. You might want to find out how much insurance they have on the factory. Did the fire department say who called it in?"

I should have known he'd listen. "No, I'll check that out first thing tomorrow. Thanks, Frankie. What's this case you're working on?"

"My client thinks one of his managers has a couple of thieves in the plant. I'm keeping an eye on things. Did Dave have an address on that Chet Dowling guy? I didn't have a chance to look into it."

"He did, so you can take that off your list of things to do. I'll visit the Dowlings in the morning."

"Who hit you?"

"I have no idea, but Josh found me. He said he saw me walk past the barn on my way to the woods, and when I didn't come back, he thought he'd better check. That could be true, I suppose."

"You don't think so?"

"I don't know what to think. My brain is on overload. I'll find out what I can about the fire and pay Chet Dowling a visit. I suppose the fire could be unrelated to the kidnapping."

"Maybe, the fire is a coincidence but what about the slashed tires? Do you think that's unrelated?"

"I don't know!" I snapped at him and regretted it at once. After all the help he'd given me, Frankie didn't need to be on the receiving end of my foul mood. "I'm sorry. The lump is making me a little crabby. Do you want to have dinner tomorrow? I'll make us a surprise." It would be a surprise for both of us because I had no idea what I'd make. Before I could ask Frankie if he liked fried bologna sandwiches, he made a better suggestion.

"Why don't we go out, Mattie, my treat. You need to stay focused on this case until you bring Mrs. Quigley home, and I need to eat."

"You're a good kid."

"I know."

*

Something pushed the air out of my lungs, and even in my unconscious state I recognized Sebastian's announcement that it was time for breakfast. My eyes opened to two delightful golden green orbs staring at me from atop my chest. I gave Sebastian a scratch behind the ear before a pain in the back of my head reminded me of the previous evening's events.

Because of that pain and to Sebastian's chagrin, I took the can opener and food into the bathroom and closed the door to avoid the game. After setting down the great cat's food, I put on a pot of coffee and returned to the bathroom to turn myself into something that resembled a private investigator. The coffee had just finished perking when I came back to the kitchen. I used the first sip to take an aspirin, and as a precaution, dropped the bottle in my purse. While Sebastian bathed, I dressed, gathered my notes, and as I headed out the door, kissed the top of his furry little head. He didn't wait for the door to close to clean the spot I kissed. You gotta love cats.

My first stop was to see if Chet Dowling was living at the address Dave gave me. It was on Chicago's Northwest Side in a well-cared for, blue-collar neighborhood with plenty of old brownstones and a few wood frame houses. The house I found at the supplied address was a two-story frame building with a tidy yard and a variety of flowers and bushes out front. I climbed the stairs to the porch noticing that they kept the building in good repair. The paneled exterior looked recently painted.

"Can I help you?"

"Are you Mrs. Dowling?" I asked the slender brunette who opened the door. She confirmed my question while shifting the baby she supported on her hip. I hoped the bundle belonged to them and that they'd had no more problems. Before I could say anything else, a toddler showed up and tugged on the hem of Mrs. Dowling's dress. "Are these your children?" I asked. She responded with a smile.

"This is Amy." She lifted the tiny human and pointed with her elbow at the slightly larger male version hiding behind her dress. "And this is Davie."

"Davie? Why did you name him Davie?"

My inquiry surprised her and she lowered her eyebrows to give me a second look. "Who did you say you were?"

"Oh, I'm sorry. My name is Mattie Draper. I'm a private investigator trying to find Mrs. Quigley. Have you heard she's been kidnapped?"

Unlike a few members of the Lake Oak community, Mrs. Dowling made no attempt to suppress her emotions. Her expression changed rapidly to one of concern. "Yes, we heard. Please come in. I'm Linda, Chet's wife. He's sleeping. He works second shift, but he should be up soon." She pushed the door back and nudged Davie out of the way. I found a chair and stood in front of it while the trio made their way across the room as a unit. Davie clung to Mrs. Dowling's leg, and apparently accustomed to walking that way, she maneuvered them to the couch with the skill of a city bus driver at rush hour. "Has there been any word?" she asked when they'd settled.

I told her there hadn't and sat in a comfortable stuffed armchair across from the couch. "One of the reasons I'm here is because last night someone started a fire at the Q & S plant."

She caught on to the purpose of my visit. "You think we're involved?"

"I don't have enough information to think anything, but it would help a great deal if Chet could tell me where he was around ten o'clock last night." I was fairly sure that they wouldn't have hired a babysitter to attempt arson as a couple.

She released a breath and relaxed into the couch, giving Amy a gentle squeeze and patting the top of Davie's head. She was about to speak, but instead smiled at a voice from the doorway of a nearby room. "I was at work. At least twenty people can vouch for me." I turned to the voice. "I'm Chet Dowling," he said. "Who are you?"

"Chet, this is Mattie Draper, a detective looking for Mrs. Quigley."

He joined his family on the couch. They were a good-looking group, but I saw anger in his eyes. Although as I studied him, I realized I'd have the same look if a stranger disturbed my sleep to accuse me of starting a fire after I worked all night. I smiled at the kids and saw that Davie bore a strong resemblance to Chet. "They both look healthy and happy. Were there any complications after your first loss?"

"No." Mrs. Dowling answered. "We had no problems, thank heavens. Now I see why you asked about Davie's name. His name is David Chester, and we did name him after David Quigley." Mrs. Dowling could have been a detective the way she figured things out so quickly. I'd have to remember her skills if I ever needed an assistant and she needed a break from the kids. I figured I could call in a few years. "Once we had time with our grief we realized Mr. Quigley wasn't to blame. He didn't know what the toxins could do. Even now not many people are aware of the dangers. After all the problems we caused him, he still helped us and wrote a good work reference for Chet. Did he tell you about the money?" I nodded and Linda continued. "It gave us time to recover our senses and our lives. We bought this house and rent out the upstairs, which helped us make it until Chet went back to work."

"Did David Quigley ever mention to you why he gave you the help?" The adult Dowlings shook their heads in unison and little Davie joined them. "He and Diana can't have children, children that they both desperately want. Your loss devastated them."

Mr. and Mrs. Dowling's heads dropped. This time Davie put his hand on the side of his mom's face and patted it softly. I discreetly wiped the corners of my eyes as Linda Dowling spoke. "We didn't know, and now this horrible kidnapping. Miss Draper, is there anything we can do?"

I retrieved my purse, which I had dropped onto a coffee table covered with toys and baby bottles. "Chet, I don't want to go to your company asking questions. People have a bad habit of assuming the worst. Could you ask your co-workers to sign a paper, or call me to vouch for your being at work last night at ten?"

He looked at me for a few seconds and then stood. "Come to the factory with me at three and you can ask them yourself. I'd appreciate it if you didn't mention the trouble I caused for Mr. Quigley. I have no record, but it would sound bad."

Frankie wouldn't have agreed with my decision, but that was all I needed to hear. If nothing else turned up, I'd check deeper into Chet Dowling, but I had to go with my gut on this one. My gut told me the Dowling family members were too happy with their lives to involve themselves in a crime as nasty as kidnapping, particularly a kidnapping involving David and Diana Quigley.

I stood and dug in my purse. "Here's my card. Call if you remember anything from your days at Q & S that might help. When we have Mrs. Quigley home safe, I know that she and Mr. Quigley would love to meet Davie and Amy."

Chet took my card and left the room for a few seconds, returning with a piece of paper on which he'd written two numbers. One said home and one said work. "Here's our phone number and the number at the plant. They can come and get me if you need to call. If there's anything we can do, please ask."

As glad as I was to find the Dowlings doing well, I was back to square one. I needed a new suspect. Frankie had asked what I found on Josh Spencer. I didn't tell him I hadn't investigated Josh because he seemed like a good guy. The time had come for me to find out if I was right.

Chapter 10

I couldn't resist cootchie-cootchie-cooing little Amy Dowling before I left. Her joyful smile made me smile, which made Chet and Linda smile, which made Davie join in with another cootchie-coo to his sister's chin. Leaving the cheerful Dowling tribe made my next stop even harder. Kathleen showed me to the dining room and Mr. Quigley. He didn't look good. My concern about his health grew. "Morning. Have you had breakfast?"

He drew his head up and stared. At another time the look would have put me on the defensive, but right then, I could see he didn't need or want my comment. He was paying me to find his wife, and so far, I hadn't found squat. He returned his gaze to the paper and I swallowed a sigh.

"The fire chief called," Dave said via the newspaper. "It was arson. They'll investigate further and call me if they find anything that will help. He wasn't hopeful. In the meantime, the plant will have to shut down today and won't be in full production for at least another two days. What else can go wrong?"

I could see that Mr. Quigley didn't care if the plant closed. He cared about his wife's return. I wondered if the news about Chet Dowling would cheer him up a bit. "I just came from meeting with Chet and Linda Dowling. They still live at the address you gave me. He couldn't have started the fire. He works second shift and his coworkers will testify that he was there until eleven." That was the truth. I just hadn't confirmed it yet. "Seeing him and his family I'm convinced that there's no way he's involved in Diana's kidnapping." Dave didn't comment, but when he raised his eyes I saw that the news came as a relief. "There's something else you should know. The Dowlings have had two healthy children since they lost their first. They named the oldest boy Davie, after you. They're grateful for everything you did and didn't do. I doubt he'd name his child after you and then do a thing as horrible as kidnapping Diana."

His eyes filled and he dropped his head to the table. I knew men didn't like people to see them cry so I went to find Mrs. Allen. I wondered, as I squeezed Dave's shoulder and left, if he could be that good of an actor. I found it hard to believe, but there was always a chance I was wrong.

Mrs. Allen was in the kitchen. "Good morning," I said.

She pulled her hands from the sink and dried them on her apron. "Oh, Miss Draper. Do you have news?"

"I'm afraid not. Were you able to discover if Mrs. Quigley had any other meetings?"

She reached in a pocket and handed me a piece of paper. "She had no other meetings on her calendar for Monday, but I thought you might want this. It is a list of the women on the board of the art museum and their address and phone information." She pointed at the note. "They are all important ladies in Lake Oak, but I know they would want to help Miss Diana."

After scanning the list, I put it in my purse. "Thanks, Mrs. Allen. Let's hope they can do just that. You've worked here the Quigleys since their marriage. They move here right after that, right?"

"Yes. I worked with the kitchen staff for Mrs. Quigley's mother and father until Miss Diana stole me away." She covered her smile. "I enjoy working for Miss Diana much more. She's...."

I raised my hand like a traffic cop and finished the now familiar phrase, "…a good person. Yes, I know. Are you familiar with Diana's jewelry?"

"Most of it. I keep the pieces cleaned and organized for her. She throws everything in the jewelry box, and once or twice a month I untangle the necklaces and earrings. She has expensive pieces in the safe. I don't see those often." She frowned and crossed her arms. "Why?"

"I found an earring in the woods last night. A clip-on, silver with a moon and a star."

"It sounds familiar. Can I see it?"

I stared at the upturned palm of her extended hand. "I'd love to show it to you, Mrs. Allen, but someone hit me over the head and took it from my pocket."

"Someone hit you over the head!" She yelled and took a step back, although I wasn't sure why. "When did this happen?"

"Last night, after you left. I went to the woods to look around. Josh found me."

"Then it is a good thing he was there. Maybe you shouldn't go walking in the woods at night with these crazy things going on." The way she stood with her arms crossed shaking her head reminded me of my grandmother. The same curly white hair capped her wrinkled face, and although a smile from Gram felt like a reward, a frown could make me feel three inches tall. Mrs. Allen's frown packed a similar punch.

"You might be right, Mrs. Allen. I couldn't take too much more head thumping. Would you happen to know where Josh came from?"

"Do you mean was he born in this country or somewhere else? He was born here."

"No, I meant where did he work before Mr. and Mrs. Quigley employed him?"

"Oh, I can't remember if I ever heard where he worked. One day Mrs. Quigley brought him in and introduced him as the new gardener and stable hand. Mr. Peterson, the old gardener, had health problems and needed to quit. Maybe Mrs. Quigley ran an advertisement and he answered, although she usually told me about things like that."

"I'd better ask him." I left her to her dishes and went to the garden. I didn't want to learn that Josh kidnapped Diana, and as I scanned the picturesque yard, I continued to have my doubts. I understood why Josh had said outside work was good for a person. The smells and colors in his garden were inspirational. "Hey, Josh!"

"How are you feeling this morning, Mattie?"

"Like my head and a rock went ten rounds and the rock won. Do you have a minute?"

He glanced at the garden as if asking permission. It must have said okay. "Sure, what do you need?"

"Who hired you?"

"Mrs. Quigley."

"Did you apply for the job?"

His normally passive expression tensed into a frown. "Am I a suspect?"

He didn't want to be a suspect. I didn't want him to be a suspect. Unfortunately, that wasn't up to either Josh or me. "Josh, until Mrs. Quigley is found, everyone is a suspect, including Mr. Quigley."

Josh remained still for a few seconds and then lifted his right arm and dragged the short sleeve of his tee shirt, taut against his muscular shoulder, across his forehead. That must have given him enough time to consider what I'd said. He relaxed. "That makes sense. I'm sorry I overreacted."

I almost smiled since I would hardly call a frown overreacting. "Not a problem, Josh. Tell me about it."

"I was sitting outside the art museum one day with a friend and heard Mrs. Quigley tell some of the other ladies that she needed a new gardener and stable hand. I didn't have a job at the time." He turned from me to the garden and I wondered if it embarrassed him that he'd been unemployed. "I knew I shouldn't approach her with the other ladies around, so I waited until she walked to her car. I might have scared her at first because, well, because I was dressed the way I am now."

He pointed at his jeans and tee shirt. He wouldn't have scared me looking like that, but I could see where a wealthy lady by herself might be a bit nervous. "She told me to come and have a look at the gardens. I showed up a couple hours later and she explained what she wanted done and asked if I could do it. When I told her I could, she took me to the barn to meet Vagabond. I have a way with horses. I always have. Once she saw I'd get along with Vagabond, she hired me. Mattie, I'd never do anything to hurt Mr. or Mrs. Quigley."

I believed him, but Frankie would expect more than simply his word. "What did you do before you came here?"

His firm square chin dropped and he turned to the garden again. This time, I had no doubt it was to avoid my eyes. "I spent two years in jail on a fraud charge."

I tried to imagine what fraud a gardener could commit and came up empty, so I made a joke. "You planted plastic geraniums?"

I was glad he smiled, but it disappeared quickly. "I worked for a stockbroker until the feds caught the company selling phony bonds. I was the newest employee and they blamed me for the whole thing. I wasn't involved, but it came down to the big bosses' words against mine. I wondered if they'd hired me as a fall guy in the first place. I didn't have experience and thought it was too good to be true. I was right."

"Sheriff Brown would have discovered that you spent time in jail."

"He did. He questioned me at the station for a couple of hours the afternoon Mrs. Quigley disappeared. After I answered their questions they told me I could go, but not to leave town. One of the deputies was keeping an eye on me before that stuff started up in Chicago. I haven't seen him since."

It irritated me all over again that the sheriff and agents hadn't shared their information. It also made my job twice as hard. Since there wasn't much I could do to change that, I let it go. "Were you ever a gardener before you worked here?"

"No, I read books in the prison library. I did handle horses as a kid. I grew up on a farm in Iowa and we had a few. I told Mrs. Quigley I was in prison and why. She said we would try each other out for a few months and see how it went. I've been here ever since."

"Did Mr. Quigley know you'd been in prison?"

"She said she couldn't see any reason to tell him unless there was a problem."

"Thanks for being honest with me, Josh." His hesitant nod told me he wanted to know what I'd do with the information. "Mrs. Quigley said she wouldn't tell Mr. Quigley unless she found a reason. I can give you the same promise." He looked relieved. Of course, since the person who could back up his story wasn't around to do so, I would need to do more digging on Josh. "Do you want to point me in the direction of the Jeanine and Gregory Sandburg Estate?"

Dave had phoned Mrs. Sandburg, Diana's mother, to let her know I'd be dropping by, which I figured was why the gate was open. It turned out that Dave's parents, Art and

Arlene Quigley, were staying with the Sandburgs until Diana returned home. I wondered how two sets of parents could live in the same house and not strangle each other. I wondered that until I meandered up the drive. Compared to the Sandburg Estate, Dave and Diana's place was a cabin in the woods. Eight sets of parents could have stayed there and not seen each other for a day or two.

Rachel told me that Diana's sister, Renee, had moved back to the palatial home after her divorce. She also said she'd replaced the companionship of her hubby with that of a bottle. Dave also mentioned that Renee hadn't been happy for the last few years.

Of all the doors I'd faced in my short career, I'd never pounded on one with a large brass doorknocker, especially one pulled open by a butler. It took me a second to respond. "I'm Mattie Draper, a private investigator working for Mr. Quigley. I'd like to speak to Mr. and Mrs. Sandburg. I believe they're expecting me." Pleased that I'd managed a coherent introduction, I watched him nod and back up, pulling the two massive white doors inward to expose the marble floor of a large foyer. I figured that meant I should come in and after waiting as he re-secured the fort, I followed him into an enormous sitting room with more furniture than my apartment and office combined. I'm sure I don't need to mention who had the better stuff.

"Miss Mattie Draper," he announced to the four occupants, and faded from the room. An older couple sat on one of the couches and I assumed they were Arthur and Arlene Quigley. Dave bore a strong resemblance to his mom. Arthur Quigley kept tugging at his shirt collar, which told me he didn't usually sit around in a suit and tie. Both Quigley's struck me as people who were comfortably retired and spent most of their summer in shorts and tee shirts.

They were in their late sixties with gray hair. Mrs. Quigley's thick waves sat in a neat pile on her head. She'd probably had it done before they came up north. Mr. Quigley had scant hair on top and kept the remaining thin strands on the sides combed back around his ears. They looked friendly. I hoped that was true, because the faces at the other end of the room were considerably less congenial.

They were Jeanine and Gregory Sandburg, and unlike the Quigleys, both Mr. and Mrs. Sandburg appeared quite comfortable in their expensive, nearly formal clothing. They were around the same age as their guests, but it seemed likely that neither had ever worked up a sweat from scrubbing floors or mowing the lawn. Mr. Sandburg approached with his hand out. "How do you do, Miss Draper, I'm Gregory Sandburg. Please come in and have a seat. Would you like something from the bar?"

I almost said it was too early, but noticed a woman seated at the bar with a glass of good cheer in her hand and a bit of a glaze in her eyes. That had to be Renee. "Water would be good, thanks." I chose the chair nearest the door and sat. It wasn't that I wanted to be ready to make a quick getaway, but they weren't the friendliest group of people I'd ever had to interview. Okay, I sat there because I wanted to be able to make a quick getaway.

The butler must have been hanging around nearby because he appeared out of nowhere with a glass of water and placed it on the table next to my arm. It was a little startling to have him pop up unexpectedly. Sebastian often showed up without warning, but he was less than a foot tall and had padded paws. "I understand that you were all at the party at Dave and Diana's house the night before Diana disappeared." A group nod suggested the interview wouldn't take long. "Did anyone notice if Diana behaved in a strange manner, or appeared worried?"

"She couldn't have been worried that she'd be kidnapped since it hadn't happened yet." Renee made the comment with a slight slur that suggested she'd downed a cocktail or two before my arrival. Even tipsy, she bore a strong resemblance to her sister, at least what I saw in the painting. She was tall and had reddish hair, brown eyes, and a smart mouth. Her remark was inconsiderate, especially in front of her parents and her sister's in-laws.

Mr. Sandburg agreed. "Renee, you might want to finish your breakfast upstairs," he told her. I watched her grin behind the glass as she took another drink. She didn't act at all concerned about her sister's abduction.

"There is a possibility she did know, Renee. It's happened before. A neglected spouse fakes their own abduction for attention," I said.

Red crept up under the group's collective collars, and Mr. Sandburg rose to his feet. "How dare you!"

Then Mr. Quigley stood. "Diana would never do such a thing. She had no reason to fake a kidnapping. You think my son is such a monster that his wife would go to those lengths for his attention?"

I lifted my hands and held them in front of me to deflect the incoming anger. "I'm just telling you that it's happened in other cases. But you should know that I don't care what you think of my questions or me. My job is to find Diana and if that means asking questions that you don't want to hear, I'm sorry, I'll be asking them. Did anyone notice if Diana seemed upset at the party?"

The husbands returned to their seats and Mrs. Quigley spoke. "Diana did seem troubled toward the end of the evening, but when I asked her if she was all right, she said she was fine, she just wished Dave would think a little less about work. I saw him talking to Jeffrey and figured they were discussing the business. He's always been that way, working too much, but Diana would never do this to him."

Mrs. Sandburg cleared her throat and glared at Mrs. Quigley, a look that might have meant she didn't want family matters discussed with a stranger. Arlene Quigley responded to the warning quietly. "Jeannine, don't you want your daughter found? We have to tell Miss Draper everything we can."

I prepared myself for another "how dare you," but instead, Mrs. Sandburg put her face in her hands and seemed to be crying. Mr. Sandburg, put his arm around her and patted her back as if he thought it helped. I hate when people pat me on the back. "Maybe this would be easier if I talked to you one at a time." I knew I'd better speak to Renee first. I wanted to catch her while she was still coherent. "Is there a place you and I can talk, Renee?"

She stood without a word and waved me to follow her to what turned out to be the library, another enormous room. I dropped into a chair and watched as she set her glass on a stunning wood end table without a coaster. It wasn't my place to say, but she needed to work on her manners.

"So Miss Draper, who do you think took her? Dave's brother, Robert? He's nearly broke. What about Josh Spencer, that hunk gardener of hers? I've heard a few things about his past, but in all honesty, I wouldn't object if he offered to help me mount a horse."

"Miss Sandburg." I had planned to ask her why she hadn't kept her married name, but I realized I didn't care. "Maybe you don't understand how serious this is. Your sister has been kidnapped, and many kidnap victims end up dead."

"I know she's been kidnapped," she hissed. "You're the one who suggested she wandered off on her own."

I wondered if Miss Sandburg was giving me a one-woman good suspect, bad suspect performance. But she was right. I had mentioned that Diana could have faked the kidnapping. I wrote Robert Quigley in my notebook to collect myself and get back on track. "If I knew who took her, Miss Sandburg, you can bet your…, you can bet that Diana would be home."

"Call me Renee. You don't have to watch your language for me, Miss Draper. What's it like to work as a female private investigator? Do you carry a gun?" I don't often show people my gun, but since it was possible I was interviewing an individual with an unbalanced personality, I lifted my jacket and revealed the semi-automatic Colt 45. "Wow, that's cool. Are you ever afraid? Have you ever been in a shootout?"

If she'd been sober, I would have thought she was behaving silly on purpose. Whatever she was, it was time to take charge of the conversation. "Renee, as much as I love discussing my work, I'm here to find your sister. You're not upset that she's missing and possibly dead?"

In a single breath, the excitement on her face turned to boredom. "She's not dead. Bad things don't happen to that woman. Diana has little angels flying around her."

I figured Renee was the only one who saw the angels. "Dave told me they couldn't have children. Since they really want them, I would consider that bad."

"Yes, that's true. She felt terrible when she found out. Unlike me, she wants kids."

I tried to picture the woman pouring milk instead of scotch. It wasn't working. "Okay, well, now about Josh. What did you mean when you said you heard things about his past? What things?"

"That he'd been in jail."

"Did Diana tell you that?"

"No, I heard that particular bit of gossip from Joe Sumner at one of their parties. He doesn't like Josh much.

I'm sure it's jealousy. If he wanted, Josh could pick Joe up with one hand and toss him across the room." She sat thoughtfully for a moment. "I wouldn't mind seeing that."

So much for Josh's past being a secret. I wondered how Joe found out and how many other people he told. "Did you hear Diana say anything odd or out of character at the party?"

She crossed her long legs and swung the top one up and down while she sipped her drink. I was admiring her pants, which looked like silk, when she responded. "I don't remember a great deal about that night. It was a party, after all. I thought I saw her talking to Joe at one point. That would have been odd because she can't stand him. I had to freshen my drink, and when I came back, she was with Robert Quigley. Maybe she was talking to him in the first place. That makes more sense."

"Do they look alike?" I asked.

"Who?"

"Do Joe and Robert look alike?"

"They don't look remotely alike." She stood and left the room.

Chapter 11

I remained in my seat after Renee's exit, wondering if we'd finished the interview. That was okay. I didn't expect much help from her fogged brain. As I stood to join the other family members, Renee returned with a fresh drink. She placed it next to the empty glass and parked herself. "Where were we?"

I sat. "Did you drink excessively at the party?"

"Excessively is relatively relative, isn't it? At least it is for this relative." She smirked, and I waited for a real response. "No more than usual, I suppose. Why?"

"I'm wondering how reliable a witness you are. Can you think of anything Diana might have said or done that made you think she was upset? Did she mention any problems she was having in her relationship with Dave?"

For the first time since we sat down to talk, her face grew serious. She looked out the window rather than at me. "Diana asked me if my divorce had been difficult. I told her my ex and I didn't like each other much by that time, but I still found it painful. When I asked her why, she shook her head and said she'd heard something she didn't believe, but would find out more the next day." Renee spent a few seconds studying her drink. When she spoke, it was with what I thought to be genuine concern. "I wondered if she and Dave were having more problems than just him working too much. I'd heard that complaint a couple of times lately, but Diana loves Dave. She always has and always will. She went against Mother and Father's wishes and married someone they considered beneath her station. I have to admit, it made me jealous to see how much they cared for each other. After going through my horrid divorce, it hurt even more." Renee might have had a snootful of gin, but she meant what she said. I put my notebook in my purse and stood, which jarred her back to the conversation. "Is that it, Miss Draper?"

"Call me Mattie. Thanks for your time, Renee. I'd like to talk to you again." I assumed I'd have to meet her before breakfast and possibly reintroduce myself.

"Sure." She hung her leg over the arm of the chair and I wondered what was on her mind as she stared out the wall of windows. She did the spoiled rich kid well, but she had a good brain soaking in all that alcohol. Did her divorce make her jealous enough of Diana to kidnap her? That wasn't easy for me to imagine.

Renee's interview had been strange, but both sets of parents behaved the way one would expect family members to behave in a crisis. I talked to Dave's parents first. They were cooperative but had little to add to Mrs. Quigley's earlier remark.

Mrs. Sandburg had regained control and though she might preside over the family, her love and concern for her daughter was evident. I felt sorry for her. She tried to keep her emotions under wrap. That made it harder for her to deal with Diana's disappearance than for the others. I learned a long time ago that when you hold pain in, it turns dark and nasty.

Both Mr. and Mrs. Sandburg admitted that they weren't pleased when Diana announced she was marrying Dave, but they found him to be an honest and hardworking young man who adored their daughter. Mr. Sandburg voiced his concern that their pushing Dave to succeed had been partly responsible for the couple's problems. Jeanine Sandburg agreed in her stoic way. I left the estate convinced that neither they, nor Art and Arlene Quigley were involved. I wasn't as ready to say that about Renee.

When I entered the Quigley dining room, I saw Dave drop the phone in the cradle with an even more pained expression, not a small feat considering how miserable he looked. "What is it?"

"The chief called with the final report. He said whoever set the fire didn't use a great deal of accelerant. It didn't appear that they wanted to burn the place down and he wondered if it hadn't been a prank that got out of hand. He also said the person that reported it never gave a name. The dispatcher thought it was a woman, but the voice was muffled."

"Maybe whoever did it knew what happened three years ago and lit the gluing room to implicate Chet. He was the first person I thought of when I saw where it started. If the arsonist does work for you, they wouldn't want to be out of a job by burning the plant down, so they kept it small and called the fire department right away. I'm guessing most of your employees have been with you for a while, right?"

"Some were with me in my first plant, before I merged with Sumner, but we hire new people on occasion. Why would a person from the plant start a fire if they didn't want to burn it down?"

"I'm not sure. I'm not even sure there's a connection to the kidnapping, but I don't want to ignore any possibility. Listen, Dave, I found an earring last night when I was looking around. It was a diamond studded silver clip-on with a moon and a star. Do you remember seeing Diana wear anything similar?"

"It sounds familiar. Can I take a look?"

Just as with Mrs. Allen, I stared at the extended hand. I didn't want to tell the head-bashing story again, but I didn't have much choice. "I'm afraid not. Right after I found it, someone hit me on the head and took the earring."

"Someone hit you on the head? Are you all right?" He realized what he said and took a breath. "Of course, you are. I'm sorry. Mattie, what's going on around here? Did you see who did it?"

"No. Josh found me and helped me back to my car. That's when we met you yelling at your tires."

The memory of his behavior obviously embarrassed him. He let the remark go. "That explains why Josh wanted to know if you were all right."

"Right. I was a little unsteady at first."

"When I heard him ask if you were okay, I thought maybe he'd offended you somehow. You know, flirted, but I couldn't deal with another problem."

I didn't bother to tell Dave that it wouldn't have offended me if Josh had flirted. For the briefest moment, I wondered if I wasn't attractive enough for the gardener. After hearing my own thoughts, I told my brain to take five. "Does he flirt with people often?"

"No, I've never heard that he has. I'm glad you weren't seriously hurt. Why do you think the kidnapper would have been in the woods?"

Before I could answer with the most common phrase in my vocabulary these days, "I don't know," someone pounded on the front door. I moved forward in the chair to stand, but Mrs. Allen announced the visitor in something other than her usual friendly tone. "Mr. Quigley is here." A person that I assumed to be Dave's brother, Robert, pushed passed Mrs. Allen as she left, but remained at the entrance to the dining room.

"Hey, Dave. What's happening?" He leaned on the doorjamb, his condition not unlike Renee's earlier that morning. It was possible he'd slept in his suit.

"What the hell is wrong with you, Rob? You come in here drunk and yelling like an idiot when Diana's missing?" Dave turned to me. "Mattie, I know you have questions for him, but could you please take him to another room."

I stood and grabbed my purse. I wasn't looking forward to having a discussion with the clown, but the least I could do was get him out of Dave's hair. "I'm Mattie Draper, Mr. Quigley, a private investigator. I'd like to ask you a few questions."

"Hey, I'm all ears, baby."

What people call me doesn't normally matter, but Robert worked his way under my skin and I wasn't about to let his comment go. "Maybe you didn't hear me say that my name is Mattie Draper, not baby." As he followed me out, I looked back to see Dave shaking his head.

The chair I selected in the living room was one of a pair of stuffed high backs. I didn't think it would be wise to sit on the couch in case he decided to join me. Rob remained standing. He looked a little like Dave, but I saw very quickly that there were major differences in their personalities. "Thanks for talking to me, Mr. Quigley. Do you know Diana well?"

"Call me Rob. Yes, I know Diana. She's a snob and doesn't talk to people she considers beneath her unless she has to. My late wife had money, but she didn't walk around with her nose in the air."

I wondered if she should have. She might have smelled the garbage before she married him. "When did your wife die?"

"Two years ago, in a car accident. Christina was a lovely woman and wealthy, but now I'm finding she hadn't been quite wealthy enough."

I glanced at the Persian rug, grateful I hadn't eaten lunch. It would have taken all my concentration not to lose it. "I've heard that you're running out of money."

"Who told you that?" He seemed curious, not upset.

"Renee Sandburg."

He nodded on the way to a table to grab an ashtray. I waited while he extracted a pack of cigarettes from his pocket and lit one. "Was she drunk, or was it before breakfast?"

The expression "pot calling the kettle black" came to mind. "My question is, was she right?"

"I'm running a little low, but I'll figure things out. I always do. I asked him for help." His long Quigley chin pointed toward the dining room. "My dear brother offered me a job with Q & S Design. I didn't want a job, I wanted money."

Abandoning the cigarette in a different ashtray, Rob made a visit to the bar. No wonder people drank so much in Lake Oak. There were bars everywhere. The glass he brought and set on the table contained an amber liquid that, in my present state, looked enticing. "Would $100,000 be enough to help you figure things out?" I asked.

"I'd call that a good start. Why? Do you have extra cash you want to give away, sugar?"

"Did you kidnap Diana Quigley?"

The drink disappeared in one gulp and Robert Quigley stood in front of me. "I like that in a detective—and a woman as a matter of fact—right to the point. No, Miss Draper, I didn't kidnap Diana. I don't have a freezer big enough to store an icicle that size. Is that all you wanted to know?" He returned the glass to the bar and left the room.

I hoped he went out the front door and tried to recall who had said they had a hard time picturing him as Dave's brother. I remembered. It was Rachel who'd said it at breakfast, and she'd nailed it. When Robert Quigley was drinking, he was obnoxious.

Chapter 12

My interview with Rob brought me no closer to finding Diana. I felt gloomy and sorry for myself until I remembered that Frankie promised to take me to dinner. Good company, good food, and someone to help me make sense out of a notebook full of non-sense sounded like the perfect pick-me-up.

I was right. Frankie took me to a great little Italian restaurant in the neighborhood. He loved their lasagna and I was partial to their ravioli. Cheese or meat, it never mattered. That night I had both. He bought a bottle of the house Chianti and until we devoured every bit of pasta, we discussed a variety of topics, but none that had to do with kidnapping or Diana Quigley.

Finally, I wiped my mouth, pulled out my notebook, and watched Frankie push his plate away. We hunched over the table and went to work. "Okay, Mattie. Who's first on your list?"

"That changed this afternoon. I met Dave's brother, Robert Quigley. He was generally offensive and fairly loaded. According to Renee Sandburg, who may be an equally unreliable source, Robert has spent a large portion of the fortune he inherited from his late wife and is running short on cash. He admitted that, and told me he'd asked Dave for help and was insulted when he offered him a job instead of money. What has me confused is that he had nothing even remotely nice to say about Diana Quigley. If he did kidnap her, wouldn't he at least want to pretend he liked her, or that Diana's kidnapping upset him?"

"Not necessarily. If he'd bad-mouthed her all along, people would be suspicious if he suddenly became a concerned brother-in-law."

"That makes sense." Frankie's little nudges often put me back on track. "Frankie, is there a possibility you can talk one of your buddies in blue into finding information on Robert Quigley? He makes a good suspect and he and Dave aren't particularly close."

"I'll see what I can do. What were you saying about Josh being in prison?"

"He said it was for fraud, but maybe it was something else."

"I doubt that he'd tell you he was in prison and then lie about the crime. It's too easy to check. I'm a little concerned that he found you in the woods while you were doing your internal star gazing." Frankie waited for my reaction to his joke, and dragged his mouth into a lopsided smile when I frowned.

"You were saying, Mr. Ficaro."

"Could he have seen you go to the clearing from the barn like he said?"

"He could. It would have been easy enough to spot the flashlight beam." The wine hit the spot and I forced myself to take a sip and set the glass down. "I suppose he could have been the one that hit me."

"What puzzles me, Mattie, is why anyone would care that you found Diana's earring. If she lost it during the kidnapping, what difference does it make? We know she's missing."

"I gave that some thought, Frankie. What if it wasn't Diana's earring?" He poured us both a little more wine, which I wasn't sure I needed. My recent exposure to excessive consumption made me want to take it easy.

"What do you mean?"

"Just what I said. What if it wasn't Diana's earring? It's possible there's a woman involved in the kidnapping. I don't think a woman could have kidnapped Diana alone unless she used a gun, but one could be involved. If she lost an earring, then recovering the one I found would make sense. She'd be protecting her identity. Am I right?"

The proud teacher smiled and asked the obvious question. "What females do we have who could be involved?"

"There's Renee. I suppose she could do it if she stayed sober long enough, but Diana's her sister. Could a person do that to her own blood?"

"Don't trust anyone, Mattie. They'll beat you if they win your trust. Who else?"

"We have Sandra Sumner. She and Joe live next door. Sandra is supposed to be Diana's friend. She said she was on a flight to New York when the kidnapping occurred. Of course, I only have her word for that. Is there a way I can check the plane schedules and passenger lists?"

"I have a buddy who can run a check on the airlines for you, but that could take a day or two. How does it look for Mrs. Allen's assistant, Kathleen?"

"I suppose it could be her if she worked with a partner. She wouldn't be physically capable of abducting someone Diana's size without help, or as I said, unless she had a gun."

"Maybe Josh and Kathleen are working together."

I groaned. "Yes, maybe Josh." Then I thought of a fact that made Kathleen less likely. "Kathleen couldn't afford jewelry as expensive as that earring, Frankie. Even if she had one really nice pair, I doubt she'd wear them during a kidnapping."

"That's a good point."

"And if I'm right, the same would go for Linda Dowling if we keep her and Chet on the suspect list. That earring wouldn't have come from her jewelry box."

Frankie agreed. "Are you sure Mrs. Allen isn't involved?"

"I'd sooner suspect my own mother."

"Careful with that, Mattie, I've met your mother." He didn't smile, but I knew he was kidding and he confirmed it. "I'm teasing. Have you contacted the ladies on those boards Mrs. Quigley is on?"

"Not yet. I'll get on that. Maybe one of them is close to Diana and she told that person something she didn't want to tell her family. Before I talk to the ladies, I want to have a conversation with whoever is in charge at the art museum. Oh, and I meant to tell you, Renee made a comment in passing that I remembered later. At the party, Diana told her that she'd heard something she didn't believe but would find out more the next day. They were discussing Renee's divorce and Renee wondered if Diana was thinking about divorcing Dave. It didn't mean anything to me then, but that could imply that things were not as hunky-dory with their marriage as Dave wants us to believe." The wine began to transform from the warm liquid in my stomach to a thickening fog in my head. "We'd better call it quits for tonight, Frankie. My brain is ground chuck."

"That doesn't go too good with Chianti. Do you want me to come home with you?"

"Did you bribe me with dinner and have another activity in mind?"

"Don't make it sound that way, Mattie. I always have another activity in at least a part of my mind when I'm with you. I can't help it, you're irresistible, but I'd never ask you to do anything you didn't want."

"I know, Frankie. Right now what I want is to find Diana. Then we'll figure out what I owe you and how I can repay it. How does that sound?"

"That sounds good. I'll check with my friend about the airlines tomorrow and see if I can find anything on the sheriff's investigation. You might want to discuss the earring with Diana's sister and Mrs. Sumner. Can I walk you home?"

"I'd like that. I have to remember to take my jackets to the dry cleaner tomorrow morning. Do they do one day turnaround?"

"They do, but it costs extra."

"I'll have to pay it. This is my last jacket and it's nearly ready for the cleaner, too. I suppose I notice it more because of how well those Lake Oak folks dress."

"Give me the jackets when we get to your place and I'll take them to a friend of mine. He can have them ready for you in the morning. Then you can have that one done, too." He pointed at the sleeve of my jacket, which appeared to have sopped up some of the marinara sauce my napkin missed.

"How will you do that?" I asked studying the mess.

"He owes me a favor."

"Half of Chicago owes you a favor, Ficaro. If you don't mind taking them, I'd appreciate it." I owed him big time, but Frankie was a gentleman and a man of his word. He wasn't kidding that he wouldn't pressure me. He'd asked me to his place a few times to watch his new color television. He might have had more in mind than watching *The Ed Sullivan Show,* but we'd only known each other for about a few months and I hadn't decided where my relationship with him stood in that area. He never pushed. I liked Frankie and liked learning new things about him. Besides, I didn't say no, I said not yet.

*

I slept through the night and by the time Sebastian jumped on my chest I felt good for the first time since someone increased my hat size. Frankie showed up in time for a cup of coffee. The jackets looked great. I wondered what he had done for his dry-cleaning friend that be worth cleaning them in less than twelve hours, but I knew better than to ask.

While we had our coffee at the kitchen table, Sebastian wandered in and curled up under Frankie's chair. Sebastian was not normally a people cat, but for some reason he liked Frankie. The only thing I could figure was that Frankie gave him food when I wasn't looking, but both cat and human denied it. "Hey, Mattie, my friend found a couple of scraps of paper in the pocket of one of those jackets." He dug in his own until he found them.

"I don't remember…. Oh, I know. I found these in the garden the first time I went to the Quigleys' house. I thought they were trash. What do they say?" He hadn't read them so I unfolded the first one and saw that whatever writing had once been there had faded. When I opened the second note, I read it again to make sure I had it right.

Diana, meet me at the clearing at nine thirty.

When I didn't say anything, Frankie asked to see it. I put it in his hand and watched him read. "Frankie, she could have dropped this on her way to the barn and it blew into the garden."

"Interesting. What does this tell us?"

He was quizzing me, but I was fairly sure I had the right answer. "She left of her own free will with a person she knew." I watched his slow nod. "Who would have to give her a note to meet her? Why not ask her in person, or call on the telephone?" If Frankie knew the answer, he kept it to himself. "Maybe she went to meet a person she didn't want other people to know about," I suggested.

Frankie flattened the note on the table and pointed. "That would be a good assumption. This is a guy's handwriting."

"How do you know?"

"It's sloppy."

"My handwriting is sloppy and I'm not a guy."

"No, Mattie, you're not a guy, and yes, your handwriting is sloppy, but you're what they call the exception that makes the rule. Women take more time with their writing. Most women that is."

"She could be having an affair." Rather than discussing my sloppy handwriting or my gender, I returned to the case. "Maybe with Josh. He's eight years younger, but that painting made it clear that she's still a beautiful woman." I pulled the hand brake on that particular train of thought. "That doesn't make sense, though. If she wanted to have an affair with Josh, she wouldn't have to kidnap herself. Hell, they could meet in the barn or his cabin. And he wouldn't have to write her a note. No, no, no. She wouldn't have to kidnap herself even if it wasn't Josh. None of this makes sense."

"What do you want to do?"

"I need to get handwriting samples from everyone involved. I have Dave's on his contract."

"You can't tell people what it's for or they'll disguise their writing and that will be easy because you don't have much to go on."

"You're right. I'll figure out a plan on the way to Lake Oak. What do I owe you for my jackets?" His eyebrows danced up and down and I wondered why I asked.

After Frankie left, Sebastian returned to the bedroom and I called my sister Mary Anne. Their small horse ranch was up near Kenosha, Wisconsin. "Morning, Mary Anne. Are you in the barn?"

"How did you know?"

"Either that or the kids are making strange noises in the house."

"No, the kids went into town with Rick. What's up? Are you still playing Nancy Drew?" She knew her kidding bugged the hell out of me, but that was our relationship, and if I made a fuss, she'd do it even more. She'd sent me a magnifying glass and deerstalker hat to be funny. I didn't tell her I liked them.

"Yes, I'm still working as a private investigator, and I have a couple of questions for you concerning my case. I'm looking for a kidnapped woman. She's a horse person, but the morning of her kidnapping, she went riding without her boots. Her stable hand and housekeeper both said she didn't usually do that."

"Huh. If she did something she didn't usually do, she might have had different plans."

"That's what I thought. You have a little Sherlock in you, yourself, Sis. What reason would she have to ride without her boots? They're black leather and they go up to the top of my calf. She's taller than me, but not by much."

"Do they have laces?"

"No laces, zippers, or anything. The leather feels expensive, and inside it's stamped 'handmade in Italy.'"

"They're probably dress boots. Expensive dress boots from the sound of it. And you say she wore them all the time?"

"Yep. They're her only pair and the only riding she does is for pleasure."

"It sounds like she just likes them. If I were going for a short ride and had limited time, I might jump on without my boots. Dress boots are not easy to put on or take off. Regular shoes don't stay in the stirrups well and there's nothing protecting your calves, but if she were going a short distance over terrain familiar to her and the horse, she'd be okay. Was she a good rider?"

"Definitely a good rider and that particular morning she only went a short distance. What I can't figure out is if that was the kidnapper's idea or hers. Next item. The police say they found a rope tied across the path. They believe that she didn't see the rope and it pushed her off the horse. The thing is, the horse continued to run for quite a ways, and horse and rider were supposed to be simpatico."

"If it was an inexperienced rider or they were new to each other, the horse might have gotten spooked when she fell, and run off."

"Are you listening to me, Mary Anne? They weren't new to each other. I told you they were buddies."

"When I fall off one of our horses, the first thing I do is reassure the animal that everything is okay. If she wasn't hurt in the fall and they were as close as you say, she would have done the same. Do you know if she was conscious?"

I sighed. "I can't even find evidence that she fell, but let's say she did. Do you think the police theory could be wrong?"

"It sounds to me like you think so."

I sighed. My sister wasn't giving me the answers I wanted. "Thanks for your help, Mary Anne. Give Rick and the kids a hug for me. Maybe when I finish this case Frankie and I'll come up for a visit."

"That sounds good. We'll give Rick and Frankie a beer and send them to the back porch. They can reminisce about the military, which always seems to make them happy."

"They'll love it. See ya'." Mary Anne was right. Frankie and Rick enjoyed talking about their days in the service. Frankie doesn't discuss his time in Vietnam with me, and I don't share my opinion of the mess we're in over there. Too many young guys in my neighborhood have gone over and not made it back. The ones that do are having a tough time getting into the swing of regular life. I have yet to hear one decent explanation from a politician or the Pentagon as to why we're fighting. War protests are getting bigger and more frequent, and I suspect the Democratic Convention is just a sample of what's coming.

I drove up Lake Shore Drive considering what Mary Anne had said about it being all right to wear shoes if it was a short ride. If Diana knew she'd only be riding to the clearing, she might have thought she wouldn't need the boots. If the reason she didn't want to wear them was how difficult they were to take off and put on, she could have been meeting for an activity where boots were optional.

I didn't want to think about that, but it was within the realm of possibilities. A morning ride would make a good cover for a rendezvous. She could be gone for an hour or so and no one would be suspicious. I told myself that there was also the chance that her reason for meeting someone was innocent. What innocent reason would she have to meet someone in the woods?

I had to assume that the note was written by the kidnapper and that meant I had to find out who wrote it. To do that meant convincing people to give me samples of their writing. I'd stopped at the office and checked David Quigley's writing on the contract. He'd filled out his address and other information, so there was enough to tell that it wasn't close. I had Rachel's sample because she wrote the list of names for me, not that she was a suspect. Her writing was in line with Frankie's idea of how women wrote—neat and careful. Okay, so I had two samples. How did I get the rest? I could ask people to write down their thoughts about the case. Hey, Josh, could you give me a short essay on who you think kidnapped Mrs. Quigley? Of course, he'd just think my experience in the woods had knocked a couple more screws loose.

I arrived at the Quigleys' without any clever ideas for obtaining handwriting samples and found Mrs. Allen's and Dave's cars in the drive. I wondered if Diana had her own car. There was a building at the side of the house that could have been a garage. Maybe it was in there. Did Josh or Kathleen have vehicles? If Kathleen kidnapped Diana, she had help moving her. She wasn't more than five two. If she and Josh were in on it together and neither one had a car, how would they have taken her? Maybe they only took her out to Josh's cabin behind the barn. I still hadn't looked there and needed to do that soon. The note's discovery threw a wrench into a few of my theories. It also made Diana Quigley a suspect in her kidnapping.

Chapter 13

"Hello, Mrs. Allen. How's Dave holding up?"

"Not so good, Miss Draper. He still is not sleeping much that I can see, and he barely touches his food. Have you found anything?"

I sat at the kitchen table and said nothing for a minute. I needed to trust someone and since I had complete faith in my mother, even if Frankie didn't, I picked Mrs. Allen. "I found a clue, but you have to promise not to tell anyone. That includes Mr. Quigley. Okay?" She agreed and I retrieved the note from my purse. As I did that, another piece of paper dropped out and I saw the home and work phone of Chet Dowling. I felt a shot of relief when I saw that his handwriting was not at all similar to the note. I put Dowling's note in my bag and laid the message to Diana on the table.

"What is this?" she asked as I unfolded it in front of her.

"I found this in the yard. It must have blown into the garden. Do you recognize the handwriting?"

"No, but this says Miss Diana should meet someone at the clearing. Do you think this is from the person who took her?" She pointed at the paper.

"I do. I also think she knows the person. I need handwriting samples from everyone even remotely connected to Dave and Diana to compare with the note. If I tell people why I want the sample, they'll disguise their writing." I knew a few of them would just tell me to go to hell.

Without a word, Mrs. Allen rose and picked up a sheet of paper from the counter. She returned to her chair and tapped on the page as she placed it in front of me. "That is a shopping list and a sample of my handwriting that I wrote before you showed me this." The tapping finger moved with even greater enthusiasm to the note. "You will see that I did not disguise it to fool you." She folded her arms and gave her head a firm nod.

I'd never believed that Mrs. Allen kidnapped Diana, but her effort to prove her innocence would have convinced even the doubtful Franklin Ficaro. "I know you didn't kidnap Mrs. Quigley. I hope everyone is as cooperative as you."

"I can get samples of writing from Josh and Kathleen. They give me lists of what they need. That's two more. I can tell you by looking at this, neither of them wrote it, but I'll get the samples. I also know it is not Mr. or Mrs. Quigley's handwriting." She pursed her lips, frowned, and looked as though she wanted to say something, but hesitated. I gave her what I hoped was a look of encouragement and she forged ahead. "I don't mean to sound pushy, Miss Draper, but we need to get moving on this." My mouth dropped open. "I'm sorry. I didn't mean to offend you. I know you're doing everything you can, but you must let me help."

"What do you have in mind, Mrs. Allen?"

"Have you contacted the ladies from the art museum board yet?" I shook my head and waited. "They might know something, but if you haven't had time to do that, I could talk to their help. I know most of the cooks, housekeepers, and maids in Lake Oak."

"A friend of mine recommended that I start calling them, too. Until I can do that, go ahead and talk to the maids and housekeepers. It's a great idea, Mrs. Allen." Her head bent, but not enough to hide a satisfied smile. "While you're doing that, I want to contact the person or persons Mrs. Quigley planned to meet at the museum the day she disappeared. Would you know who that was?"

"She keeps a list of contacts for the different committees. She told me once that the man she works with at the art museum doesn't like her. I thought that her feeling might have been the same for him. I'll be right back." She left and I listened to her heavy steps pound up the staircase. A few minutes later, Mrs. Allen entered the kitchen and dropped in the chair, red faced and out of breath.

"You didn't have to run up the stairs, Mrs. Allen," I told her.

A warm smile dimpled her round cheeks and she patted my hand. "Miss Draper, if I had run up those stairs, I would have needed to take a little snooze before I came down." That was another good reason to remove Mrs. Allen from the suspect list.

After supplying the name of the museum curator Diana planned to meet, Mrs. Allen rested and I went to look for Dave. I found him in the dining room. "Why do you spend so much time in here, Dave?" I asked.

I wasn't sure if he'd heard because he fingered the newspaper silently, still watching the door. When he answered, it was as if I wasn't there. "I didn't spend enough time with Diana, but we always ate breakfast together. I keep thinking if I wait, she'll walk in that door and kiss me on the cheek while I pour her a cup of coffee."

His moving response tied a quick knot in my stomach. I felt for the guy, but I had to remember that everyone was a suspect until Diana came home. Frankie warned me often enough about being too trusting, and he was right that my job was to deal with facts, but I also know the value of intuition. As I left Dave to talk to Peter Fielding, the curator at the Lake Oak Art Museum, I told myself that I would deal with facts but stay open to those intuitive nudges I've found useful over the years. I hoped one of those things could help me find something soon to put Diana Quigley at the breakfast table where Dave could pour her a cup of coffee.

Lake Oak isn't very big, and most of the public buildings, city offices, and small businesses are located on an aptly named street, Lake Oak Boulevard, that runs through the center of town. I had no trouble finding the art museum and parked the Chevy across the street, remembering to feed a few nickels into the meter. The police might be busy, but I was betting the local meter maid wasn't involved in controlling protestors.

Once inside, I saw to the left of the door a desk occupied by a receptionist and to the right, a ticket booth. A sign on the ticket booth indicated it was the entrance to the gallery.

The young woman at the desk looked about twenty and wore the same bored expression I often wore behind a desk. "Hi, my name is Mattie Draper. I'd like to speak to Mr. Peter Fielding."

"Do you have an appointment, Miss Draper?" She asked the obligatory line and twisted a black curl around her finger. I leaned forward and scanned the empty column under the day's date.

"Nope, I don't see me scheduled. As a matter of fact, I don't see anyone scheduled. Please tell Mr. Fielding that I'd like to speak to him about Mrs. Quigley's kidnapping. I'm a private investigator working for Mr. Quigley."

Her attitude disappeared in a hurry. "You are? Wow! I can't believe someone kidnapped Mrs. Quigley. She's very sweet, but I don't think Mr. Fielding shares that opinion."

"Fielding doesn't like Diana Quigley?"

"They have very different opinions about art. I'll tell him you're here." She didn't pick up the phone, but rather left her desk and walked to the end of a long hallway. She wore a short skirt with high boots and a colorful tie-dyed blouse that I noticed kids were wearing lately. I could hear them having a discussion, but couldn't understand a word.

She returned to the desk and stuck out her hand. "My name's Carol." I shook it. Young women did that more often these days. "He'll see you now, Miss Draper. Good luck." She glanced down the hall adding, "He's a jerk."

"Thanks for the warning." I shot her a smile and followed the path she'd traveled moments earlier. The door stood open, so I walked in and waited for him to acknowledge my presence. I'd never met Peter Fielding, but studying his bent head, he reminded me of someone. I thought it might have been a character from a book. When I realized which character, I had to keep myself from laughing. He was the image of Ichabod Crane from Washington Irving's story about the Headless Horseman.

He looked much the way I remembered Irving described the teacher Crane—more like a scarecrow than a man—with narrow shoulders and a small head with huge ears and a long nose. He looked gaunt or at least undernourished and his flesh was the color of the skin on Frankie's bongo drums. The brown tweed jacket he wore looked too big and the padding in the shoulders was better suited for a quarterback than a scrawny museum curator. That might have been why his head looked too small for the rest of his body. As he continued to write, I noticed the talon-like shape of his bony hands and thinning brown hair that hung well over his collar. He wasn't the kind of guy I'd take home to meet Mom.

A full two minutes passed and he continued writing, pointedly ignoring me. I hated when people did that. He knew I was there but played his little power game. There wasn't time for games with the schoolteacher from Sleepy Hollow. "Mr. Fielding, I'm a private investigator and I'd like a word with you about Diana Quigley. My name is Draper, Mattie Draper."

He raised his head and looked over his black framed glasses, doing that body scan thing. It was the same once-over Sandra gave me. The sour look on his face told me he'd reached a similar conclusion. "Don't tell me, Miss Draper, you're another one of Mrs. Quigley's little projects."

I had no idea what he meant, but the way he said it told me it wasn't a compliment. Since he clearly didn't plan to offer me a seat, I took the one in front of his desk without an invitation.

"Did you know, Mr. Fielding that over forty percent of people who are kidnapped wind up dead? If you don't want to help find Mrs. Quigley, the police might look at you as an accessory to murder."

"If the police wanted my help, why haven't they come to talk to me?"

"Surely a man in your position reads the paper and knows that there's a little excitement in Chicago right now. The local boys want to make sure nothing happens on the quiet streets of Lake Oak." I paused. "So what did you mean when you said another one of her projects?"

"Oh, that gardener she hired." He waved his hand as if shooing away a fly, or an unwelcome visitor. "Diana and her kind like to give handouts to worthless bums and let them go on believing society owes them a living. They suck us dry."

"If you mean Josh Spencer, he's worked hard for her for three years. She didn't give him a handout."

"Well he may have fooled her, but I know his type. It wouldn't surprise me at all if he was the one holding her for ransom."

My regard for a number of the good citizens of Lake Oak continued to plummet, not that they'd care. Peter Fielding was a bitter, unhappy man with a grudge. "I'm not sure you could do the job Josh Spencer does, but why do you despise Diana Quigley?"

"Do you know who I am, Miss Draper?" I stared at him, half expecting to hear him say Ichabod Crane. "I'm the curator of this museum. That makes me the curator of the dullest art museum in the country, possibly the world, because of the Diana Quigleys of this village. Each time I suggest a change that will build our reputation, she and her wealthy little club on the board vote against it. I've tried talking sense to her, but she's completely unreasonable and determined to have things her own way. While she enjoys her pretty pictures, I rot in this dreary museum."

"Why don't you quit if you're unhappy? Can't you find a job at another museum?"

"You obviously know nothing about the art world, Miss Draper." He folded his arms and confirmed his contempt with a sneer. Sometimes you meet people who should only exist in fiction. His dramatics made me wonder if he'd been a theater major before switching to art. "I can't walk into another museum and fill out an application to become a curator," he informed me. "I must be invited, and that won't happen until we become reputable."

"Is Diana the one keeping you from making necessary changes?"

"The others vote along with her because she's the only one of the group that has even a modicum of taste. That's a scary thought, isn't it?"

I considered a snappy comeback, but decided it was counterproductive. To appease my irritation, I pictured him running, unsuccessfully, from the Headless Horseman and asked another question. "If Diana Quigley was out of the way you would be able to make the changes you need to move on to a bigger museum. Is that the way it works?"

"Well, yes." He pulled a handkerchief from his jacket to pat his forehead. I was sorry he did that. I wanted to see sweat drip down that long, hooked nose. "I hope you're not insinuating that I had anything to do with her kidnapping. I'll have you in court so fast you won't know what hit you. Slander is against the law."

I had the urge to fold my arms, sneer, and tell him that he knew nothing about the world of private investigators. Instead, I stood and gave him one last look of disgust. "Thank you for your time, Mr. Fielding. If you think of anything that might help find Diana Quigley, please, give me a call." I put my card on his desk, turned toward the door, and shared one last thought. "You might want to keep your fingers crossed that Diana Quigley is found alive. I'm not slandering, mind you, I'm just telling you how the law will see it when I share my information with them. My guess is that they'll see you as one hell of a good suspect."

Outside his door, I took a couple of deep breaths and continued to suck air as I returned to Carol's desk. By the time I reached her, I was smiling. Some people are so peculiar that smiling is the only thing you can do. Ichabod Fielding was one of those people. "Boy, you weren't kidding that he's a jerk, Carol." I pulled out another card. "Could you give me a call if you think of anything that might be important to finding Mrs. Quigley? A good place to start might be by keeping an eye on your boss."

"Sure, Miss Draper. Do you think he could have had anything to do with it?" The mass of curls bounced as she tilted her head down the hall. "He despises her."

"Call me Mattie. Of all the people I've met during my investigation, he's the one I'd most enjoy seeing in a pair of handcuffs."

"Ooh, I'd like to be around to see that happen."

I left the museum and found two full minutes left on the meter and a meter maid waiting for it to expire. My smile did little to cheer the officer as she shoved her ticket book in her bag and made a disappointed exit. Avoiding a ticket was a good sign. Maybe my visit to the museum would be the break I needed.

Part of me suspected Fielding was somehow involved, but I based that less on evidence and more on a powerful contempt for the man.

Chapter 14

Fielding made my skin crawl, but I was glad to have met Carol. I've often wondered how many employers knew about the complex network of women who ran their offices. If a female revolution took place, secretaries held secrets to nearly every corporation in the country. That was power.

Mrs. Allen opened the front door and as I stepped inside, I heard two male voices involved in what sounded like a boisterous and jovial conversation. I didn't think Dave was in the mood to entertain. "Is that Dave in the living room?" Mrs. Allen informed me that it wasn't, and her stiff jaw and raised chin said she wasn't pleased with whoever it was.

"It is Joe Sumner and Robert Quigley. They have been in there since right after you left. Mr. Quigley joined them when they first arrived, but stayed only a few minutes. He does not feel like drinking and laughing. If you ask me, they should both go home."

"You're right, Mrs. Allen. But before they do, I'll listen in on their conversation."

She left for the kitchen and I found a nice high back chair near the door of the living room, perfect for eavesdropping. For the first ten minutes I listened to Joe's opinion of what was wrong with the Cubs' management. Robert, who didn't have much of an interest in baseball, finally changed the subject. "So, who do you think snatched the ice queen?"

I recognized Joe's laughter. "Hey, I tried to thaw her out, but she wasn't interested. She doesn't know what she missed." Ice clinked and I assumed he took a drink. "Rob, I don't want to bad-mouth your brother or anything, but do you think it's possible he paid a professional to do kidnap Diana? From what I've been hearing, he's going to need her money if he wants to keep the business going."

"Dave needs money?" Robert Quigley sounded confused and seconds later added, "I don't think so, Joe. I would have heard if Dave needed money."

"There have been rumors at the company that he and my dad are negotiating a big contract and they plan to sink a lot of money into redoing the plant to handle it. If they make it, the company will be in great shape, but things haven't been going well, and now this fire has stopped production."

"What do you mean rumors? I know you don't spend a lot of time at Q & S, but doesn't your dad tell you what's going on?"

"Dad doesn't think I have much business sense."

"If Dave doesn't have the money, how will he pay Diana's ransom?"

"That's what I'm saying. If he kidnapped her, he won't need to pay the ransom. He pretends to pay a fictitious kidnapper and then in a few weeks, he sends an anonymous tip to the police about where her body is. He inherits her money, plus collects her insurance and he hasn't spent a dime. You're familiar with how inheritance works, aren't you Robert?"

"Shut up, Sumner."

"Okay, I'm just saying that he might need money as badly as you do."

"I doubt that." Robert sounded angry, but he didn't elaborate.

"I can't believe you spent your wife's fortune. That was a lot of dough."

"I spent enough. I'm talking to a guy about investing what I still have so I can make something on it. I just have to stay away from the cards and dice for a while."

"Consider yourself lucky, old man. At least you don't have anyone draining your bank accounts faster than you can make deposits. No one besides you that is. Now that I think about it, Robert, your financial situation makes you a good suspect for kidnapping Diana. Are you sure you didn't snatch her?"

There was a long silence. When Robert finally spoke, he ignored Joe's remark and asked him how he got away with spending so little time at work. He seemed anxious to change the subject, but Joe didn't notice. "You mean the antique furniture factory?" Joe's loyalty to his father's company was touching. "I work as few hours as necessary to keep Dad off my back. I have my own plans for the business, and if your brother did kidnap Diana and is caught, I'll be in charge soon enough. When that happens there'll be plenty of changes. In a year or so I won't have to show up at all."

That sounded like motive to me, but the most appalling part of their conversation was that they were having it in Dave and Diana's living room. Both of them sounded more than capable of kidnapping Diana.

I still had my ear to the room when I heard my name and almost jumped out of the chair. "Hi, Mattie. Has there been any news?" I stood and grabbed Dave's arm to lead him away. He didn't need to hear the discussion. "Are they still here?" He pointed at the living room. I told him they were and he suggested we go to the back porch where it was shady, cool, and devoid of visitors.

"That's a good idea. Then I can tell you everything I know about museum curator, Peter Fielding."

Dave and I talked for almost an hour. I gave him as much information as I could. I was 90 percent sure Dave hadn't kidnapped Diana, but that 10 percent kept him a suspect and I remained cautious.

Dave said he'd heard Diana mention Peter Fielding in connection with the museum and knew she didn't care for him, but he'd never met him. I filled him in on why Fielding had such animosity toward Diana and told him that I was interested in the curator as a suspect. I ran out of new information at about the same time Dave ran out of energy. I could see as I stood he was ready for a nap. I hoped he could.

I headed through the house to leave by the front door and heard nothing from the living room, but when I stuck my head in, I saw Joe. Unfortunately, he saw me. "Hi, Mattie. How's the case going?"

Robert wasn't around. A conversation with one of them seemed tolerable, so I went in and sat. "Slow, I'm afraid, Joe. Do you have any thoughts?"

"Now that you mention it, I do. I was in here with Robert Quigley—Dave's brother." I tried for a look of surprise and hoped he bought it. "He wasn't a big fan of Diana and he's running out of his late wife's money. He said he asked Dave for a loan, but he turned him down. Maybe he figured out a different way to get it from him."

I'd been staring straight ahead at the bar and listening to Joe's thoughts. Robert hadn't moved down much on my list, but I wondered about Joe's motive in pointing a finger at him. I turned to the younger Sumner. "How about you, Joe? What would you gain by Diana's kidnapping?"

"It wouldn't make sense for me to take money from the company. I'll be half owner soon and there's not much of a future for the owner of a bankrupt furniture manufacturing plant."

"That's true. I can't see much sense in that. Dave told me you have ideas you plan to introduce when your dad retires. He didn't sound interested. Are you hopeful that will change?"

"Definitely. Dave will come around when he sees the profits, especially if it costs him a small fortune to get Diana back."

Forcing Dave to spend a large sum of money was the second motive I heard for Joe. "You told me you flirted with Diana at a party and she hasn't spoken to you since. How long ago did that happen?"

"A month or so. It was over at our place. Like I said, I was drunk."

"You must have said something pretty offensive for her to hold a grudge."

Joe answered that question the same way he answered many questions—with a shrug. "I couldn't tell you. I don't remember much about the party, but after that, she stopped talking to me and never did say exactly how I offended her. She can be a prude though, so it wouldn't have taken much. Keep in mind I wasn't one of her favorite people even before the encounter. That just made it worse."

I leaned back to digest the disclosure. My grandma used to say that money didn't bring people happiness. It might be nice to find out on my own, but judging by the Lake Oak group, she was right. Joe rose. "I have to take off, Mattie. Call me if I can help."

"I will, Joe. Do you mind giving me your home phone number? I don't have it." I handed him a business card and my pen and thanked him as he wrote. He might have thought my gratitude was for the phone number. It was for his handwriting sample. "Maybe you will be able to help."

When I heard Joe close the front door, I took the note from my purse to compare it with the writing on the card.

Portsmouth 73049

The writing bore a resemblance to the note, but there wasn't enough to be sure. They made it look so easy in the movies.

I drove to the city and stopped at my office. Sometimes I found it helped just to sit at my desk to feel like a private investigator. Frankie said that clients had to believe you were a professional. I had to believe that, too. After a few minutes of soaking up the dusty, cluttered atmosphere, I took the handwriting samples downstairs to the currency exchange. They have a plain paper copier that gives you a copy for two cents. Years of working with messy, smelly mimeograph machines and fragile carbon paper had made me doubtful that you could make a copy by pressing a button. But there it was. Maybe someday machines *would* run the world.

I put the notes I'd collected on the glass and copied everything onto one sheet. It would be easier to carry that in my purse than all the little scraps. Back in my office, I put the loose samples in a folder in my desk, and when I finished my filing and organized my notes, I realized nothing sounded better than a cold beer.

I told Frankie if I didn't see him at the office, I'd meet him at Benny's at seven. I didn't arrive until seven-thirty and was surprised that Frankie wasn't there, but I wasn't surprised to see that the boilermaker crowd occupied their usual stools.

Between seven and eight every Saturday evening, Benny had a boilermaker special. He sold a shot of whiskey and a glass of beer for fifty cents, and he sold a lot of them. Some of the older guys dropped the shot glass in the beer before drinking the mixture, but most of them downed the shot and washed it back with the beer. My stomach doesn't appreciate that kind of assault and I usually stick with a beer. "Hey, Benny, has Frankie been in?"

"Not yet, Mattie. Do you want a draft?"

"That would be good." I pulled a dollar from my wallet and my notes from my purse. Benny took the bill and left two quarters and a beer in front of me. That's why most of the guys went for the boilermakers. Beer was fifty cents even without the shot.

I'd organized and reorganized my notes and still hadn't made sense of them. Joseph Sumner was aloof, but he had charm. I wondered what his relationship with Sandra was like if he hit on Diana Quigley. Of course, he claimed to be drunk. An invitation in that state had more to do with physical urges than matters of the heart.

Peter Fielding had my attention. I hadn't seen anyone that full of hate in a long time. I wondered if he would have tried to temper it if he had kidnapped Diana Quigley, but that amounted to the same thing Frankie said about Robert. He couldn't suddenly claim to be concerned when everyone knew he hated her. I guessed that most of Fielding's hatred came from his own shortcomings, because I doubted that Diana was responsible for all his problems at the museum.

I had no idea how much time had passed, but I looked up when Benny said my name and handed me the phone. He responded to my raised eyebrows with, "It's for you."

It had to be Frankie, no one else called me at the bar. "What's up, Frankie? Did you get a better offer?" I clutched the phone to keep it from dropping when I heard him say he'd been shot.

Chapter 15

"I'll be right there!" I shouted and shoved the phone at Benny. "I'll be right there!" I said again as I dumped my belongings in my purse. "I'll be right where?" I screamed at the bartender.

"He's at Pres, Mattie, room 302." While I stood there screaming, Benny had the good sense to find out what room Frankie occupied at Presbyterian-St. Luke's Hospital.

"Thanks." I meant the thanks for Benny, but the guy I ran into as I flew out the door he held, smiled, tipped his hat, and said, "You're welcome."

It was lucky for me that the police had their hands full with other matters. I would have been paying for a handful of tickets for my speedy trip to the hospital, and another one for the parking spot I found across the street.

I rode the world's slowest elevator to the third floor and jumped off shouting at the nursing station, "Where's room 302?" I must have looked crazed because they pointed down the hall without saying a word to stop me. Or maybe my jacket flew open and they noticed my gun.

"Frankie!" I gasped at a figure with a bandaged head and a leg cast hoisted in the air.

"I'm over here, Mattie." Frankie's voice came from around a curtain and when I pushed it open, I saw the detective sitting up in bed looking as healthy as ever. "I couldn't have called you if I looked like him." He nodded toward his roommate.

"What happened?" I slid the chair closer to the bed and sat as I took his hand.

"I'm a little embarrassed to tell you."

"What? I've never done anything dumb."

Frankie knew when not to answer a question. "Well, this time it wasn't me that made a dumb move. At least I don't think I did. It's this riot. Things are tense on the streets and everyone is tired. I went to Grant Park to talk to a friend of mine on the force. As we were exchanging pleasantries this kid ran by and oinked. Before I realized it, my buddy had pulled his gun. I stuck my arm out because the kid couldn't have been more than fourteen or fifteen and was definitely unarmed. I don't know what he was thinking, and it surprised us both when the gun hit my arm and went off. Bottom line, he shot me in the foot."

After the few seconds it took for the story to sink in, I tried my hardest not to laugh. My efforts failed. "Frankie, in all your years as a PI have you ever been shot?"

"Nope. First time. Mattie, I'd prefer you didn't tell everyone what happened. I'd still like to be thought of as a hard-nosed PI."

I leaned over and kissed him. "People know you're a hard headed PI. That won't change. What story do you plan to tell about your foot?"

"I believe what I said was hard-nosed. I won't need a story. It's not that bad and I'm fine to go home but because a member of the CPD fired the shot, they won't release me until tomorrow. A department mouthpiece stopped by and said it has something to do with insurance regulations. They're afraid I'll croak. I won't, but I will have to spend a few days at the office until I can drive." He pointed at his right foot. "No gas pedal for a day or two. How's the case going? Did you match the handwriting samples?"

"No. Mrs. Allen said she'd take care of Josh and Kathleen. I tricked Joe into giving me a sample, but I can't tell much."

"Let me see it." I dug through my purse and handed him the page of samples I'd copied. I had added names to each sample, but Frankie wasn't exactly overwhelmed. "It doesn't tell us much, does it? Joe's is similar, but a judge would never issue a warrant on that."

"Frankie, whoever is doing this is putting the screws to Dave. It stinks that he's making him wait this long for the call."

"The kidnapper's in no hurry. I even wondered if he didn't call off the first drop on purpose. He could've guessed the police would have been there and used them as the excuse. That might have been his first attempt to frustrate Dave. The longer he takes, the more desperate it will make Dave and he knows that. That's to your advantage though. That gives you time to find Diana Quigley. And you have to find her, Mattie. No matter who has her, when he gets the money, if she knows him, he'll have to kill her."

"I know, and that scares the hell out of me." Frankie heard by my voice that David Quigley wasn't the only one getting desperate. "Maybe I should tell Dave to hire a more experienced investigator to handle this. I don't want to be responsible for Diana's death."

"Who can he hire? The best PI in the city is flat on his back. He'll have to settle for the second best. Mattie, you're handling things fine. Inside jobs are the toughest to crack. They know everything you're doing. Besides, the Sheriff's Department must be working on some leads."

I wasn't sure about the last comment, but I was ready to talk about something else—anything else. "Hey, where's your car?"

"CPD towed it to my garage space at the apartment since I won't be driving."

That gave me an idea that I hoped the best detective in the city would go for. "Frankie, you won't be running around by yourself for a while. Why don't I pick you up tomorrow when you check out of here? You can take a ride with me to Lake Oak and meet some of the players. That is if you think you'll be able to handle it. I know you. You'll sit in your apartment whining all day."

"You're right about the whining. I chewed out the poor nurse who told me I had to stay overnight. I'll be more than up to it, and you could use my help. But for tonight, there'll be no waltzing Matilda for me." I socked him in the arm for the suggestion that I needed his help, not for the waltzing Matilda line. "Ow! Have a little respect, Draper. I'm an injured detective."

"Who would have thought after getting it shot you'd still be able to put that size eleven foot in your mouth? I'll pick you up tomorrow."

*

It took almost all morning to complete the paperwork required to release Frankie. The city had two lawyers present and a ton of stuff that needed Frankie's and his doctor's signatures. The poor guy who shot him felt awful even though Frankie tried to tell him it could have happened to anyone. He didn't believe it and neither did Frankie. I didn't say anything to either of them, but I was glad he hit Frankie's foot and not the fourteen-year-old kid. I knew Frankie felt the same way.

As we merged onto Lake Shore Drive to head north, Frankie took out a notebook. "Okay, Mattie, here's a piece of good news. Tommy, the officer who shot me, feels bad and promised to do some research for us, aaannnddd…" He stretched the word to a couple of syllables. "He has a connection at the Lake Oak Sheriff's Department. He'll get us the information they have so far."

"Wow! That is good news. I wonder what you could have finagled if he hit you in a vital organ?"

I thought Frankie was going hurt himself he laughed so hard. "Good one, Draper. That was funny. We'd better work on the case before you start thinking you're another Carol Burnett." Frankie was a happy guy and laughed at almost anything, so I didn't take his comment too seriously. When he was back in control, we went to work. "I need my own list of the suspects. Tell me each name and what you think their motive might be."

"Robert Quigley, Dave's brother, he's running out of the money he inherited from his late wife." I waited for him to finish writing. "Josh Spencer, the gardener and stable hand, he might be tired of working. A hundred grand would let him retire. Am I going too fast for you?"

He frowned. "Have you checked his cabin yet?" I shook my head hoping I wasn't going to get a lecture. "You should do that, but the man would have to be pretty stupid to hide her there. He doesn't sound stupid."

"No, he's not, but I am. I should have checked it the first day. He did tell me the police searched it, but since the police won't talk to me to confirm that, all I have is Josh's word."

"Don't beat yourself up. You've been handling a lot, and that would be a dumb place to stash her. We'll see what Tommy manages to find out. Who's next?"

"We have the friendly curator at the Lake Oak Art Museum, Peter Fielding. He doesn't like the amount of control that Diana Quigley has at the museum and thinks she's in the way of advancing his career. From Q & S Design we have Jeffrey Sumner, half owner of the business. Maybe he wants the whole enchilada. Then there is Joseph Sumner,

Jeffrey's son, who has his eyes on taking over his dad's share when he retires. He suggested that Dave might be more willing to discuss his ideas for a new line of furniture after he paid Diana's ransom. Then again, I also heard him tell Robert that he thought Dave might have kidnapped her himself. And that is a possibility, so there is David Quigley."

"You don't have any women suspects."

I had a habit of thinking women wouldn't do certain crimes. I'd seen enough of us behave badly to know that wasn't true. "You're right. Okay, there's Renee Sandburg, Diana's sister who drinks too much and told me she resents Diana and Dave's relationship. Sandra Sumner, Diana's friend and neighbor, who as far as I can figure is a world-class snob, but I haven't found a motive for her. Then there's Kathleen, also without an obvious motive except money. She might be working with Josh and both of them are tired of working for rich folks. Who am I forgetting?"

"Both sets of parents."

"I doubt it, Frankie. How does your foot feel?"

"It's a little uncomfortable, but you forget, Mattie, I'm a Marine. A bullet wound to me is no more than what a mosquito bite is to most people."

Frankie made the mosquito bite comment as we drove into the Q & S Design plant. I didn't remind my recovering friend about what happened when we visited my sister in Kenosha, Wisconsin. He wound up with a few mosquito bites and whined so much you would have thought they were bullet wounds. "Here we are, Detective. I'll drive around back and show you where the fire started."

When I stopped the car and went to help him out, he waved me away. The stubborn Marine pulled himself through the door, took a step on his bad foot, grimaced, and reached in for the cane the hospital gave him. "I'm ready."

I led the way to the back of the plant. "It started here?" he asked. I nodded. "Why do you suppose they chose this spot? What do they do here?" Frankie lifted his cane to point to the charred building.

"That's the gluing room. The epoxies used in there are flammable, so if they were planning to burn down the plant, that might be a good spot to start it. What's interesting is that the call came in almost immediately. Look around, Frankie. There are no houses or buildings of any kind. Who would have seen a fire that had just started at the back of the plant?"

"And I'm guessing that the person who called the fire department didn't leave a name."

"Correct."

"Do you think it's connected to the kidnapping, Mattie?"

"I think it is. I don't know how, exactly, but I think everything that's happening to Dave and Diana Quigley is connected. I just had a thought, Frankie. Chet didn't know they had a separate gluing room. When he left the company, they did the gluing in the main plant."

"He might be in contact with an old coworker."

"Possibly, but I think we should cross the Dowlings off our list. Chet was at work when the fire started."

"He could have paid someone to do it. For right now, Mattie, don't take anyone off."

He was right. If I hadn't had Frankie to keep me in check, I'd have few suspects. "I'm sure you're getting tired, Frankie. Let's go back to the car and finish this discussion."

Once settled in the Chevy, Frankie picked up his list and I offered another female suspect. "You'd better put Diana Quigley on there. She might have done it for the attention. A number of people heard her complain about being lonely because Dave works so much. Maybe that earring did belong to her and whoever is helping with the deception took it from me. If Diana did plan this, she has to be staying somewhere, so someone else could be involved."

"That someone could have started the fire, and Diana could have made the call. The note implies she knew the person she was meeting. When you think about it, if Diana resented the time Dave spent at work, she'd have more reason than most to start a fire." He didn't give me time to suggest that if she did want the fire, she wouldn't have called the Fire Department before he changed the subject. "You said Diana modeled?"

"Yes. She retired eight years ago. From what I understand, she was fairly well known."

"That's an exciting life to leave at twenty-five. It might make it even harder for her to be alone."

"You're right, it might, but rigging up a phony kidnapping is a dramatic way to motivate your husband to pay attention."

"Not too dramatic if the spotlights on the runway in the bedroom have dimmed."

I didn't argue with him, but I didn't agree with him either. "I guess I don't want to believe Diana planned this. Frankie, let's head over to the Quigleys'."

"Before we do that, take me for a quick tour of Lake Oak so I can get an idea of the layout."

I agreed and we left for our first stop—the Lake Oak Art Museum. It wasn't as large a building as many of the other nearby structures, but it was formidable. I wondered what the gallery was like. I had seen only the front area and Fielding's office. "Hey, Frankie, do you think you can hobble for a bit to look at artwork? If not, I can go myself."

"Sure, I'll go in, Mattie. I feel good. What do you think you'll find?"

"I don't know yet," I told him as we left the car. "This Peter Fielding guy is one unhappy curator. Do you remember

Ichabod Crane?" Frankie gave me a strange look. "You know, from *The Legend of Sleepy Hollow*." He didn't know. "His problems all started when he met this wealthy woman and wanted her fortune."

"Is that what you think Fielding wants?"

"I don't think he wants Diana's fortune, but he wants one of his own. It's just a hunch, but keep your eyes open for a smashed pumpkin." Frankie stopped and stared forcing me to explain. "In the story, the horseman throws his head at Ichabod, but all they ever found was a... never mind." I paid the four dollars for both of us, and we walked toward the gallery. I needed to get that story out of my head.

Carol saw us from the reception area and hurried over. I made the introductions. "Hi, Carol. This is Frankie, an investigator and good friend. Frankie, this is Carol."

"Nice to meet you," he told her.

"You too, Frankie. Mattie, whatever you said to Fielding yesterday sent him flying out of here. He stayed gone for the rest of the day, or at least until I went home." She turned and looked down the hall. "He's coming. I'd better get back to my desk." She made it to her chair as he came out of the hall, but when he opened his mouth to talk to her, he noticed Frankie and me.

"What are you doing here?" The look on his face as he stormed toward us ended all hope of removing the Ichabod image from my brain.

"Is this how you welcome all the visitors to your museum? We paid our admission fee and want to explore the gallery." I waved our ticket stubs. "Frankie, this is Peter Fielding. He's curator." Frankie stuck out his hand and Peter shook it, but quickly let it drop. "Mr. Fielding, I heard that Mrs. Quigley was excited about some new paintings you were expecting. Are they on display in the gallery?"

His sour expression didn't change, but his body stiffened. "I don't know what you're talking about, Miss Draper. We have no new paintings. Now if you'll excuse me, I have a meeting." He turned and hurried out the front door.

Carol watched our exchange and shrugged at my quizzical look. I felt Frankie tap me on the shoulder. "What was that about?"

"The day she disappeared, Josh heard Diana tell Vagabond their ride would be short because she'd planned to be here when some new paintings arrived. I wonder why Fielding doesn't know anything, or if he does, why he won't admit it."

"Maybe he kidnapped her, not to collect the ransom, but to get her out of the museum. If she's out of the way, he can make the decisions. These paintings could have been her idea and he decided he'd had it with her. He gets rid of her and the artwork at the same time."

"I hope you're wrong about that, Frankie. If you have it right and he didn't take her for the ransom, the chances are good he's killed her." Frankie's face said he knew that was a possibility.

We approached Carol's desk. "Carol, what meeting did Fielding have scheduled today?"

"He doesn't have anything marked."

"Huh, that's interesting. Do you know about any new paintings?"

"I thought there were supposed to be four delivered last Monday, but I never heard if they arrived. I work Tuesday through Saturday. Do you want me to check into it, since you scared Mr. Fielding away again?" She was enjoying her boss's discomfort.

"That's a good idea. Thanks. Also, do you have a sample of his handwriting?"

"Sure." She dug in a drawer for a few minutes and pulled out a note. "Here. Will this help?"

The slip of paper I took from her hand didn't say much, but I could see similarities to the note. "This could help. I'll be in touch. Give me a call if anything interesting happens. Do you still have my card?" She waved it in the air. "If you need to contact me during the day, call the Quigley estate. Do you have their number?" With her nod, Frankie and I left for a tour of the gallery.

I liked what I saw, and if Diana had a part in the selection, she had great taste. I wondered what kind of paintings Peter Fielding wanted to hang. As we returned to the car, I was considering the possibility that Fielding had kidnapped Diana. "There's a chance he took her, isn't there?"

"There is, especially since as soon as you asked him about those paintings he looked like he'd been shot with the freeze gun of Flash Gordon's bitter enemy Captain Cold."

"You read *Flash Gordon* comic books, Frankie?"

"Nah. I just remember that from when I was a kid."

Chapter 16

My astonishment at there being usually only two residents inhabiting the enormous Sandburg Estate returned as Frankie and I pulled up outside the gate. I stared at the massive structure while filling him in on its owners. "According to Rachel, the Sandburgs are old money and not crazy about their daughter's working class in-laws. People are funny, aren't they, Frankie? Everyone has about the same number of bones, muscles, teeth, and eyeballs, but a person with money is supposed to be better."

"People use all sorts of things to make themselves feel like they're better than someone else—money, race, religion, and if those don't work, they use muscle. None of it matters much once they start shoveling dirt over your pine box." He tossed an imaginary shovelful into the floorboard. "Hey, didn't you say that Diana's sister, Renee, was jealous of Diana and Dave's relationship?"

"That's what she told me. Keep in mind, Renee might have been in fantasyland after her fourth or fifth drink. Except for jealousy, there isn't a strong motive, but if she had a reason, she wouldn't have had to overpower Diana. Renee might have met her in the woods and the two of them walked to where she had a car waiting and she smacked Diana over the head."

"Jealousy can be a pretty strong motive. People kill for less. Do you know if Diana left anything for Renee in her will?"

"No, Dave told me their estates go to each other if one of them dies. I haven't seen the agreements, but since it sounds bad for Dave, I can't imagine he'd have made it up."

"You're right that it sounds bad for him. Even worse if there's truth to the rumor that the company is in trouble. Have you heard anything more about that?" Frankie asked.

"No, just what I heard Joe tell Robert. That and the anonymous tip to the Trib. Dave said he and Jeffery both invest a little every now and then, but they had never over extended themselves. He said that's just bad business. Since managing money is not exactly my strong suit, I wasn't going to argue."

"This is when it's hard to be a PI. The cops can subpoena company records and figure out if someone's lying. We have to keep watching our suspects until they make a mistake. I wonder if the sheriff subpoenaed Q & S records."

"I thought you were going to see what you could find out."

"I was, Mattie, but I got a little sidetracked."

"Doing what?"

He pointed at his foot.

"Oh. Right. Sorry, Frankie. Let's take a look at the Sumners' place and then head over to see Dave."

Although Joseph and Sandra Sumner's home was big enough to house all the folks in my apartment building, after seeing the Sandburg estate, Frankie wasn't impressed. By the time we arrived at the Quigleys, we'd both had enough of suburban architecture. "Why do you think people need so much room, Frankie?"

"They might think all that extra space protects them."

"From what?"

"The usual stuff—crime, sickness, death."

As I pulled close to the front door so Frankie didn't have too far to hobble, I thought about why he and I were there. "It really doesn't, does it?"

"Nope."

My brain had enough to work on without worrying about being safe in a crazy world. "I keep wondering who has the most to gain by Diana's kidnapping."

"That's what you should be wondering. Who do you think it is?"

"If the rumors are true, David Quigley has the most to gain, not by Diana's kidnapping, but by her death." I let my thoughts continue in that direction. "He could have easily come home from work and met her in the woods. Maybe they were playing a game of some kind to add spice to their relationship. You know, a secret rendezvous. Experts tell couples they should do stuff like that to put the spark back in their marriage."

"Is there any reason in particular you've been reading about spicing up relationships, Mattie?"

I ignored him and went on. "The note could have been part of a game. He tells her not to tell anyone at the house about the meeting and when she arrives in the clearing, he kidnaps and then kills her."

"You said that wasn't Dave's handwriting on the note, but if they did set up a romantic rendezvous, it could have been Diana's, although I still think a guy wrote it."

"Mrs. Allen said it wasn't Diana's writing." I stopped my runaway brain train of ideas. "This is way too far out. I can't see Dave and Diana needing to have a secret meeting. Diana's only complaint was that he worked too much."

"Anything's possible, but I agree about it being a stretch. Could the person you talked to on the phone have been David Quigley?"

"I couldn't tell. The voice sounded strange, like the caller wanted to disguise it. Can you call your own phone from your house? I know Dave was there."

"You can if you have more than one phone line."

"I answered the phone, but I don't remember if there was anything special about it."

Why don't we check that first?" Frankie said while I knocked on the front door.

Mrs. Allen pulled it open. "Hi Mrs. Allen, this is my friend and fellow investigator, Frankie Ficaro. Frankie, Mrs. Allen." After exchanging greetings, Frankie and I headed toward the dining room. When we passed the hall phone, I pointed it out to Frankie. It had multiple buttons. The Quigleys had more than one phone line.

We found Dave in the dining room and I introduced him and Frankie before removing myself. "If you don't mind, Dave, I need to use your phone to call art museum board members. One of them might know more about Peter Fielding and the paintings." Dave nodded and I left them, glad that Frankie was there. He was a good person to talk to when you're feeling low. He was for me.

Armed with Mrs. Allen's list of board members, I went to the phone in the living room. It was a much nicer space without Rob and Joe. The first person I called was a Mrs. Lawrence Kendall. A young-sounding female answered on the third ring and put me on hold to inform Mrs. Kendall. A short time later, Mrs. Kendall picked up. "How can I help you, Miss Draper? Diana Quigley is a wonderful woman. I was stunned to hear about the kidnapping. Has there been any news."

"Nothing yet, I'm afraid. Mrs. Kendall, do you know anything about the paintings that Diana expected at the museum on Monday?"

"I know they are a great addition to our collection. I'm afraid I can't tell you who the artists are, if that's what you mean."

"No, that's not it. I talked to the curator and he expressed less than charitable feelings for Mrs. Quigley and her taste in art. He also told me there weren't any new paintings. I guess I'm wondering if he might be involved in her kidnapping." I heard Mrs. Kendall gasp. "Is there anything you can tell me about him that would help me prove or disprove that theory?"

"I'm sorry, my dear. I don't know anything that can be of help, but you should talk to Helena, Helena Hayworth. She often worked with Diana on selecting the pieces and has had a few run-ins with Mr. Fielding. Do you have her number?"

I scanned the list and saw a Mrs. Rutherford Hayworth. "Yes, I do." I wasn't sure whether I should ask someone in Mrs. Kendall's class for help, but I figured I had nothing to lose. "Mrs. Kendall, it would be useful to me and Mr. Quigley if you could talk with other board members and see if they have any information while I give Mrs. Hayworth a call." I prepared myself in case I was out of line and she slammed the phone in my ear.

"I'd be happy to do that, Miss Draper. Can we reach you at Dave and Diana's house?"

"Yes, that would be great. Thank you." I dialed the number for Mrs. Rutherford Hayworth and it surprised me that she answered herself. And when I told her the reason for my call, she offered to do whatever she could. I considered that it might be time for me to revise my opinion of "the haves."

Mrs. Hayworth said there were four paintings scheduled to arrive at the museum last Monday. She described them in detail and volunteered to drive me there and point them out.

I agreed to go, but Frankie decided to stay at the house. I had a feeling he enjoyed lounging around the Quigley estate. His apartment was not much bigger than mine.

A white Lincoln appeared in the drive with Mrs. Hayworth at the wheel. Minutes later she and I wound through the small village to the museum. She told me to call her Helena and made her opinion of the skinny curator quite clear. I followed her into the museum where we didn't have to pay to enter. I guessed that was because of Helena and not me. As she stopped to talk to the person at the ticket counter, I wandered over to Carol's desk. "Did Peter come back?"

"No, and he hasn't called or anything. What's going on, Mattie?" she asked, but didn't take her eyes off the approaching Mrs. Hayworth.

"We want to find the paintings Diana said were going to arrive last Monday. Mrs. Hayworth said she'd recognize them."

Helena and I went to the gallery where I watched her spin on her heels looking for the paintings. "They're not here!" she shouted. "I don't understand. He promised to have them framed and hung by Thursday. Where is that little pipsqueak?"

I loved the description of Fielding, and refrained from mentioning Ichabod Crane as I followed her trail of smoke through the gallery and past Carol's desk. We stomped down the hall to Fielding's office, but as Carol said, he wasn't there. We stomped back. "You tell Fielding to call me as soon as he shows up. That man will be a curator in hell before he ever works in this state again!" Helena stormed out the door. I followed close behind, asking Carol over my shoulder to call me when and if Peter showed up.

Helena had calmed considerably by the time she dropped me off at the Quigley estate. I promised I'd let her know when I heard anything. I also suggested that she not meet with Peter Fielding alone. I didn't trust the guy. She agreed, but not easily. I was sure she could have out wrestled him, but he might have a weapon.

After filling Dave and Frankie in on what happened, I told Frankie he needed to go home and rest. The gunshot wasn't serious, but it was a gunshot, and the human body, even one belonging to a Marine, was not designed to serve as a target. "What do you plan to do next, Mattie?" he asked after climbing out of my car in front of his apartment. I joined him on the sidewalk.

"The first thing is to see what I can find out about Peter Fielding." I almost smiled when he pulled his mouth to the side. A warning was forthcoming.

"I don't need to tell you to be careful, do I?"

"You don't need to, but you could anyway, so I know you still care." I kissed him on the cheek. "I'll talk to you later."

I closed the door to my apartment, removed my shoes, and wiggled my weary toes with joy. Before Sebastian and I made it to the kitchen, I answered the ringing telephone. I figured it was Frankie giving me another warning, but it wasn't. "Mattie, it's Carol at the art museum. You told me to call if anything came up. I was on my way home from dinner and remembered that I'd left the book I've been reading at my desk. When I came in the front door I heard noises, but there were no lights on."

"Was it a robber?"

"That's what I thought at first. The noise was coming from the back so I went into the bathroom where a big window looks out to the alley behind the museum. I saw Fielding loading paintings into the trunk of his car."

"Doesn't he usually do that?" I asked because I didn't have a clue.

"No, I've never seen him take paintings out. Besides that, paintings are in crates when they come to the museum to protect them from damage. These weren't crated. I couldn't see much, but I saw him throw at least four unprotected canvases in his trunk. He took off in a hurry. Do you think those were the missing paintings?"

"I'd have no way of knowing, but Peter Fielding is definitely up to no good." It wasn't necessarily about the abduction, but he was up to something. "Does he live in Lake Oak?"

"Yes. Do you want his address?"

I took his address and thanked her for calling. "Okay toes, back in the torture chambers you go," I groaned as I slipped into my shoes. With no time for games, I took the cat food and opener into the bathroom to open it, and after giving Sebastian a bowl of food and a kiss, I headed out the door. "I'll be home soon," I promised.

I had considered calling Frankie to tell him I was off to visit Fielding, but knew he'd want to come along. He'd been on that foot too many hours and I decided to call him when I returned. I did however check my weapon. It wasn't as good company as Frankie, but it was protection.

The address Carol gave me was easy to find. The houses in his neighborhood weren't as big as the estates, but they were big—two and three story English stone and cedar buildings. I still couldn't believe how much room people needed. Frankie might be right about wanting to feel safe. The front doors were imposing, heavy wooden slabs with a tiny window, or no window at all. They all had spacious yards with large old trees and manicured bushes and lawns. In fact, the entire block was neat and tidy. I began to understand the tradeoffs of city living. The trash around my apartment wasn't pretty, but it reminded me that I wasn't alone, and it also reminded me that the world wasn't perfect.

With no lights visible in the front of Fielding's house, I crept down a gravel driveway along the side. At the back, I peered through a small garage window and saw Fielding shaking out a blanket. He was about to cover paintings stacked on the floor in the back seat of his car. I walked to the opened garage door and looked in, but he'd disappeared. In seconds, I felt an arm around my neck.

Fielding wasn't strong. Between the self-defense classes I'd taken and growing up fighting with my brother and sisters, I could easily overpower him. Our exchange started at the front of the garage where I noticed, as he pushed me against it, that the hood of his car was warm.

I made my body limp and when he thought I'd surrendered and relaxed, I grabbed his arm and twisted. We did a slow shuffle to the rear of the garage where I spun him, pulled his arm behind his back, and pushed upward until he yelled. "Ow! You bitch! Let me go!"

"What are you doing with those paintings, Fielding? Are those the ones Diana selected for the gallery?"

"That's none of your business. Let me go. I'm going to sue you. I'm going to…"

His voice was really irritating. "Where's Diana?"

Before he could answer, if he planned to, someone shouted from the door. "Put your hands on top of the car. Now!"

Chapter 17

I recognized Sheriff Brown's crusty voice and released Fielding to put my hands on the car. Fielding, however, turned and started shouting. "This insane woman attacked me. I demand you arrest her."

While his ranting occupied the sheriff, I saw that he hadn't had time to cover the paintings. I wondered if there were more and moved slowly to look in the open trunk. There were no paintings, but I caught sight of something shiny. With nothing to lose I grabbed it and dropped it in my jacket pocket. It looked like a necklace.

"Hey, get up here and put your hands where I can see them!"

I moved forward with my hands in the air and faced the sheriff. "Peter Fielding stole these paintings from the art museum and he might be involved in Mrs. Quigley's kidnapping."

The sheriff recognized me and smirked. "Ah, you're Draper, the female PI from Chicago. Do you really think you're going to find Mrs. Quigley alive? Or maybe you're milking David Quigley for what you can get. It would be my guess, Miss Draper, that since Mr. Fielding is the curator of the museum, it's perfectly fine for him to take paintings. It isn't, however, fine for you to attack him. I don't know what they call that in Chicago, but here in our little village, we call it assault. What does he have to do with Quigley?"

"Those are paintings Mrs. Quigley selected for the gallery and he didn't want them there. He told me that Diana Quigley is making his life miserable. If you don't believe me, Sheriff, ask Mrs. Hayworth. She can identify the paintings and tell you about his relationship with Diana."

That stopped him. "Mrs. Rutherford Hayworth?" When I said yes, his smirk returned. "Is that a fact, Miss Draper? Well, I don't suppose you have a number where we can reach Mrs. Hayworth, do you?"

"Yes I do, Sheriff, in my car. I went to the museum with her earlier because she wanted to make sure Fielding had framed and hung these paintings. When she saw they weren't there, she tried to find Fielding to have him explain why. I'd say this explains it." I kept my hands raised but pointed at the back seat and turned to Peter. "Did you return Mrs. Hayworth's call?" Fielding didn't answer and the sheriff looked less than happy. His squad car was parked right behind the garage. He used his radio to call one of his deputies and ten minutes later, the deputy took Fielding and the paintings in his car and the sheriff took me.

On the way to the station, we stopped at the Chevy for my purse. When we arrived, I sat at a table in their interrogation room—a five by five cubicle with the table and two chairs. The sheriff put a phone in front of me and reapplied his sneer. "Call Mrs. Hayworth." I could tell he thought I was bluffing. I took the list from my purse and picked up the phone. Dialing was not easy in handcuffs. While I waited for her to answer, I studied the list, which I'd managed to lay flat while making the call. My first little bit of pleasure since I encountered the sheriff was the grimace he made when he saw whose phone numbers I had.

Mrs. Hayworth answered. "Hello, Helena. It's Mattie." The sheriff's discomfort increased when I called her by her first name. I explained the situation and when I'd finished, expressed my irritation at the cuffs by clumsily replacing the handset. "She's on her way." I told him. It took every bit of professional training, plus biting the inside of my mouth, not to stick out my tongue.

"She's coming here?" He ran a hand over the back of his clean-shaven neck and took off his Stetson as he slumped into the chair. "Oh, shit."

"Don't you want to ask Mr. Fielding if he knows where Mrs. Quigley is?"

"Don't tell me how to do my job, Draper. Even shorthanded we'll have this solved before you. Then you'll see that women aren't cut out for this work."

"Sheriff, I would be absolutely delighted if you found Mrs. Quigley before me. Whether you like it or not, we're on the same side."

While we waited for Mrs. Hayworth, I mentally thumbed through my notes until I found the phone conversation with Carol. She told me that when she looked from the bathroom window to the alley, she saw Peter Fielding loading paintings into his car. When I arrived at his house more than an hour later, he still hadn't removed them. He'd left the museum earlier, but I knew because of the warm engine, he'd only recently returned home. Of course, he could have stopped for dinner.

Then I remembered that Carol said he put the paintings in his trunk. When I saw them, they were in the back seat. Why would he move them from the trunk to the back seat? I tapped my stubby nails on the table until the sheriff gave me a dirty look. The answer popped into my brain. He had to make room to put something in the trunk. Something that wouldn't fit in the back seat or that he didn't want seen. I wondered if that was Diana's necklace in my pocket.

I heard Mrs. Hayworth's voice and watched the sheriff jump to his feet and hurry out to the office. "Mrs. Hayworth, please sit down."

She ignored his invitation. "Have you asked Fielding if he kidnapped Diana Quigley?" Her tone was not nearly as polite as mine had been. I couldn't see from the little room, but I could hear well enough. The sheriff asked Fielding what he knew about Mrs. Quigley's disappearance.

"I don't know anything about what happened to Diana Quigley. That woman in there is crazy and you should lock her away for good. Now, Sheriff, I'd like to go home."

"Be quiet, Fielding. You're not going anywhere," Mrs. Hayworth said. "Sheriff, where is Miss Draper, and where are the paintings?"

The deputy brought me from the room and when Helena faced the sheriff her face had a red glow. "Why is she wearing handcuffs, when he," she pointed at Fielding, "is sitting there like a guest?"

While the sheriff removed my handcuffs, the deputy brought in the paintings that Fielding had in his car. Mrs. Hayworth was so enraged when she saw them she shook. "Not only did you remove these without authorization, but you removed them without protection. Mr. Fielding, I repeat what the sheriff asked. What do you know about Diana Quigley's abduction?"

Fielding turned to the sheriff for help and saw immediately that he was on his own. "For your information, Mrs. Hayworth, I didn't see any reason to put time and energy into crating junk."

I assumed that was his tasteful way of turning in his resignation. Mrs. Hayworth allowed her outrage to escalate. She wanted an answer. "I asked you a question young man. Did you kidnap Diana Quigley?"

The hate in his eyes would have wilted a lesser person, but Helena didn't blink. "No, I didn't kidnap her. I heard about the kidnapping right before the paintings came. I decided since Diana Quigley was out of the picture, I'd find a buyer and acquire works of art that would give me the reputation I deserve."

I'd been leaning quietly on a desk, but when I heard his remark, I stood. "I don't know what reputation you hoped to achieve, Fielding, but what you are right now is an art thief and kidnapping suspect." I turned to the sheriff. "Do you plan to question him about the kidnapping, or take his word that he didn't do it?"

The sheriff ignored me but told his deputy to put the sputtering Fielding in a cell. He told Mrs. Hayworth that he'd question him and inform her of the outcome. He also asked if she wanted to press charges against Fielding for taking the paintings without authorization. I could see that what she wanted was to hang the curator and possibly the sheriff, but instead, she asked to use his phone. When she finished, she told him the board would meet in the morning and she would contact him as soon as they'd voted to press charges.

I wasn't sure what the sheriff had planned for me, besides ignoring me completely. I asked Helena for a ride to my car if the sheriff had no further questions. She agreed, wearing a look that defied him to hold me. When he didn't argue, we left.

"Do you think Fielding kidnapped Diana, Mattie?"

"He certainly has enough anger, but I'm not sure he has enough strength. He tried to grab me when I went to talk to him, and I broke loose easily. I doubt he is strong enough to have kidnapped her alone, but I do believe he's somehow involved." I told her that he'd moved the paintings from the trunk to the back seat and lifted the necklace from my pocket. It had a white gold chain with a single diamond in a simple delicate setting. "I found this in the trunk. Have you ever seen Diana wear it?"

"I'm not sure. It does look familiar. You decided against giving it to the sheriff?" I told her I did and crossed my fingers as I waited for her response. "Good thinking."

"How long has Sheriff Brown been in office?"

"About eight years I believe, and I can imagine what you're thinking, Mattie. How? I wish I knew. Maybe I should investigate him on my own. A few years back there were rumors about him taking bribes, but I never heard any more about it. Forgetting the sheriff for a minute, if that necklace does belong to Diana, what do you think Fielding has done with her?"

"He probably had her at his house until Frankie and I paid him a visit at the museum. We may have scared him and he moved her. Maybe the sheriff will be able to get more out of him." She turned, wearing a rather doubtful frown and I considered my words. "What was I thinking?"

When she dropped me at my car, I thanked her and promised to keep her posted on my progress. I sincerely hoped I'd have progress to report. Helena had told me during the ride that the board planned to meet early the next morning to consider pressing charges against Fielding. She added with a twinkle in her eye that the vote would be unanimous. She also said she planned to have the paintings framed and hung in the gallery so Diana could see them where they belonged when she returned home. People really did like Diana Quigley.

I reached my apartment a short time after midnight, exhausted, but conscious enough to know I'd better call Frankie. "Hi, did I wake you?"

"Nah. I went to sleep right after you dropped me off. I'll probably be awake for the rest of the night. Where were you? I called earlier."

I told him about my confrontation with Peter Fielding and the sheriff, and described the necklace. "I think Fielding moved the paintings from the trunk to the back seat in order to take Diana to a new location." After I filled him in on all the details of my adventure, I added that I was glad I became an investigator.

"Why do you say that, Mattie?"

"Driving home tonight I realized that I'd rather end up dying doing something that mattered, than living a long safe life."

"I knew you'd be a good investigator, Matilda Draper. I'm glad you feel good about what you're doing. Just remember that I'd rather you kept yourself alive while you were doing it, okay?"

"I'll do my best, Mr. Ficaro," I promised him. "I'll do my very best."

I went to bed and fell right to sleep. My body recognized that I'd need all the strength I could muster. Before Sebastian and I dozed off, I informed him that my first stop in the morning would be a visit to the Lake Oak Sheriff's Department. We were both sure that Sheriff Brown would be delighted to see me.

*

Frankie never did get to sleep and called me first thing in the morning. I think he and Sebastian had talked because he called only minutes after the stout kitty's wake up romp. I dragged myself to the parlor to answer the phone and hoped I sounded more awake than I felt. "This is Mattie Draper."

"Mattie, it's me," Frankie said. "I'm bored. Do you need a slightly wobbly assistant today?"

"Sure, Frankie. I plan to go to the sheriff's office as soon as I shower and dress. I'll pick you up on the way. How's that sound?"

"Great. I'll be waiting on the stoop. I gotta get out of this apartment." The poor guy was used to being on the move. If he woke during the night and wanted to work on a case, he jumped in the car and worked on the case. Not being able to drive made him crazy.

The entire trip north, we debated the best way to talk to the sheriff. I didn't like the man any more than he liked me, but he had a big advantage, he could put me in jail. When we arrived at the station, I asked Frankie to wait in the car. If the sheriff did or said something dumb, Frankie might, in my defense, do or say something dumber. He agreed quickly. That told me he felt the same way.

The sheriff's face didn't light up when he saw who opened the door, but I ignored him and stared at the empty cell. "Why did you release Fielding?"

"Not that it's your business, but I had no reason to hold him."

"You may not think he's a suspect in the kidnapping, but you know damn well Mrs. Hayworth and the board are pressing charges."

"They haven't yet, and there was no reason to hold him. He's an upstanding member of the community, which, may I add, you are not. Is there anything else?"

"Did you tell him to stay in town?" He told me no and wore that nasty sneer I'd grown extremely tired of seeing. "This is only a suggestion, Sheriff, but if you should ever find Fielding or his car again, you may want to check his trunk for evidence that he had Mrs. Quigley in there. I'm sure he had her at his house and moved her after I showed up at the museum."

"Well, I'll certainly take that under advisement, little lady."

He had a real problem and I had more important things to do than bringing him into the twentieth century. "Sheriff, when this is over, you might be sorry you didn't listen."

"I doubt that, Miss Draper."

I heard the door open and saw him stiffen. "Hello, Mrs. Hayworth," he stammered.

"He released Peter Fielding," I informed her with way too much enthusiasm. The response made its way from a less developed part of the teenage Matilda Draper brain—a part that felt a sense of satisfaction when someone other than she faced an angry authority figure. I knew that because of the excited *na-na-na-na-na-na* sounding in my head.

Mrs. Hayworth glared at the sheriff. "You oaf. Bring him in this minute. We're pressing charges." She and I took a seat while the sheriff ordered a deputy to pick up Peter Fielding. Helena was upset but hopeful that the deputy would bring him in and we'd find Diana. We heard through the crackling radio that they'd found no sign of Peter or his car. His house was unlocked and the back door open, but the deputy said it didn't look cleared out.

If it hadn't been such a serious matter I might have enjoyed staying to watch the sheriff's discomfort. There wasn't time to gloat. I suppose there never really is. I left Helena to handle the sheriff because, judging by her face, she had quite a bit to say to the inept lawman. Frankie and I headed for the Quigley estate.

"How did it go?"

"He released Fielding."

"Geez, the guy is a real goofball. Did he get his badge from a box of Cracker Jacks?"

I wanted to laugh, but all I could manage was a sigh. "He might have, Frankie. He might have."

Chapter 18

As we pulled into the Quigley drive, I remembered I'd promised to let Carol know what happened. When Mrs. Allen opened the door, I abandoned Frankie to use the phone in the hall. Noticing its multiple buttons, I wondered again if Dave had anything to do with Diana's disappearance.

Carol had been waiting for my call.

"Mattie, what happened? When I came in this morning I saw that Mr. Fielding's office had been cleared out."

"They released him from jail. If his office is empty, they must have let him go after Mrs. Hayworth and I left last night."

"Jail! Did he kidnap Mrs. Quigley?"

"The sheriff doesn't think he did, but so far, he and I haven't seen eye to eye on anything." I told her the paintings she'd seen Fielding removing were the ones Diana had chosen. I also told her that, as she probably guessed, he was no longer curator. Since he'd cleared out his desk, he knew that too.

"I think he kidnapped Diana, but doubt he could have done it by himself. I need you to think about people he's met or spoken with in the last few weeks. One of them might be in on the kidnapping."

As I asked her to think about that, I realized that if Fielding put Diana in the trunk, he'd have needed help, even if it were Diana that helped him. He could have given her drugs that kept her too stoned to fight but left her lucid enough to stumble to the car and climb in the trunk, no doubt at the point of a knife or nose of a gun.

Carol's voice brought me back to the present. "I will, Mattie. I'll do whatever I can to help."

"I figured I could count on you. I'll call if we hear anything. In the meantime, think about the people he's been meeting. Talk to the woman who works Sunday and Monday. She might have seen something." When we said goodbye, I called Peter Fielding's home phone. As I expected, he didn't answer. The sheriff probably hadn't told him to stick around, and even if he had, I didn't think we'd see him again. I had to find out from Dave if it was Diana's necklace burning a hole in my pocket.

Dave and Frankie sat in the dining room. I wasn't surprised to find that Frankie had convinced him there was hope. "Hi, Dave. How are you doing?"

"All right, Mattie. Frankie told me about this Peter Fielding guy at the museum. Do you think he could have kidnapped Diana?"

"He's interested in making a name for himself as a curator and believes Diana is in his way. I think he's involved." I pulled out a chair and joined them as I drew the necklace from my pocket. "Dave, have you ever seen this?" I laid it in his hand.

"It's familiar. I think it might be Diana's. Where did you find it?"

"In the trunk of Fielding's car."

Dave turned white. Without a word, he stood and left the room with the necklace.

"What do you think, Mattie?" Frankie asked.

"He went to see if Mrs. Allen can confirm that it belongs to Diana." No sooner had I said that when we heard Mrs. Allen let out a cry in the kitchen. Dave returned clutching the necklace.

"Where is Fielding?" His hand trembled.

"I called his house, he's not there, or not answering. His secretary at the museum told me he cleared out his office."

Dave held the necklace against the side of his face and Frankie reached over and squeezed his arm. "Dave, I know it doesn't seem like it right now, but this is good news. This is the first physical evidence we've had that Diana is alive. If she weren't, this guy wouldn't have had her in his house and had to move her. He's scared, and that's going to help us get Diana back. Don't give up."

I saw Dave sorting things out in his head. I also saw that Frankie made him feel better, at least a little. I hoped he was right about finding Diana. "Dave, I'm convinced that someone is working with Fielding and it makes sense that it's someone close to you. I know you don't want to, but right now, we have to assume that's true. Let's bring everyone we think is suspect, or anyone we think can help, to the house tonight and see what we can learn. If that's okay with you, I'll start calling. You should too."

"I can't have a party with Diana missing."

"Not a party, Dave. It'll be more like a meeting. We want to hear their thoughts about what we might be missing. Besides, someone knows what's going on, and we have to find out who that is. They won't tell us outright, but we can make them nervous. That might force a mistake."

Dave agreed and I brought out my list of names and numbers. With the two phone lines we were able to call everyone in a short time. I contacted Rachel last. She said she'd be delighted to come "I need you to keep your eyes and ears on people for me. I want you to watch for unusual behavior while you mingle. It's more of a job than a visit, but it might be interesting and it would certainly be helpful."

"Sounds good to me, Mattie. I know you've guessed what a good information gatherer I am. You've just had the good sense not to call it gossip. I'll see you tonight." As I hung up, Mrs. Allen came in.

"Mr. Quigley said that everyone he called will be here this evening, Miss Draper. Will you and Frankie be joining us?"

Her blue eyes glistened when she asked, and I realized that in the short time he'd known her, Frankie managed to win her heart. Even a woman in her sixties couldn't resist the detective's charms. "Mrs. Allen, if you can call him Frankie, then I insist you call me Mattie."

"Very well, Mattie, and I will insist that you call me Anna, please."

"I'd be honored. Yes, Frankie and I need to run home and change and we'll be back by seven."

That made her smile. "I wanted also to tell you that I talked with a few of the housekeepers and maids. No one heard or saw anything suspicious, but they all promised to call people that I don't know and then they will call me."

"Good work, Anna. Who's helping you this evening?"

"Kathleen will be here and Josh will help. This will be good for Mr. Quigley. He needs to be with other people and Frankie is good company for him."

"Anna, Frankie is good company for everyone." Her white curls shook in enthusiastic agreement.

As Frankie and I headed to the city to clean up for the gathering, I considered my closet. It wasn't a pleasant task. "I'd sure like to look professional when I'm talking to this group." I figured that fell on deaf ears because Frankie rarely thought about his wardrobe. I was wrong.

"You said last week that you wanted to buy a few of those pantsuits ladies are wearing, Mattie. Can't we pick one up on the way home?"

"I won't be expanding my wardrobe until I solve this case." I depressed myself further continuing the mental scan of my sparsely populated closet.

Frankie didn't give up. "I have an idea. I can buy you an outfit today, and you can pay me when you solve the case."

"You're assuming that I'll bring Mrs. Quigley home alive."

First he scared the hell out of me by slapping the dashboard, and then he spoke loudly and with rare impatience. "Listen, Draper. How can you solve the case if you don't believe you can solve the case? Stop talking that way and borrow the damn money to buy a pantsuit."

I glanced toward the passenger's seat. My usually calm and collected friend and mentor looked angry. "Okay, Frankie. I'll borrow the damn money for a pantsuit, and work on this case knowing I can solve it. How's your foot?"

Frankie was about to say something, but lowered his raised eyebrow and let me change the subject without an argument. "Good enough to travel without the cane this evening."

"Why don't you bring it along just in case and you can leave it in the car if you don't need it."

"Hey, that Sears store might have a pantsuit." I pulled into the parking lot where he pointed and realized it was Frankie's turn to change the subject. He wouldn't be bringing the cane tonight.

We went right to the women's department and in a few short minutes I found a nice looking beige pantsuit. I wore a perfect size twelve and didn't have trouble buying things off the rack. When I came out of the dressing room to see what Frankie thought, he whistled. Every woman in the area turned to look, first at him, and then at me. Frankie never cared what people thought and I hoped to learn to be the same way. I put a hand on my hip, swung it to the side, and threw him a kiss. He loved it and the women went back to minding their own business.

Fifteen minutes later I stood in the shower, using the time to evaluate the soundness of my theories and the stream of hot water to soften a few brick hard muscles. I felt relaxed and renewed as I climbed into my new clothes. The blouse I chose was one Mary Ann had given me for my birthday a few years back. It was a rose-colored silk, tailored like the pantsuit. I had a pair of beige open toed pumps that matched perfectly, and a handbag that went with the shoes. When I stood in front of the mirror, I liked what I saw. The new clothes gave me confidence. Frankie would have said it shouldn't matter, but, to me, it did.

He was waiting outside his apartment when I drove up, wearing navy slacks, a light blue jacket, and no cane. It amazed me that he could find things to fit across those shoulders. The jacket fit great and looked even better. We whistled at each other when he settled in the passenger's seat, I said, "You look prettier than me."

"You're right, Draper, but not by much." He gave me the once over, winked, and pulled a notebook from his pocket. It never bothered me when Frankie eyeballed me. I guess that's something only a close friend or family member should try, and even then, not all of them. "Okay, Mattie, let's go over the guest list for this shindig."

"We're expecting all the suspects on our list except Chet and Linda Dowling, and of course, the missing curator. Chet couldn't take off work on such short notice. He did tell me something interesting on the phone. After my visit, he talked to a friend who still works at the furniture factory. Do you remember I told you that one of the plant employees said they were having a number of accidents? Chet's friend mentioned them, and told him they were on the increase and getting pretty strange."

"What did he mean by strange?"

"There were machine parts coming loose that shouldn't, and tools going missing. Chet wouldn't tell me who told him, but he's been with the company since they opened. He said they've had more accidents in the last six months than they've had in all the time he's been there. They didn't report them all to Dave and Jeffrey. They told them about the ones that affected production, but they took care of the others amongst the workers. They're afraid for their jobs and they don't want the place shut down."

"That makes sense. Mattie, can your friend Rachel get you a list of new employees? People that started in the last year."

"I'm sure she can. I think we can trust her, and I'm glad, because we can't even trust Jeffrey Sumner at this point. I'll ask her to do it on the sly."

"That's a good idea. Speaking of the Sumner family, my friend from the airlines couldn't find a Sandra Sumner on a flight from Chicago to New York on the twenty-sixth. He checked the twenty-fifth to be sure and nada."

"I suppose she could have flown to another city first and then on to New York, or even flown under a different name. I'll have to ask her tonight. I wonder if Peter Fielding is still in town. The sheriff could have told him to beat it." Too many leads were going nowhere. We were running out of time and I felt frustrated. "It'll be a week tomorrow that someone took Diana, Frankie. We have to find her."

"Do you want to swing by Fielding's place and check it out before we go to the house?" Frankie asked.

"Not tonight. I want to see what we learn from this gathering. If it is Fielding, he has a partner and it could be one of our guests. I asked Carol to make a list of people Fielding met with at the museum. That might help. Rachel is coming tonight to be an extra pair of eyes, and Josh will be helping Mrs. Allen serve beverages and stuff. He'll keep his eyes and ears open too." I wondered if he'd dress for the event. With the Sandburgs present, he might. "I'll bet he looks good in a monkey suit." I said it without thinking. When I saw Frankie's slightly unhappy face, I realized I should have kept the thought to myself. "Just an innocent comment, Ficaro. He's too young for me."

"He's only two years younger."

"Those are important years." Frankie didn't look convinced, but he knew I wasn't going anywhere. "Well, we're all dressed up with someplace to go. Are you ready for what should be an interesting evening?"

"I am. Are you?"

"I'd mingle with Lyndon and Ladybird if it would help us find Diana Quigley."

Josh opened the front door and I saw that my guess about him looking good in a tuxedo was right. He looked great. "Hi. Josh Spencer, this is my friend, Frankie Ficaro." They shook and Frankie asked Josh if he'd take him out to the stable later to meet Vagabond. Josh agreed and when Frankie went in, gave me a smile and wink. He just wanted to tell me that I looked good. I smiled and winked right back to deliver the same message.

While Frankie went to look for Dave in the living room, I went to the kitchen to chat with Anna. She and Kathleen were preparing trays of food. "Good evening, ladies." Kathleen wore a black maid's uniform and Anna wore a dress with pink and purple floral print and a matching pink apron. I wondered if she'd dressed so colorfully for Frankie.

"Hello, Mattie. You look very attractive this evening. You won't be detecting in that outfit."

"You look great, too." I nodded at Anna and smiled at Kathleen. "Let's hope the only detecting I do is watching and listening. Any excitement this afternoon?"

"No, nothing I saw. Is Frankie here? I should take out a tray of snacks." She tipped her head toward the living room.

"I can take them out for you, Mrs. Allen," Kathleen volunteered.

"No, I will take it, Kathleen." Anna said quickly. "I want to see which kind Frankie likes so I can make him some to take home. Is that all right, Mattie?"

The guy was so smooth. "Of course. Frankie loves to eat." When Anna left, I spoke to Kathleen. "Have you remembered anything that might help?"

"No, Miss Draper, but there was something that happened at the last party that I thought I should remember and haven't yet. I'll keep thinking."

"That's all I can ask. Thanks Kathleen." I left to join the others in the living room. It was nice not to feel underdressed for a change.

As I left the kitchen, I heard a phone ring and saw Joe answer it in the hall. I watched him greet the caller and then stand in silence, apparently listening. His eyes pointed in my direction, but I had the feeling they didn't see me.

"Yes, I'll tell him." He put the phone down wearing a confused frown. When he looked up and saw me he said, "That was the kidnapper."

Chapter 19

They say clothes make the man. I'm not sure what they're supposed to do for a woman, but my classy new pantsuit had no affect my impulsive behavior. I grabbed Joe's arm and almost yanked it out of its socket. "What did he say?"

"He said he was going to arrange for the drop-off, but he'd call back when Dave wasn't so busy."

"He knew there was something going on here tonight?" Joe nodded. "And you're sure it was a man?" Another nod. "Okay. I'll tell Dave. Joe, you'd better call Sheriff Brown." I looked at the phone and ran into the living room taking a mental picture of everyone there. I found Dave and Frankie together. "Dave, Joe just talked to the kidnapper. He said he'll call back."

"Did he say anything else?"

I explained the message and watched his jaw clench. "Dave, whoever is doing this is trying to make you crazy. It's a game to him." Dave's mom and dad must have heard about the call. They joined us. Frankie and I left them to console Dave and found an empty corner. "Frankie, did you see anyone leave the room a few minutes ago?"

"No, I didn't notice. I was talking to Dave. Why?"

"When Joe told me who was on the phone, I thought that would eliminate everyone here, but I remembered the second line. Someone could have called from another room in the house. The person said he'd call when Dave wasn't so busy.

Either he's watching the house, which would be pretty hard to do undetected, or he knew this was happening. It has to be someone in this group."

"The call eliminates Joe." Frankie said.

"Not necessarily. Joe told me he talked to the kidnapper, but how do I know that's true? He could have had someone call. He could be working with Fielding, and that was him on the phone."

"You're getting good at this stuff, Mattie."

"Not quickly enough, I'm afraid, Frankie. I'm off to find a comfortable chair and have a drink. Maybe the kidnapper will sit next to me and confess." I turned toward the door when I recognized the sheriff's voice in the hall. "I'm surprised he responded this quickly for a phone call."

Frankie had a theory about why that was true. "He showed up for the free food and to impress on these folks that he's doing his job."

"I wonder if we should give him the necklace."

"What do you think the sheriff would do with it? He doesn't think Fielding is involved in the kidnapping. He probably wouldn't believe you found it in his trunk. Besides, there's no way Dave is going to let it out of his sight. Did you tell him not to mention it to anyone?"

"Yes."

We turned back to the entrance to watch the sheriff giving orders. "We need a list of everyone who's been here for the last hour. The phone call eliminates you all as suspects."

I started to raise my hand to tell him about the two phone lines but Frankie put his arm around me and blocked my attempt. "Don't bother, Mattie. The more you try to help the sheriff, the more he'll look in the opposite direction. Plus, he may not be appreciative. You don't need him making your job any harder." He was right. I didn't need the sheriff's department throwing any monkey wrenches into my slow moving investigation.

Josh poured me a scotch on the rocks and I found a comfortable chair. The liquor tasted so much better than the stuff in my kitchen cabinet I wasn't sure if what I had at home was really scotch. I took another sip, leaned back, and gave the room a slow scan.

A subdued Renee Sandburg occupied a chair on the opposite wall. Not only was she quiet, but she also wasn't putting them away at her normal pace. I didn't think she would come to talk to me, so I gave up my chair and wandered over for a visit. "You're quiet tonight, Renee. Is anything wrong?"

When she lifted her head, I saw her eyes were red rimmed, and I guessed the reason was tears rather than booze. "Do you think someone's killed her?"

That was not the Renee Sandburg I had spoken to a few days earlier. I took the adjacent chair. "No. He wants money, and the deal is that Dave talks to Diana before he delivers the money. Are you worried that she's been killed?"

"I know I sounded unconcerned the other day, but I love Diana. I've been angry about my divorce, and it just seemed that life always goes her way. I thought this kidnapping thing would be over in a day or two. That Dave would give him whatever he wanted and she'd be home. I never believed for a minute that she might be killed." Her eyes were ready to overflow. I crossed the room and brought her a handful of tissues. "She's my kid sister. I don't want anything to happen to her."

I'd be nuts if someone kidnapped one of my sisters. "Something has happened, Renee, and now we need to figure out how to bring Diana home. Were you in here before the sheriff showed up?" She said she was. "Did you notice anyone leave or enter in the last twenty minutes?"

Renee lifted her eyes and studied the faces. "Josh left for a short time, to get more liquor from the basement I think. I heard Sandra tell Joe she had to use the powder room, and I saw Jeffrey Sumner come in a few minutes ago, but I don't know when he left. Oh, Mrs. Allen went to the kitchen. Why are you asking if someone left?"

I wondered if Renee realized how much more observant she was when she wasn't ninety proof. "Just trying to keep track of everyone." I pointed my glass at hers. "What are you drinking, Renee?"

She looked at the drink as if she'd forgotten it was there. "I don't know. Josh poured me something. Mattie, let me know if I can help."

"Do you have the same phone number as your mom and dad?" I hoped she didn't.

"No, I have a private line. Let me give you my number."

I whipped out my notebook and pen so fast, I startled her, but she wrote her number and I tucked everything back in my pocket. I'd check her handwriting later. "Thanks. Keep your eyes and ears open."

Renee was full of surprises. She'd set the glass on a coaster and had not taken a drink. I had to find out if she was putting on an act. Was she the concerned older sister, or so controlled by alcohol that she would destroy her younger sister's life, or maybe even kill her?

To my delight, when I found my way back, the comfortable chair remained empty. As soon as I filled it, Sandra Sumner parked herself next to me. "Isn't it awful that the kidnapper hasn't released Diana?" I told her it was and took a sip of my drink. "Maybe Dave shouldn't have invited us all here. What if it scared him off?"

"Don't you think Dave is doing what he thinks is best to bring Diana home?"

A look, somewhere between impatience and doubt appeared briefly on Sandra's face. It disappeared when she leaned in and spoke just above a whisper. "Diana is my dearest friend, and I told you before that she and Dave were having more problems than just Dave's long hours. She asked me not to tell anyone, but she was having serious thoughts about divorcing him. It surprised me, because to tell you the truth, I've always been a little envious of their perfect marriage."

"Why did you wait until now to mention this, Sandra?"

"Because I had no idea that it would go on this long, and Diana trusted me with that information. You do realize that if Diana told Dave she wanted a divorce, he might kill her for the inheritance."

I wondered why people didn't judge a kidnapping serious until it went on for a certain amount of time. I also wondered how many days made it serious. "Yes, that's a possibility. Do you own a pair of silver earrings with a moon and a star? They'd be the clip-on style."

"No, I don't. If I can help you with anything else, let me know."

How had she thought she'd helped? "You can tell me one thing. Your name wasn't on any passenger lists for flights to New York on the twenty-sixth. Do you know why that would be? Did you fly under a different name?"

Sandra's mouth dropped open and she stared. "I gave you at least a dozen reasons why Dave might have killed her and you're asking me why you can't find my name on a list. I knew I was right the moment I laid eyes on you. You're not capable of handling this job and you're too embarrassed to admit it, or maybe you're taking Dave for whatever you can get. If Diana is killed, it will be your fault." She'd have been shouting but she didn't want others to hear. She stood and gave me a look of pure disgust. "If you'd bother to stay up on things, you'd know that many contemporary women use their maiden names when they travel." She stormed out of the room.

What I learned from that conversation was that women used their maiden names when they traveled and that Sandra Sumner had a temper.

Seconds after Sandra left, Joe replaced her. An extremely tired part of my brain hoped he'd confess so it would be over. No such luck. "I heard what Sandra said, Mattie, and I apologize. I'm sure you're more than capable of handling this case. I'm afraid Diana and Dave's marriage isn't the only one having problems. Sandra and I have been having a little stormy weather ourselves. She may be Diana's friend, but she's jealous of her and Dave's relationship. It doesn't help matters that I'm attracted to Diana."

I raised a questioning eyebrow. "Hitting on her at the party wasn't because of the booze?"

"No. Diana's a beautiful woman, and from what Dave has said over the years, she's a wonderful wife."

"You don't think Sandra is?" I wondered about the direction of this conversation. I also wondered if he and Sandra ever talked to one another.

"Oh, Sandra's a good wife, but she's high maintenance and needs a great deal of excitement. Often when I come home from work, all I want to do is take it easy and she's ready to party."

Everything I'd heard about Joe suggested any exhaustion would have come from avoiding work rather than doing it. "I can understand that. How long have you and Sandra been married?"

"Six years, and they haven't been bad." I followed Joe's eyes to where Sandra stood across the room with Jeanine Sandburg. "Sandra isn't the only one who's jealous of Diana and Dave's relationship. They make it look easy. They're comfortable with each other." He stood. "I didn't mean to use you as a marriage counselor, Mattie, but thanks for listening."

I was about to ask him how I served as a marriage counselor when noise from the hall ended our discussion. Robert Quigley made his way, rather clumsily, into the room. "Hey. How's the party?"

"What a jerk," Joe muttered as he went to intercept the newly arrived guest. I watched him put his hand on Robert's shoulder and escort him to a chair. Frankie sat in the now empty seat next to me. It looked as if I might not have to move all night. Eventually, everyone would stop by.

"Who's that?" Frankie asked.

"Robert Quigley, Dave's brother. He doesn't understand that Dave isn't in a partying mood these days." I was considering how he could care so little about his brother when something dawned on me. "Frankie, he wasn't here when the call came."

"Are you thinking he made it?" I nodded. "Did Joe say if the caller sounded drunk?"

"He didn't say. I'll ask him."

Frankie scanned the area before asking another question. "Did you find out if anyone was missing from the room when the call came?"

"Renee Sandburg told me that Josh, Jeffrey Sumner, Mrs. Allen, and Sandra left the room before the call. Have you heard anything?"

"There was one interesting bit of information. It seems that Joe Sumner is afraid of Vagabond." I tilted my head and waited for further explanation since I couldn't figure how that related to the case. Frankie explained. "Jeffrey Sumner told me that when he still owned Vagabond, Joe wouldn't go near him. Apparently, the horse didn't like him. I think Jeffrey might have been trying to tell me that if Joe kidnapped Diana, he wouldn't have been able to tie Vagabond to a tree."

"Protecting his son, just in case. Well, he has a good point, but if Diana went to meet Joe, she could have tied Vagabond to the tree. Josh mentioned that possibility. The thing that's wrong with that picture is that Diana couldn't stand Joe."

"Speaking of Vagabond, I went to the barn with Josh and he could have easily seen you walking back there. That doesn't mean he didn't follow you, though. He took me to where he found you. I think you were right about the horse trotting to the clearing. I also think the rope went up afterward so the investigators would think just what they did, that it was put up to knock her off Vagabond. If we go with the assumption that Diana knew who she was meeting, my guess is there was no rope, and she stayed in the saddle all the way to the clearing."

"That was one theory I considered and it's as good as any. You met Vagabond?"

"I did. He's a great horse."

"You didn't have trouble getting along with him?" I didn't have to wait long for his smirk. "Of course, you didn't. Why then, when we were at my sister's, wouldn't you ride? I thought you didn't like horses."

"I like horses. I just don't like riding them. I feel the same about buses."

I chuckled at the big guy and decided it was time to get back to the case. "After Jeffrey put in a good word for his son, did he have anything to say of interest?" I located him across the room talking with Dave.

"I asked him how business was and told him I heard that he and Dave made large personal investments for an upcoming contract. He said he had no idea what I meant. They had no new contracts in the works."

"Did he sound believable?"

"He did. Of course, that doesn't mean much, but I thought the news surprised him. He's an easygoing guy and doesn't let much about the business upset him. Maybe you get that way when you're close to retiring."

"Or maybe you go the other way and think that you have to control things for as long as you can."

"Possibly, but that's not what interests Jeff. He wants to buy a few horses and enjoy life."

"He did say that. Whether the rumors are true or not, the financial state of Q & S Design is an important part of this case. We need to get a look at their records. With all your connections, Ficaro, why don't you have friends at the Internal Revenue Service?"

"The fewer people I know over there, Mattie, the happier I am."

"I suppose I could just ask Dave to show me their books. I think he'd understand that I have to do my job." I lifted my glass for a drink and saw Rachel talking to Robert. I hoped she was getting an earful. Frankie took off and I had a two-minute break before voices rose behind me. I turned and saw that Rachel had moved on, and Mr. and Mrs. Quigley stood in front of Robert's chair. "What the hell is wrong with you? The last thing Dave needs right now is you coming in here drunk and acting like a fool," Mr. Quigley told his son.

"This ought to be good." Rachel's voice reached me as she sat in the busy chair. I checked another person off on my list of visitors.

"Hi, Rachel. I saw you talking to Robert. Did he tell you anything interesting?"

"Not really, but I had the strangest feeling he wasn't as drunk as he seemed. Every time I asked him a serious question, he was suddenly too drunk to answer. It was weird, like he wanted company, but he didn't want conversation."

Robert's voice carried over most of the room. He could still carry on a conversation. It might not have been coherent, but it was loud. "I don't care what Dave needs. He certainly doesn't care what I need. Leave me alone." Something hit the ground and shattered. Robert had knocked the ashtray off from where he'd positioned it on the arm of the chair. Josh appeared with a small brush and dustpan to clean up the glass, but Robert didn't notice the ashtray was gone and flicked his ashes on the chair. A disgusted Mr. & Mrs. Quigley joined the Sandburgs. The four appeared to have had enough and were ready to leave. Both couples had a kid with a drinking problem and a missing loved one. A loved one that I had to find.

Chapter 20

Rachel distracted me from Robert Quigley with a question. "I heard Joe say that the kidnapper called." I told her she'd heard right. "What did he say? Will he release Diana?"

"Rachel, between you and me, I think we need to find her before Dave pays the ransom. If it's someone close, which I'm sure it is, they won't let Diana identify them."

"Damn. I feel so helpless." Her tone and expression were grave.

"I know what you mean." I needed to change the conversation to keep that same feeling from overwhelming me. "Did you pick up anything of interest while mingling?"

"I overheard Joe and Sandra going at it. She accused him of hitting on Renee. I never saw Joe and Renee talking, but of course, that doesn't mean he didn't approach her. What a fun group, huh?"

"Fun wasn't the first word to pop into my head. Can you think of a reason why Jeffrey Sumner wouldn't want me to talk to Joe alone? When I first came to your office and asked to see Joe, Jeffery invited him to join us instead of sending me to his office."

"I'd guess it's because Jeffery knows about Joe's reputation and wanted to spare you the groping and innuendo. Most women in the office avoid being alone with

Joseph Sumner. The same is true with the women at the plant if he shows up there."

"He has a reputation as lecherous? Huh, I can't imagine Sandra tolerating that kind of behavior."

"Sandra may not be aware of it. I've never seen him hit on anyone when she's around. As far as Joe being a letch, I have personal experience."

I was about to ask more when I noticed something interesting at the other end of the room. "Rachel, don't turn right away, but when you have a chance, glance back to where Robert is sitting. This is indeed an interesting group."

Rachel knew how to observe. She waited a minute and then stretched in a yawn and lifted her head to see what I meant. Rob and Renee were involved in what appeared to be an intimate conversation. When she'd seen enough, she turned back with a look that was both miffed and bewildered. "I can't believe Diana's sister and Dave's brother would be necking like teenagers while Diana is in danger." Her second glance at the couple brought another surprise. "They're gone. Did you see where they went, Mattie?"

"Out that side door. Have you heard any rumors about those two having a relationship?"

"Yes, but not a cozy one. When they're both drunk, they usually end up in a shouting match that is unintelligible to everyone else. I didn't think they were close, especially that close."

"Maybe tragedy brought them together." I didn't believe that for a minute. "I need to find Frankie. Have you met him?" Rachel's smile said she had.

"He's a wonderful person, Mattie. I expected him to be tough and surly, but he's a teddy bear. I saw Mrs. Allen offering him snacks a little earlier."

Frankie could charm the skin off a snake. "I don't imagine Anna had any difficulty getting Frankie to eat. I'll check the kitchen. Maybe he's having better luck gathering clues. I'll talk to you later, Rachel. Keep your eyes open."

When I entered the kitchen, Anna rose from the table and blushed like a schoolgirl. "Oh, hello, Mattie. I was giving Frankie something to eat."

"I'm glad someone's keeping an eye on the detective." I commandeered a chair and smiled at the happy pair before asking Frankie a question. "Did Renee and Robert make their way through here?"

"Not that I saw. Did you see them, Anna?"

She shook her head and picked up the plate of snacks. "No, I saw them in the living room earlier, but that was the last. Would you like some of these, Mattie?" I took a sampling of the offered hors d'oeuvres and watched Anna push the plate in front of Frankie and ask if he'd had enough to eat.

"I did. Thank you, Anna." His playful wink rekindled her blush.

After Anna departed with the tray I turned to Frankie. "You are such a schmoozer."

"That's what makes me a good detective, Mattie. Anna is here every day and sees almost everything that goes on. She may not remember certain events until we coax her mind into cooperating. If you know what you're doing, it doesn't take much coaxing."

I'd been watching the two of them with an elbow propped on the table and my chin resting in my hand. I lowered the hand to his arm and shook my head at his pleased smile. "I hope you don't think that toothy grin would do much in the way of coaxing me."

"No, Mattie, I'm well aware that persuading you would take more than a smile. By the way, as far as suspects go, your mom is far more likely than Anna. Why did you ask about Renee and Robert?"

My hand still rested on his arm so I pinched it. "I'm telling mom that you said that. Renee and Robert were having a cozy chat in the living room and then they disappeared. That was right after Robert's father gave him a piece of his mind for coming in drunk. By the way, Rachel said she had the feeling he pretended to be more loaded than he actually was."

"Hmm, I wonder why he'd do that. Did you have a chance to ask Joe if the caller sounded drunk?" I shook my head. "If it was Robert, he may be trying to establish that he couldn't have made the phone call because he was soused."

"I just thought of something, Frankie. I'll be right back." I found a light switch at the top of the stairs leading to the basement. After answering my question, I returned to the kitchen. I was not pleased.

"Why did you go down there?"

"I wanted to see if they had a phone in the basement. Renee said Josh went to bring up more liquor right before the kidnapper called."

"I take it there's a phone."

I nodded. "I know it's dumb, but I don't want it to be Josh who kidnapped Mrs. Quigley. She gave him a job and a second chance. I'm beginning to realize I don't read people as well as I thought I did. When I spoke to Renee earlier, she seemed sincerely sorry for her behavior and appeared frightened for Diana. After seeing her socializing with Robert and almost as drunk as him, I'm thinking she's a good actress and a good liar."

"Mattie, you know darn well that there are people who make lying an art form. You grew up on Chicago politics."

"I know, but I put politicians in a class by themselves. Could Renee and Robert have planned this? He might hate Dave that much, and Renee might feel the same way about Diana. If they pulled it off, Robert would have the money he needs and Renee would have revenge." My involuntary shiver stopped further speculation. "Boy, I have a hard time imagining someone could do this to their sibling."

This time Frankie patted my arm. "People do things that are hard to understand, Mattie. It isn't pleasant, but it happens, even in families."

"Right." I hated my naive beliefs, but my family meant a lot to me. "The earring could belong to Renee. I see I need to talk to Miss Sandburg again."

Dave, Frankie, and I sat in the dining room after everyone left. "How are you holding up, Dave?" I asked. Nothing short of Diana's return would make him feel better, but he still had hope. Frankie had a hand in that.

"I can't allow myself to think about what Diana is going through." He rubbed his hands rapidly up and down his folded arms and changed the subject. "What did we find out this evening? I mean, what, besides that Robert is an ass, which isn't a news flash."

"Dave, do you have any sense of who it might be?"

"To be honest, Mattie, at first I wondered if maybe Josh might have done it. He'd been in prison."

"You knew about that?" I was surprised that Diana would have told him after she promised Josh.

"I knew. Diana didn't tell me, but Sandra heard from someone at the museum. I'm guessing now that it was Fielding. I talked to Diana about it and she felt bad that she didn't tell me, but she'd promised Josh. I understood."

"Do you still think Josh is involved?"

"No. He seems happy here, and why would he wait three years to do this?"

"He is happy, Dave."

Frankie nodded and we turned in unison, surprised by a knock on the front door. Since Josh, Anna, and Kathleen were gone, I answered and had another surprise. Renee Sandburg entered, excited and sober. "Mattie, I'm glad you're still here. I need to talk to you."

I moved from the doorway and pointed her to the empty living room. Without thinking, she headed toward the bar and then changed course and found a chair. "What is it, Renee?"

"I played nice with Rob tonight." My eyebrow must have risen. She frowned. "Nothing happened. I pretended to be drunk and tried to hit on him, but all the booze must have pickled his libido. When he didn't respond, I took him to the porch and asked him straight out who he thought might have kidnapped Diana."

"What did he have to say?"

"He said, 'someone smarter than me.' When I asked him what he meant, he said 'nothing' and grumbled something I couldn't understand."

"Anything else?"

"Yes there is, and I that's what I came to tell you. I told him I was drunk at Dave's birthday party and didn't remember much. He said he didn't even remember leaving. The cops found him in his car the next day. He couldn't remember if he'd driven off or pulled off the road into some brush right outside Dave and Diana's place, but he did and his car was barely visible. When a passerby reported seeing it, the police checked and found Rob sleeping. They woke him and sent him home." She barely took a breath before continuing. "He didn't seem to think that falling asleep in his car was a big deal and changed the subject before I could ask any more about it. That's when he asked me if I ever wished Diana wasn't in the picture so people would pay attention to me. I didn't respond because, pitifully, my answer would have been yes." She glanced at the bar and then at her hands.

"Renee, have you quit drinking?"

"I decided to try, at least until Diana comes home. Mattie, I'm not proud of what I've become. I know you see me as the poor little rich girl, and I guess that's what I am, but I want Diana home. I'll keep asking questions and bring you anything I learn. Okay?"

As I was about to respond it struck me that Renee was a beautiful woman, not as breathtakingly striking as Diana, but still quite attractive. The booze hadn't begun to have an effect on her looks so she still had the Sandburg women's beauty. I'd noticed earlier in the evening that even at her age, Mrs. Sandburg was every bit as good-looking as her daughters were. "That would be helpful. Did Joe hit on you earlier this evening?"

"Joe Sumner?" I nodded. "He wouldn't dare, especially with Sandra around."

"That's what Rachel said."

"If Sandra caught Joe hitting on someone she'd take him for every penny she could get."

"Why would Sandra have thought Joe hit on you? Did she see you two together?"

"No. I don't think much more of Joe than Diana does. I don't know why she thought that, unless he told Sandra he hit on me to get a rise out of her."

"Or she made it up to get a rise out of him. Renee, do you own a pair of silver earrings with a crescent moon and a star? I'm guessing they're expensive."

"I don't, but that design sounds familiar. Maybe Diana has a pair and I've seen them on her. I'm not completely sure since I've had blurred vision lately. Why do you ask about the earrings?"

I explained the event in the woods and when I saw her eyes widen and her mouth open, I held up my hand. "I wasn't badly hurt, but I never saw who hit me. Josh showed up and helped me to the house."

"Diana could have lost it in the struggle."

"That's true, or another woman may have been involved in her abduction and she was the one who lost the earring."

Renee's newfound sobriety allowed her brain to figure out what that statement suggested. "You thought it might be me because I acted like a jerk."

She'd lowered her head to avoid looking at me so I had to do more than nod. "I thought you might have been involved, Renee, but now I'm not so sure. If you truly do plan on staying sober, I'd appreciate you bringing me any information you find."

Her head shot up. "I will, and I'll be sober. I'll do whatever I can."

She meant what she said. It amazed me that when people communicated from their heart, their responses were almost childlike, and that usually meant honest.

"I'm tired," I told Frankie. "If you weren't still wounded, I'd make you drive home."

"I can drive if you want, Mattie. My foot is fine." He leaned closer to get a better look. "You do look beat. Pull over." I did, and minutes later we were on the road with Frankie behind the wheel. "What did Renee have to say? That was a surprise visit."

I didn't answer until I'd moved around in the passenger's seat and found a comfortable spot without a spring nudging at my bottom, which is bonier than Frankie's is. "She said the earring isn't hers and she wants to help find Diana."

"She may want to help, but she won't do you much good with a bag on."

"She's not drinking. She said she wouldn't touch the stuff until Diana came home. And speaking of having a bag on, she said Rob couldn't remember leaving the party the night before Diana's abduction." I explained to Frankie how the police found him and that he said he couldn't remember a thing.

"Blackouts are a great alibi if you can find someone to believe you."

Frankie sounded more than a little peeved but I didn't ask why. "Rachel told me that she overheard Joe and Sandra fighting. Sandra accused Joe of hitting on Renee."

"Are you surprised?"

"Not about Joe, but when I asked Renee, she said Joe didn't hit on her and that he wouldn't as long as Sandra was around. I'd better look into that. Joe and Sandra's relationship is rocky at best, but it's also strange."

"Tomorrow I'll see if Tommy learned anything, but then I have to meet a client. And you'll have to work without me."

"I'll try, Frankie, but it'll be tough."

"Who do you like for this, Mattie?"

I hoped he wouldn't ask, because depending on the time of day, I liked someone different. "I don't think Dave did it."

"I agree, and, like I said, I'm sure Anna isn't involved."

"Boy, did she fall for you!"

"Nah. Anna thinks of me the way she does her six sons. They're scattered around the country these days and she misses taking care of them. I help her feel closer to them. That's why she keeps giving me food."

Frankie could be that for people, someone they needed. I suspected he was becoming that for me. "Okay, Mr. Charm. Rob is still way up there for me, but I doubt that he and Renee are in on it together. She said the reason she got cozy with him was to pump him for information. I believe her. Peter Fielding is my favorite, but it has to be with a partner." Frankie directed his eyes my way, but not his head. I knew what he wanted to hear. "I haven't eliminated Renee as a suspect, but right now all I have is suspects, besides Anna, and my mother." I saw his smile. "I had to eliminate someone."

"Like you said, Dave doesn't look good, so that's two. After seeing the parents, I agree about them, too. And there's no real motive. If Fielding kidnapped Diana to get her out of the way, his partner, whoever that is, had to have another motive, which we're guessing is money, right?"

"Right. Fielding wants her out of the way and the partner wants the money. Maybe neither one of them thought they could do it alone. Fielding can't kill her until his partner collects the dough and the partner is in no hurry. He wants to make Dave miserable for as long as possible. What member of this group would Fielding have known that could deal with his reptilian personality? He's not a real likable guy."

"They wouldn't have to like each other. Dave said he didn't know Fielding, but Diana obviously did. Are any of the others involved in the museum?"

"I told Carol to think about the people she's seen spending time with Fielding or those who called more than usual. I also told her to check with the woman who works on her days off. I'll stop at the museum and see what she has to say tomorrow."

"Sounds like you have an interesting day ahead of you. I bet you're gonna miss my smiling face."

"You'd be right."

"Mattie, don't mess with the sheriff. I know his kind. They play real dirty."

"Thanks, I'll stay as far away from him as I can." Unfortunately, it wasn't far enough.

Chapter 21

First thing the next morning I went to the art museum and found Carol at her desk smiling. "You look pleased."

"Mom is always saying that you don't know how dark the night is until you see the light of dawn. I didn't know what she meant until I came to work this morning and realized Mr. Fielding wouldn't be here. What's happening with him, Mattie? Is he in jail?"

"Not yet. The sheriff lost him. Helena Hayworth visited the good sheriff and let him know what she thought about that. Did she call you yet?" She hadn't. "She's having the paintings brought over. She wants them framed and hung before Mrs. Quigley returns. You don't do that, do you?"

"No. She'll hire an outside vendor. There are a few in the area. Is there any word on Mrs. Quigley?"

The word "no" stuck in my throat, so I shook my head. "Have you had a chance to think about people who came here to meet Fielding, or that he talked to on the phone regularly? It could be anyone, even if they have no connection to the Quigley family."

"I thought about it. He rarely talked to anyone except Mrs. Quigley, Mrs. Hayworth, and a couple other board members. The conversations between Fielding and Mrs. Quigley and Mrs. Hayworth were not usually friendly. Mrs. Quigley's sister came in with her occasionally and she talked to Fielding. I think she has an interest in art, too."

The news about Renee caught my attention, but I supposed it made sense that she'd come to the museum with her sister. I pulled out the list of board members and scanned it. I had another surprise when I saw a name I hadn't noticed earlier. "This says Sandra Sumner is a member of the board. I could have sworn she said she didn't know anything about the meeting Diana had planned with Helena and Fielding. Is that possible?"

"Oh sure. The entire board didn't plan to be here, only Peter Fielding, Mrs. Quigley, and Mrs. Hayworth. She might not have even known when the paintings were coming, but I thought she and Mrs. Quigley were friends."

"I did, too. Mrs. Hayworth didn't mention being here when the paintings came."

"She wasn't. I talked to Angie yesterday. She's the girl who works on Sunday and Monday. She said that last Monday Mrs. Hayworth called to say she'd heard about the kidnapping and wouldn't be in. Angie said when she told Mr. Fielding, he didn't say anything. She also told me that she saw him accept delivery of the paintings and take them to his office."

"Damn him. He's been lying from the get go. I wish the sheriff hadn't let him go. I'm convinced he couldn't have kidnapped Diana alone, but he could be working with someone. I need to figure out who that someone is. Who would work with Fielding? Why would…"

"Mattie?"

Carol interrupted the conversation I was having with myself. "Oops. Sorry. Sometimes my brain gets stuck in neutral but my mouth engages anyway. What were you going to say?"

"Angie also said that she'd seen Diana's sister, Renee, and Sandra Sumner talking with Fielding on occasion."

"Did you or Angie ever talk to Diana's sister when she came in?"

"No, I only saw her a few times, and Angie said she'd never talked to her."

"And neither you nor she saw Dave or his brother Rob, or even Joe Sumner in the museum?" Carol shook her head to all three names. "I'll check in with you soon, Carol. Thanks again for your help. You've been great. Do you have any idea who they'll appoint as curator?"

"I don't care who it is, as long as it's not another Fielding."

"Brother, I hope so too."

"Hey, Mattie, what did you do before you became a private investigator?"

I smiled. "What you're doing right now. Are you getting tired of typing 'Dear Sir or Madam?'" Her frown said it all. "More things are opening up for women these days. Heck, we might even have a woman astronaut riding in one of those rockets. Reach for everything you can, Carol. Life's way too short to waste. Being a secretary isn't bad if that's what you want to do, but don't settle. If you have your eyes on the stars, aim for them."

If I didn't find Diana Quigley soon, I might be free to replace Carol when she took off for the stars. I knew better than to tell Frankie about those thoughts or I'd be listening to another lecture.

During my drive to the Quigley estate, I reviewed the conversation with Carol. According to her, Sandra and Renee both came to the museum and both knew Peter Fielding. That didn't eliminate anyone, and it made me wonder if Fielding met privately with any of the men involved in the group.

Anna greeted me at the door and told me that Frankie had called and wanted me to call him. I could see by her smile that they'd had a nice chat. She continued grinning on her way to the kitchen and I stopped at the phone in the hall. "Hi, Frankie. What do you have?"

"Don't you want to ask me how I am first?"

"Hi, Frankie, how are you, and what do you have?"

"That's better. Mattie, Tommy talked to his connection on the Lake Oak force. The morning of the kidnapping they did find Robert Quigley sleeping in his car outside of the Quigley estate. They hadn't heard about Diana's abduction yet and didn't think much about him being there because of his reputation. They woke him up and sent him on his way."

"What does that tell us, Frankie?"

"It was late morning. Around eleven thirty and they said he was in bad shape. His clothes were wrinkled and dirty and the deputy said he looked like hell. When they asked him why he was there, he told them what he'd told Renee. He didn't remember a thing."

"What are you thinking? He went to the house that morning and kidnapped Diana, put her in his trunk, and then took a nap? Wouldn't Diana have made noise when she heard the police? Why would he sleep there instead of going home?"

"He could have drugged her, knocked her out, or had her tied up and gagged so that she couldn't move. The officers said they found a bottle of booze in the car and he was drunk, but being David Quigley's brother, they sent him home. If he did kidnap her, between the booze and the exertion, he might have passed out."

"Did the cops talk to him after they found out about the kidnapping?"

"Not according to Tommy's connection. Do you plan to do that?"

"Yep. As soon as I can."

"Mattie, they also said the sheriff is putting two of his deputies back on the case full time. Did you have anything to do with that?"

"I'm guessing Mrs. Hayworth had more to do with that than me, but thanks, Frankie. Do you feel okay enough to put in a full day's work?"

"I'll be fine. I have a light caseload right now. Remember that. If you need me, call."

"I will. I'll tell you what happens with Robert, too. See you later." I hung up the phone and went to the dining room to find Dave. It surprised me that he wasn't there. I found him sitting on the back porch and hoped that didn't mean he'd given up on ever having breakfast with Diana.

"Hi, Dave."

"Hi, Mattie."

He didn't ask if I had news. Another bad sign. "What's going on?"

He tried to smile, but his eyes filled and his head dropped. "What will I do without Diana? I can't imagine my life, our home. I can't imagine any of it without her."

I wouldn't leave him alone this time, even if he didn't want me to see him cry. "Dave, you will not spend your life without Diana. I intend to find her. Frankie told me Sheriff Brown has reassigned two deputies to the case full time. Between Frankie, them, and me, we'll find her, alive, and soon. You have to believe that."

He managed almost to smile. "You and Frankie are a good team."

"I think so, too." I stood and put my hand on his shoulder. "I have to get to work. Dave, try to keep positive. I know that's not easy, but Diana will be home soon." I began repeating that in my head. I've heard that people who meditate sometimes use what they call a mantra. They repeat it over and over to achieve a desired result. "Diana will be home soon" would be my mantra until that happened.

The outside of Robert Quigley's home was impressive. It reminded me of the house in *Gone with the Wind,* a huge structure with tall columns and large windows all around. It was stunning, but neglected. When Rob opened the door and invited me in, I saw that the outside was in better shape than the interior. The smell of stale tobacco and booze filled the place. It might have looked like Tara, but it smelled like Benny's pub.

He saw me examining the mess. "I had to lay off the housekeeper. I just have a cleaning crew come in once a month."

"I hope they're expected soon."

He might not have heard me. That or he ignored my comment. He wore crumpled dress slacks and an equally crumpled white shirt that he'd only partially tucked in. Probably what he'd had on the previous evening. I'd woken him, but judging by his condition, it wasn't from a good night's sleep. "You're funny, Mattie."

He did hear me. "Thank you. Do you have a few minutes to talk?" I wondered what he did all day, every day if he didn't work.

"Sure. Why don't we go to the library? I never use it. It's the only clean room in the house. My late wife was the reader in the family." I followed him and realized that nothing embarrassed the guy. He lived in his own little world and didn't give a damn what anyone thought. Frankie didn't care what people thought, but the difference was that though he didn't care, he didn't act like a jerk to prove it. "Would you like a drink, Mattie?"

I declined and watched him pour what might have been breakfast. "Robert, the Lake Oak police said they found you sleeping in your car outside of Dave and Diana's house on the morning of her kidnapping."

"I've been expecting someone to talk to me about that, but I thought it would be the sheriff, not a private investigator. How did you find out?"

"I have connections with various police departments." That sounded a great deal more impressive than it was, but I couldn't say that the cop who shot my boyfriend felt bad and passed on the information. "While you were parked, did you see anyone drive in or out of the estate?"

He studied his drink, which was probably a Bloody Mary with little bloody and a large amount of Mary. "No, I didn't see anything until the deputies disturbed my slumber and sent me home. When you're Dave's brother, you can pass go and not go directly to jail." He lifted his eyes from the drink to me. "That's from Monopoly, Mattie. Do you play?"

"I played it as a kid. Why were your clothes messed up?"

"You do have good sources, or that could have been a lucky guess." He pointed at his clothing. "I don't remember a single thing after I arrived at Dave's place. I must have blacked out."

Frankie was right about how convenient a blackout story could be. "Do you have a big enough grudge against your brother to kidnap Diana?"

He turned and put his drink on the table before facing me. "Mattie, I may well have kidnapped Diana, but if I did, I don't remember. If I called asking for ransom, I don't remember. Do I have a big enough grudge against David to have kidnapped Diana, maybe, but, like I said, I don't remember having done so."

"Maybe you should quit drinking and help your brother find his wife."

His reaction to that one wasn't as calm. His voice nearly doubled in volume. "Number one, I'm not quitting drinking. Number two, Dave doesn't want or need my help, and Number three, what makes you so damn sure that Diana's coming home? Don't you think it's cruel to let Dave keep his hopes up for something that might not happen?"

"It will happen, Robert. It's my job to find her and bring her home, and I don't start a job I can't finish. Have you ever worked? I mean held a paying job?" It had nothing to do with the case, but he'd ticked me off and I needed to settle down.

He found a crumpled pack of cigarettes in his shirt pocket and lit one with a lighter from the table. "I've had a few jobs. The last one was as my late wife's limo driver before we became a couple. I literally charmed the pants off of her."

I had calmed myself enough to ignore the remark and ask another question. "You said your wife died in a car accident. What happened? I mean was it a collision with another vehicle, or did she drive off the road?"

"It happened right here in Lake Oak. The poor dear had one too many martinis and plowed into a tree. Thankfully, she died instantly."

The poor dear remark was incredibly tasteless. What the hell was wrong with the guy? "Did investigators have an autopsy done to see if there was a physical reason she'd lost control?"

"No, there was no doubt she was drunk and drove into the tree. The insurance company babbled about suicide because they didn't want to pay on the policy, but they had no case. My wife was a happy woman."

I stood, wondering how he'd know if she was happy or not but asked if it had been Sheriff Brown who investigated the accident. When he nodded, I figured there hadn't been much of an investigation. "Thanks for your time, Robert." I let myself out. It was unsettling how little emotion Robert showed when he discussed his wife. It could have been that he didn't remember much about her, either.

I was a half mile from the entrance to Dave and Diana's house when I heard a siren and saw the lights of a police car behind me. I automatically checked the speedometer, which was well under the limit, and pulled over to let him by, but he pulled in behind me. When he stopped, I recognized the sheriff.

"Oh, this should be fun." I reminded myself that whatever happened, I'd keep my mouth shut. When the sheriff arrived at my door, I spoke through the open window. "Hello, Sheriff. What can I do for you?"

"Well, Miss Draper, I didn't know it was you."

He knew damn well who it was. He saw my car the last time he hauled me to the station. I noticed the even nastier than normal sneer on his face and prepared for the worst.

"You have a broken taillight," he told me.

"No, I don't." I opened the door to climb out and he shoved it closed.

"Stay right there and keep your hands on the steering wheel." I watched him walk to the back of my car and pull out his gun. I suspected what was coming and listened to the crunch as he used the butt of the gun to shatter the lens on my taillight.

As he ambled to the front of the car, the number of good intentions lining my already well-paved path to hell rose. I jumped out and shoved my nose in the sheriff's sneering face. "You can't do that." My brother Bill mentioned often that I needed to learn when to keep my mouth shut. As soon as the words left my mouth, I realized this might have been one of those occasions.

"I told you to stay in the car. You should have listened. Turn around Miss Draper. I'm beginning to think you like wearing my bracelets. Of course, they're worth more than any jewelry you've ever owned. Prettier, too, no doubt."

He locked the handcuffs and reached into my jacket for my gun, dragging his fingers along my breast as he did. I bit my lip instead of his hand to avoid assault and resisting arrest charges.

The station was only a few miles away and I used the time to take slow even breaths and focus on what I had to do, ignoring the sheriff's commentary on what jobs where not suitable for a woman. Private investigator was second to police work. When we arrived at the station and went inside, he unlocked the cuffs and sat at his desk. "You can go, Miss Draper. You'd better get that taillight fixed."

I wondered why he was doing this. Something more than what happened with Fielding had the sheriff ready to hang me. "Are you going to give me a ride to my car?" Yes, it was a stupid question.

"What I'm going to give you, Miss Draper, is a little friendly advice. I don't like you interfering in my town's business. I strongly suggest you go back to Chicago and leave Lake Oak affairs to me."

"Mr. Quigley is paying me to do a job that has nothing to do with you, Chicago, or Lake Oak. I intend to complete that job."

"Don't say I didn't warn you. And you'd better have that light fixed. Next time you might have to spend a day or two enjoying the comforts of a Lake Oak cell. I know I can come up with a few ways to keep you entertained."

"Can I have my gun?"

He pushed it forward on his desk and I picked it up, praying he didn't jump over. There was enough stomach protruding over his belt to assure me if it turned into a foot race, I'd be safe. That didn't stop my shiver as I turned away. Thankfully, I managed to force my mouth to remain shut.

The hike to my car gave me a chance to think and cool off. Cool my anger, not my body. August in Illinois, even in the woods can be muggy. I slung my jacket over my arm for the hike and wondered if the good sheriff might be on someone's payroll. Whose? The last person I saw was Robert Quigley and he didn't strike me as being on the best of terms with local law enforcement. He said the sheriff had decided his wife's death was accidental without an investigation. That sounded like standard operating procedure in Lake Oak. Maybe the sheriff belonged on my list of suspects.

Chapter 22

My plan, after I made it back to my car, was to go to the Quigley estate, but instead I drove to Q & S Design. I wanted to talk to Jeffrey Sumner again, and hoped he'd see me without an appointment. It was nice to find a friendly face at the reception desk. "Hi, Rachel. Is Jeffrey in?"

"He is, Mattie. Do you want me to let him know you're here?"

I checked my watch. "I only need a minute."

She called Sumner and in seconds had the answer I'd hoped to hear. "You can go right in."

"I need to talk to you when I'm finished," I said as I turned to leave. She agreed and had something to tell me, too. I went to Jeffrey's office.

"How are things going, Mattie?"

"Until Diana's home, my answer is, not good. Let me get right to the point of my visit. I have a friend who works at the Trib. She told me they received an anonymous letter saying that you and Dave have invested large sums of your own money, gambling on a new contract. Frankie told me that you said you hadn't."

"Frankie spoke the truth. He's a good man, by the way. My dad used to say that people like Frankie were comfortable in their own skin. I'd say he fits that description quite well. I wish Joseph would spend time with him."

Joe wouldn't rub off on Frankie, but I felt protective of the detective and hoped that didn't happen. "Here's the thing. I overheard Joe tell Robert Quigley that you and Dave made a big investment expanding the plant to fulfill a contract."

Jeffrey came forward in his chair. "You're sure it was Joe you heard?"

"It was, and I heard it clearly."

"I can't imagine why he'd say something that ridiculous. We aren't interested in taking new contracts. We have enough work to keep us busy into the seventies." He leaned back and sighed. "I assure you, Mattie, it is not the case. I have no idea why Joe would say anything like that to Robert." He took a thoughtful pause. "Unless Robert mentioned that he wanted to borrow money from Dave, and Joseph thought his story would convince him to back off. I'll find out."

"I only heard part of their conversation, so it's possible Robert had said something before I arrived. As long as I'm here, would it be all right if I went ahead and asked Joe a few questions?"

Jeffrey released another sigh, this one expressing even greater weariness. "He took the afternoon off to play golf. Joseph is not the most dedicated of employees. I'm sorry." He didn't say it, but I could see he found his son's behavior disappointing. I made my way to Rachel.

"Are Joe and Dave close?"

"No. Joe's friends are the country club set, and Dave has little interest in that world. Why, Mattie? What's going on with Joe?" I explained my conversation with Jeff and that he suggested Joe made up the deal to protect Dave. Rachel doubted it. "If Joe wanted to keep Robert from borrowing from his brother, it would only be to protect the company for when he took over for Jeff."

"What was it you wanted to tell me, Rachel?"

"Oh. My news is about Joe, too. His secretary told me that Mrs. Sumner came to the office this morning and had a screaming fit. She couldn't hear everything they said, but it sounded like Mrs. Sumner wants a divorce. She heard Joe tell her to calm down because they could work it out. After that, Mrs. Sumner stormed out and slammed every possible door she could leaving the building. Joe came from his office looking a little embarrassed, but he didn't say anything."

"That might be why Joe went to play golf. Maybe Sandra found out he'd hit on someone and she's had enough."

"That could be. As I said, the only thing I know for sure is that Joe goes after anyone in a skirt when Sandra's not around."

"Here's another strange piece of information, Rachel. Do you remember telling me that you heard Sandra yelling at Joe for hitting on Renee? Renee said it never happened."

"I suppose if Sandra heard Joe was hitting on someone at the party, she might have thought it was Renee because she knew Joe was attracted to Renee's sister. Or she didn't know if Renee was the target but accused him to see if he would deny it. No matter what, their relationship is in trouble."

"It looks that way, doesn't it? Thanks Rachel." I bid her adieu and as I drove to the Quigley estate, two questions filled my mind. Had Joe Sumner tried to protect Dave, and how serious were Joe and Sandra's marital problems? Joe had said there were a few. Maybe they were bigger than he'd led me to believe. Sandra's scene at the office made it look that way.

I arrived at the Quigleys' after five and immediately called Frankie at his office. "Hey, Frankie, I'm afraid I need to ask a few more favors."

"I live to do you favors."

I had to pull away from the phone to muffle my snort. "I'm glad to hear that. I need information on an accident that killed Robert Quigley's wife. It happened here in Lake Oak two years ago. The sheriff called it an accident and the insurance company tried to claim it was suicide. There are a few rumors that she was depressed. I'll talk to people who knew Christina Quigley and see if I can learn something about her."

"Tommy still feels bad that he shot me. He won't mind checking. I limp when I'm around him."

"You're bad."

"I know. How will this help, Mattie?"

"I'm thinking that if Christina's death wasn't an accident or suicide, maybe it was murder. It would make Robert a better kidnapping suspect."

"That works. How's Dave doing?"

"You taught me well, Frankie. I'm trying to keep him as hopeful as possible. What are you doing tonight?"

"I'm clear, why?"

"I must have backed into something and broke a taillight. The sheriff pulled me over and strongly suggested I fix it in a hurry. I know I won't be leaving until after dark and I don't want him to stop me again. Do you think you could bring one so I'll be legal?"

"Sure. How could he see you had a broken taillight in the middle of the day?"

"He might have been looking for something to nail me on. I'll see you later."

"Okay. Maybe I'll have information on the other Quigley family member for you by then."

Anna entered the hall and hooked onto my arm. "You look like you have not eaten. Come and have dinner. If you want to keep up with Frankie, you have to eat well." She must have received orders to keep me fed.

I sat at the kitchen table where she presented me with a big bowl of stew. I had no idea what Dave and Diana usually ate, but if they didn't like Anna's stew, they were crazy. "Anna, this is wonderful."

"Thank you. It is one of Mr. and Mrs. Quigley's favorite things. They both enjoy my cooking." Her eyes grew moist.

"Has Mr. Quigley eaten?"

"I give him a bowl earlier, but he did not eat much."

Everyone was running out of energy. "Anna, did you know Robert's wife, Christina?"

Her sad expression changed little as she considered my question. "She did not go out often."

"How long were they married?"

"Maybe four years, not long. She had much tragedy in her life as a child. Both of her parents died in a plane crash. That was why she had so much money, but except for a distant uncle, she had no other family. I think she was often sad."

So despite what Robert said, Anna thought she was depressed. I decided to visit Joe and Sandra Sumner and see how well they knew Christina. I mopped up the last of the stew with a slice of homemade bread, thanked Anna, and explained my plan to walk to the neighbor's house.

"You should have Josh show you the path that connects to their property. It is much shorter than walking around the gates."

Josh showed me the shortcut and I went next door, smiling on my journey through the woods. My neighbors in Chicago were close enough that I could hear them brush their teeth.

The path made the walk shorter, but taking the neighborly route didn't make my reception at the front door any friendlier. I forgot that in some neighborhoods you didn't drop in unannounced. Sandra opened the door wearing a look that refreshed my memory.

"Well, Mattie. What brings you here uninvited?" As she spoke, Joe stuck his head out from behind the door wearing the same look. People in Lake Oak didn't appear to wander next door for a cup of coffee and conversation.

"I wanted to ask you a few questions about Robert Quigley's late wife, Christina."

"What did you want to know?" Sandra asked. Her square shouldered, cross-armed response made it clear that she had no intention of inviting me in. It was my guess that she hadn't forgiven me for questioning her flight to New York. I reminded myself to be grateful she didn't slam the door in my face.

"What kind of a person was Christina? I mean, did she seem happy?"

"Christina Quigley?" Sandra turned to Joe who looked at her blankly until she returned her cool gaze to me. "She was quiet. Not extremely social."

"Did you two do anything with them as a couple, or see them at parties?"

Joe gave up peeking out from behind the door and stood next to his wife. "They didn't go out much," he said. "Robert came alone sometimes, but not often."

"Did he drink back then?"

"I hadn't thought about it," Joe said, "but no, he didn't drink as much. Of course, if he did, he'd be dead by now. The guy can put them away."

"Yes, I saw that. Thanks for your time."

As I turned to walk away, I remembered what Robert had said about the insurance company. "Do you have any idea why the insurance company would have thought Christina killed herself?"

Their faces didn't change, but Sandra appeared to hear something and leaned inside the door. "Excuse me a second. That's the phone." When she left, I repeated the question to Joe.

"You know how insurance companies are," he said with his stock shrug. "You pay and pay and when it's time to collect, they find reasons why you can't. I wouldn't be surprised if half the accidents in the world were called suicide by one insurance company or another."

Joe continued expounding on the shortcomings of the insurance industry until Sandra returned. Surprisingly, she had an interest in the conversation she'd missed. After making Joe repeat his entire summary of the insurance racket, she had a question for me. "So, Mattie, why are you asking about Christina? Do you think if Robert killed her, that would make him a good suspect in Diana's kidnapping, or are you just on one of your fishing expeditions?"

The only comfort I found in Sandra's remark was that my idea wasn't too far-fetched. If a man could kill his wife, he could kidnap his sister-in-law. "I suppose it's more of a fishing expedition. Thanks for your time."

"You'll be sure to keep us informed, won't you? Diana is my closest friend and I'd like to know what progress you're making."

I told Sandra I'd keep her posted and listened to a lengthy summation of how important Diana Quigley was to all of Lake Oak but especially to her. She would have continued, but I bid them good evening and directed my frustrated self to the woods. It was getting dark, and I had to find my way back to the Quigley property.

It took several minutes to navigate the unfamiliar terrain and find the path. After the lump I'd received on my last nighttime stroll, I felt a little uneasy. Just as the lights surrounding the Quigley home came into view, I realized there was good reason for my uneasiness. An arm tightened around my neck and someone pressed a wet cloth over my nose mouth. I recognized the smell. It was chloroform. I couldn't shake off the thick arm because I could barely stay conscious. I pulled at the rag and kicked at the person behind me, but something jabbed my arm. That was, as they say, all she wrote.

Chapter 23

There are folks who wake up ready to jump out of bed and greet the day with enthusiasm. I am not one of them, not even if I feel good. When I opened my eyes I did not feel good, I felt sick. Before I could focus, my stomach did a cartwheel and forced my eyes closed so I could let things settle. The slightest movement made me nauseous. I remembered the arm and the chloroform. When I tried to take a breath, I realized my attacker had tied the soaked cloth around my mouth and I was breathing fumes. Most of the liquid had evaporated and not enough remained to knock me out, but enough clung to the rag to make me sick to my stomach.

The gears in my brain creaked forward and I remembered I was returning to the Dave and Diana's house. Someone interrupted my journey. Instead of relaxing in the comfort of an overstuffed chair, I was lying in the woods with my hands and feet tied, feeling sick to my stomach and in serious pain—as if someone beat me. Some not particularly brave person had slapped me around while I was out cold. Judging by the level of pain, they did more than slap. When I tried to roll over, I let out an involuntary, muffled scream.

My eyes began to adjust and lights from the Quigleys' yard gave me some visibility, but they did nothing to help me figure out how to change my uncomfortable position. Everything hurt when I moved, so I stayed as still as possible. It was then I spotted a note stuck to a tree in front of me. I had to strain, but with the dim light I read the scrawled message"

Get out of town Draper. Next time you won't survive.

Between the threat and my extreme pain, I was furious. I planned to track down my attacker and give him a dose of his own medicine. Unfortunately, that involved moving, something I wasn't sure I could do.

My plans for revenge faded when I heard voices approaching. I tried to drag my body into the bushes, but it was useless. If he'd come to finish me off, there wasn't much I could do to stop him. A hand grabbed my shoulder and rolled me on my back. I let out another agonized scream muted only slightly by the rag.

"Mattie, it's me." I was always glad to see Frankie, but at that moment, I was overjoyed. He untied the cloth and lifted it from my mouth only to press it to the side of my head. I let out another scream. This time there was no gag. "I didn't mean to hurt you, Mattie. We gotta stop the bleeding." Frankie's words surprised me. I didn't know I was bleeding and the amount of blood on the rag said I had a pretty good-sized cut on my noggin. "Stay still. Josh went to get an ambulance."

"I'm okay, Frankie." My voice sounded like it was coming from underground. "Help me stand."

"No."

"Then at least untie me." I wasn't sure I had the energy to argue.

"No. If I untie you, you'll try to get up. You need to let them take you to the ER. If the doc says okay, then, okay."

"Do you intend to leave me tied until they arrive?"

"I should. Damn, you're a stubborn woman." He cut the ropes and tossed them to the side. "Did you see who did this? Were you at the Sumner place?"

After rubbing my wrists to get the blood moving in my fingers, I pointed to the note. "Frankie, I have absolutely no doubt that whoever took Diana plans to kill her once he has the money. We have to find her. I wouldn't be surprised if he slapped her around for the hell of it. Sadistic bastard. He tied me up, drugged me, and beat the daylights out of me. What the hell kind of person is that?"

"Let's get you fixed up first. You can't go after anyone in the shape you're in." As he said that, Josh came through the woods with two guys carrying a stretcher. They laid it next to me and although they tried to be as gentle as they could, every inch of my body hurt. I don't swear a lot, but those poor medics heard every curse word I ever knew, and some I made up. Then I passed out.

Frankie stayed with me for the two hours it took them to poke, prod, and identify where and how serious the injuries were. They determined that someone hit, kicked, and generally abused me. I could have told them that, but they weren't listening to me.

They found nothing fatal and nothing broken, including my ribs, which I thought for sure he'd cracked. I almost asked them to double check. They stitched the cut on my head and bandaged it along with various other cuts and abrasions. I had a black eye, bruised ribs, and a good-sized cut on my noggin, and another pair of ruined pantyhose. Someone gave me a shot of pain medicine and instructions on how to clean the wound and change the dressing. I had to do that every day until the stitches came out. I said I'd take care of it and asked to go home.

"Miss Draper, if the only thing they used to neutralize you was chloroform you would have been awakened by the physical attack. Do you remember anything else about it?"

Frankie, a number of nurses, and a deputy waited for my answer to the doctor's question. I tried to picture those few seconds when I struggled with my assailant. "He gave me a shot of something. I remembered thinking he didn't need to waste it, because I was passing out." I pointed to my arm where I felt a stab and the doctor studied it.

"Yes, this puncture is from a needle. We've drawn blood. We'll also run a test for narcotics. Are you sure you're well enough to leave?" I told him I was sure and thanked him. The deputy asked a few more questions and Frankie drove us to the Quigley estate. He said Dave wanted to talk to me. I didn't like the sound of that.

Dave opened the door himself when we arrived, and his jaw tightened when he saw me. When we sat in the living room he offered us a drink. "It might not be a good idea with the medicine they gave me."

I don't know if Dave even heard me, because what came out of his mouth next had nothing to do with medicine or alcohol. "Mattie, if you want to quit, I completely understand. I'll pay you for the time," he waved his hand at my body, "and everything you've invested so far."

My brain was still moving a little slow and my initial response was a blank stare. I saw that he didn't know me very well, and realized something that made me even crankier. "If you had hired Frankie and he came in looking like this, would you have expected he'd want to quit?" He reflected on what I said for a second and admitted that he probably wouldn't. "If you don't think I'm doing my job, Dave, fire me. If you don't want to do that then you shouldn't expect any less from me than you would a male detective. I plan to find Diana and bring her home, alive. If you doubt that, get another detective. If not, let me do my job. I'll deal with the bumps and bruises I get along the way."

Dave pushed out his lower lip. He appeared to admire my spunk, but I didn't feel spunky at that moment. Frankie settled matters when he gave Dave his analysis of my work and me. "Mattie's like that watch that takes a licking and keeps on ticking. She'll get the job done."

With that settled, I was ready to hit the road. I needed a good night's sleep. Dave had another idea. "Are you coming back in the morning?"

"Since I'm still your detective, I am."

"Why don't you stay here tonight? We have extra rooms." He told Frankie that he was welcome to stay, too, but he declined.

"I have a job in the morning, but Dave's right Mattie," Frankie said. "You should get as much rest as you can. You can use the time you'd be driving home and back to catch up on your beauty sleep. Not that you need it, of course."

What a guy. Bed sounded wonderful, but I needed to change my filthy clothes. Dave read my mind. "I'm sure Diana wouldn't mind if you borrowed something from her closet. You're five-nine or so, aren't you?" I said I was. "Her clothes should fit."

"I'm afraid I'm hard on clothes, Dave."

"I can see that." Although he didn't actually smile, my comment helped him relax some. "Please consider it, Mattie. I'm going to bed. The guest room to the right at the top of the stairs is nice. Lock the front door, whichever side of it you decide to stay on, and thank you."

After Dave left, I rose slowly and followed Frankie outside. I watched him replace the taillight on my car and hoped the sheriff didn't break it again. "Maybe I should have had you bring me a gross of those."

"Huh?"

"Never mind. Frankie, I think you're right that I should stay. Could you stop by and feed Sebastian?" I pulled a spare house key off my ring and he took it from my fingers.

"Sure. We don't want Sebastian to see you in this condition anyway. You gonna be okay?"

"I'll be fine and I'll call you tomorrow. What's the job you have in the morning?"

"It's a corporate espionage case."

"What's that?"

"It's been around since the 40s, but it's getting popular. One company tries to get secrets from a competitive company. There's a lot of money in it."

"What are you going to do?"

"I'm going in as a new employee to see if I can discover whose leaking information. I hope it doesn't take too long. I'll be making toothpaste. See you tomorrow, Mattie. Take it easy." He kissed a not-bruised spot on my cheek.

"Frankie, this attack means I'm getting close. I just wish I knew what I was getting close to."

*

Someone knocked on the door and I readied myself to climb out of bed and go to the living room to answer, but when I opened my eyes, I didn't recognize the surroundings. I also didn't know why everything hurt. Anna opened the door as I sat up and swung my legs to the side of the bed. I hadn't bothered to take off my clothes or crawl under the covers.

"You did take a licking, didn't you?"

I smiled. "Don't tell me, you talked to Mr. Ficaro this morning."

"I did, and he prepared me for when I saw what a mess you are, although even he couldn't have prepared me enough. I brought you breakfast. You have to eat, and when you are ready, we can find you something to wear. There is a full bathroom in this room and you can take a shower or a bath. Maybe you'd better take a bath with that." She pointed to her forehead and I touched the bandage on mine.

"Before I move off this bed I'd better take one of those pain pills they gave me, or you'll be hearing language that'll make you blush."

"Where are they?"

"In my purse." I'd left my purse in the car when I went to visit the Sumners, and retrieved it when Frankie changed my taillight. I reached for the bag but stopped in response to a sharp pain in my side. "Damn."

"I'll get them, Mattie, so that my ears aren't too shocked." She set the tray next to me on the bed and opened my purse. "How many?"

"Just one. More than that will put me back to sleep." I took a pill from her hand and a glass of juice from the tray. I definitely needed to loosen things up. It hurt to lift the juice glass.

I ate slowly. It wasn't just because of the pain. I wanted to relish the unusual experience of someone serving me breakfast in bed. I wished I were in better shape to enjoy it, but even with my injuries, I feasted on a pair of perfectly fried over-easy eggs, bacon, two slices of toast, and a delicious cup of coffee before heading into the bathroom. Frankie must have told Anna how I liked my eggs. What a pair those two were!

My intention had been to shower, but when I saw the giant tub and a shelf full of different soaps and bath products, I decided a good soak might be in order. While the tub filled, I stood in front of the mirror for a look at my face, an action I regretted. The swelling on the left side made it almost unrecognizable even to me, and I had a good-sized shiner on my right eye. No wonder Anna looked shocked even after

Frankie's warning. My hair lay in bloody clumps around the bandage and the rest of it stuck out in every direction.

Thankfully, a voice outside the bathroom door ended my examination. "Mattie, I brought you clothes." I joined Anna in the bedroom. "Here are pants and a blouse that should fit. I hope you don't mind I chose something for you."

The clothes she'd laid out were beautiful. "Are you sure Diana won't mind?"

"When you bring Miss Diana home, she may want to give you all her clothes. She will not mind and you can't go investigating in those." She pointed at my present outfit. I had to agree.

"Okay, Anna, but maybe we should find clothes that Diana doesn't wear often, so Dave isn't upset when he sees them on me."

"That's why I picked these. I had the same thought. How are you feeling?"

"Breakfast was great and the pill is kicking in. I'll take a bath and I bet I'll feel human again within the next half hour."

It was excruciating to lower my body into the tub, but once in, I leaned back and let the hot fragrant water do its job. When I closed my eyes, murky images of the attack and the trip to the hospital swam through my brain. I also remembered that Frankie was in the ER room the entire time they worked on me. I decided not to dwell on it, but it wasn't exactly how I'd envisioned our first intimate moment.

Putting my battered body and my relationship with Frankie aside, I reviewed conversations I'd had the previous day. Whoever beat me was in a rage and could have killed me. Which one of them had I pissed off enough to take out their frustration so violently? Robert Quigley was a grown-up lost little boy who wandered around in that big empty house without any idea what to do. I sensed that something troubled him deeply. Maybe kidnapping Diana Quigley or maybe, though he seemed not to care, the loss of his wife had devastated him more than he wanted to let on.

The sheriff made it clear that I should take a hike, like the sign said. Whoever grabbed me was strong, but if the sheriff had been the one who slapped me around, I'd be dead. I shivered, and for the first time thanked my stars that I hadn't been conscious during the beating.

Sandra and Joe had been no more or less aloof than any other time I'd seen them. Although they didn't enjoy mixing with the lower classes, would they beat the daylights out of me for showing up unannounced? More importantly, would one or both of them have kidnapped Diana? I couldn't picture husband or wife taking me out alone, and I felt sure the attacker was someone much bigger than either Sandra or Joe.

After a good twenty minute soak including several minutes of careful consideration on how to wash my hair, I decided the easiest way was to have Anna help. She agreed and also helped me dress. I adored her as much as she did Frankie and thought she might like me, too. Maybe since Frankie liked me, she'd figure I was okay.

She asked me six or seven times if I felt well enough to work, and when she agreed that I could leave, I drove to Robert Quigley's house. I was angry enough about the attack not to care if I ran into the sheriff. Some of my bravado might have been from the pain medication.

When Robert opened the door, he appeared truly shocked by my condition. I realized as I spoke, I had a slight lisp. "Hi, Robert, ith it all right if I come in?" He backed away, his mouth wide enough to convince me that he hadn't been the one who met me in the woods. I remembered, too, that I hadn't smelled booze during the attack. Of course, the chloroform would have masked that.

"What happened to you?"

"Thomeone beat the crap out of me." It isn't easy to convince a person you're a tough detective when you sound like Sylvester the Cat. I decided to speak slower to see if I could control the lisp. "I look better now than I did last night." I doubted that was true. "Can you tell me where you were last night? Never mind. I can guess your answer. You don't remember."

"I was here. Do you think the person who kidnapped Diana did this to you?"

"I think a few people are involved in Diana's kidnapping and one of them did this to me. Robert, why do you pretend to be completely smashed when you're not?"

He looked at me, again surprised. "You are a good detective, aren't you? How did you figure that out?"

"Actually, a few people mentioned that they thought you were faking. If you were planning a career on stage, I'd forget it. Why do you do it?"

He sighed and looked at the floor. "If I'm smashed, people don't ask me questions I don't want to answer, or they leave me alone completely. Don't get me wrong, Mattie, I am smashed half the time, but it's usually at home, when I'm alone."

"Do the questions you don't want asked have to do with your wife and her serious problem with depression?"

Chapter 24

Robert looked about to argue against my comment, but stopped. Maybe he could see that I was tired of people lying to me, or maybe he was tired of lying. He cleaned off a chair and indicated that I should sit, which I did slowly. We made quite a pair. No one had beaten him, but his physical condition wasn't much better than mine was.

I waited as he shoved a cigarette in his mouth, lit it, and leaned back, releasing the smoke in a world-weary sigh. "Yes, Mattie, Christina struggled with depression most of her life. When her parents died, the state sent her to the east coast to live with her only remaining relative, an uncle she barely knew. He, well, he made her have sex with him. He raped her is what he did, and he told her if she told anyone, he'd make sure she ended up in an orphanage. He showed her pictures of children chained to their beds and sleeping in their own waste. She believed that's where she'd go, so she never told. She was twelve when he became her custodian for god's sake. He died of a heart attack before she turned eighteen. By the time the courts settled everything, she was an adult, a very wealthy adult. Her uncle had money, too. She got it all."

"What happened then?"

"She came here. This was her parents' home." He waved a finger at our surroundings. "It was held in a trust for her until she was eighteen. She tried to live a normal life, but she'd suffered so much. Shortly after she returned, I started driving for her. In time she began to talk a little and we became friends. Then, we became more than friends. I thought she was better, that she was finally over what he did. We'd planned to travel to Europe. Then one day, I found a note. As I was reading it, the police appeared at the door to tell me she died in a car accident."

"She did kill herself?"

He released another smoke filled sigh toward the ceiling. "I went crazy. I couldn't believe she'd do it. She was better. I knew she was, but the note told me I was wrong. She said she'd tried to get over it because she loved me, but she couldn't live with the demons anymore. I should have noticed. I should have done something."

It was the second time I'd watched a Quigley man cry and the second time I struggled to understand the depth of their pain. I gave him a chance to catch his breath before I spoke. "Did you pay off the sheriff to call her death an accident?"

He confirmed with a nod and flattened his cigarette in a nearby ashtray. "It wasn't the insurance money. Her assets were worth nearly a million dollars, and they were mine. I was angry. I was so damned angry." He clenched his fists and dropped his forehead on them. "I loved Christina, and I hated her for leaving me. The life insurance policy paid another two hundred thousand dollars. I told myself she owed me that. If I couldn't have her alive, I wanted the money. I paid the sheriff $2,000 to say her death was an accident and not suicide." He fell back in the chair. "I've been dead inside ever since."

"Why do you hate Diana?"

"If I hate her, it's because she's alive."

I left wondering if Robert would ever be able to put his life together. The detachment that he showed when he discussed Christina came from a deadly combination of pain and guilt. If he allowed it to, it would consume him. Maybe he'd decided to let the alcohol do the work. He said he did black out the night before Diana's kidnapping. He was celebrating the anniversary of when he started driving for Christina—the day they'd first met. He drank nonstop the entire day.

When I returned to the Quigley estate, Anna told me that Frankie had called. I couldn't call him, but Anna said she'd assured him I was fine and then asked me if she had told him the truth. "You did. Is Dave here?" She pointed and I went to the dining room. "Hi."

He lifted his head. "How are you?"

"I'm okay. A little stiff and sore, but I was lucky."

"You don't look lucky, Mattie. Will you stay until we bring Diana home?"

I said I'd stay and then took a deep breath and told him Robert's story. I hoped it would help him focus on something other than Diana for a short time. It did. "I'll go see him. He never said a word. I had no idea he was in so much pain. No wonder he drinks."

"He didn't want anyone to know. I think he hoped that if he didn't acknowledge how hurt he was, the pain would disappear. He may not even have realized it had control over him. Dave, do me a favor when you talk to Robert. Ask him if he told anyone that he'd paid the sheriff to lie about the accident."

After Dave left, I sat at the table, my mind full of the case and the people involved. When you see people walking down the street, you don't think about their lives. You don't wonder if they're happy or angry because you're too busy with your own stuff. At first glance, you wouldn't guess the problems behind the Sandburg, Quigley, and Sumner front doors. I reprimanded myself for thinking wealthy people didn't suffer real tragedy and recovered my notes to run a line through Robert Quigley's name. Only he, Dave, and Anna had a line drawn, and that left a number of suspects. Josh Spencer was still on the list, but not by much. Frankie told me when he pulled into the drive last night Josh came running and said he was worried because I'd been gone a few hours. Frankie had Dave call the Sumners. When they said I'd left at least an hour earlier, Josh and Frankie came to find me.

Frankie hadn't had time to ask Josh any questions and neither had I. I groaned when I stood and decided to take a pain pill before I talked to him. Anna was in the kitchen when I entered. "Do you suppose I could get a glass of water? I need to appease my slightly irritated body."

"I will give you a glass of water and then you will have a bowl of soup. Okay, Mattie?"

"Okay, Anna. How will I get along without you when this case is finished?"

"You will do fine. Frankie will see to that."

Filled with soup and slightly numbed by a pain pill, I found Josh in the garden putting in new plants. He stood when I approached. "How are you, Mattie? You look a little better today."

"I know you're lying, but it's nice of you to say. I feel a little better. Thanks for alerting Frankie and helping him look for me." I didn't have time to waste with niceties. "Josh, show me your cabin so I can take you off my damn suspect list and we can get to work."

"I've been wondering when you'd ask. Come on."

His cabin behind the barn was one large room. After having waded through Robert's place, Josh's home looked incredibly neat and clean. "Wow, this place is spotless. Where did you learn housekeeping?"

"Unfortunately, I picked it up in prison."

I walked around, not that I couldn't see almost everything from where I stood. If he ever had Diana in there, he'd cleaned up any sign. "Do you mind if I sit, Josh?" There was only one chair and I took it. "Luckily for me, you were in the area for both attacks. Unluckily for you, you were in the area for both attacks." Josh stood and listened. "I don't have much time left to solve this. If I wrongly decide a person is innocent and concentrate on someone else, it could mean Diana's life. When I first took this case, it was only a job, but now I care about Dave and Diana. Josh, did you have anything to do with Diana's kidnapping?"

"No, and I want to do what I can to help. Mattie, I didn't go to jail because I'm a criminal. I went because someone set me up."

"Okay then, let's find Diana." I stood with a little too much enthusiasm. "Oh, God."

As much as I appreciated Dave's offer of Diana's clothes, I decided to run back to the city to change into my own, and, though I'd never admit it to him, to see Sebastian. After a short game of can opener, I fed my eternally growing boy and pulled out the shoebox of first aid supplies from the linen closet to work on my cut. I still had two more days before the stitches came out, but I knew better than to mess with infections. I'd just finished putting on the bandage when the phone rang. "How was your first day at the toothpaste factory?" I asked Frankie.

"Fun, but it's going to be over a lot sooner than I thought. I'm close to nailing the guy. I'll go back in a little while. What's up with the case?"

"I've been wondering if someone was paid to cause the accidents at the plant. If someone wants to destroy Dave, it would fit."

"That's a good thought, Mattie. Did Rachel get that list of new employees for you?"

"Not yet." I told him I planned to talk to her later and explained my conversations with Robert and Josh. I also told him that an inkling of an idea concerning the case had latched onto my brain. "I'll tell you more about that after I spend some time with it. I came home to change clothes and feed Sebastian, but he looked a little disappointed when he saw me at the door. I think he prefers your company."

"That's not what he told me, Mattie. He just doesn't want you to think he likes you too much. He has his feline pride. Oh, before I forget. My friend couldn't find records of Robert's wife's accident. I don't suppose it matters now because you were only interested if Robert murdered her, right?"

"Right. Thanks for checking on that, though. If Robert won't talk, I wonder if we'll find anything to nail the sheriff."

"You never know. I have to take off, Mattie. What time do you think you'll be back tonight?"

"Exactly one hour after I bring Diana home."

"That's what I like to hear. If I finish before you do that, maybe I'll come up and visit with Anna. I could use some home cooking. Be careful."

I told him I would and didn't mention that my first stop in Lake Oak would be Peter Fielding's house. Sebastian allowed a quick kiss on the top of his head, satisfied with my promise that when I finished the case I'd buy us a piece of salmon. I also mentioned that it might be time we discussed our true feelings for each other. I interpreted the quick swipe he took at my hand as a yes and headed to Lake Oak.

I parked my car in a less ritzy neighborhood a few blocks from Fielding's house and walked. My various sore and bruised body parts made me conspicuous enough and slowed me down, but I finally located the alley and Fielding's garage. Just beyond the now empty building was the back door to the curator's home, and as I'd heard the deputy say, it was unlocked. I prayed there wasn't a neighbor watching as I slipped inside.

The house had two stories, plus a basement, so I went to the top floor first. Peter appeared to be another neat housekeeper, but it didn't look as though he'd taken many belongings when he left. I found it interesting that the police hadn't searched the place and once again wondered what the sheriff was doing. Actually, what I wondered was why he was sheriff.

The artwork on Fielding's walls told me how different his taste was from Diana's, and although I'm no expert, I leaned in her direction. A black square on a white canvas with a red line on the side may have been art, but I had to admit, I didn't get it.

Nothing on the second or first floor indicated that Diana had been there, but I felt sure she had. I went to the basement where the only light came from the doorway. There were no windows, but I hesitated to turn on the overhead and took my penlight from my purse. The tiny Eveready was another of the many little items that Frankie had assured me I'd use. He was right, of course.

From the bottom step, I could see that the staircase was enclosed and a piece of the paneling that enclosed it protruded slightly. When I ran the flashlight beam along the seam, I saw that the panel ran the length of the enclosure. I gave a tug and it swung open. My little light was more than bright enough to show me that I'd discovered where Fielding had kept Diana, or if not Diana, another guest. I was about to investigate further when someone entered the house upstairs. I could hear their conversation.

"Why does he want us to search this place? That curator guy took off."

"True, but the sheriff has to tell Mrs. Hayworth we went through it with a fine tooth comb." One of them climbed the stairs to the second floor, lingered for a few seconds, and quickly rejoined his buddy in the kitchen. "I didn't see anything."

"I did. There's imported beer in the fridge and a big color television in the living room. The Cubs are playing. Let's watch a few innings before we take off."

"Let me take a look at the basement so we can say we did. Turn on the game, I'll be right back."

I climbed under the stairway, eased the panel closed, and slid to the floor turning off my flashlight. If he searched the basement as fast as he searched the rest of the house, he wouldn't spot me.

He never left the stairs. He must have looked around and decided it was clean. When he stomped back up, I made myself comfortable, guessing by the language and boos directed at the television that the Cubs were having a normal game. Since I wasn't going anywhere for a while, I turned on my flashlight to investigate the surroundings.

There were a few pieces of rope and several cloths strewn around the space, and a syringe sitting on a shelf. He probably kept her quiet with drugs. There were a number of dirty paper plates shoved in a corner and I felt relieved that he'd at least fed her. My light reflected off something in the corner and I moved it slowly to expose a pair of shoes. Probably the pair Diana wore the day of her abduction.

The deputies' radios squawked and I made out some of the code numbers the dispatcher used. It wasn't good. "10-39 to Q & S Design, J4." The message told them to head to Q & S Design with lights and sirens. There was a fatality.

I waited five minutes to make sure they didn't come back, picked up the shoes, and headed slowly up the stairs. It was the only way I could move. Sitting on a concrete floor made every muscle in my bruised body scream. The door at the top of the stairs opened to an empty house and I headed directly to the phone. I wanted to find out what was going on at Q & S Design and didn't think Peter Fielding would mind the use of his phone. I called Dave, but when Kathleen answered she told me the police had called and Dave had gone to the plant. I was about to hang up Kathleen had more to say. "Oh, Miss Draper, I remembered something I saw at Mr. Quigley's birthday party. I'd completely forgotten until the other night when everyone was here and it came to me."

"What was it Kathleen?"

"I saw Mr. Sumner hand Miss Diana a note. He gave her a drink with a note underneath the napkin. I saw him put it there. She took it out, read it, and slipped it in her pocket. She looked very unhappy."

"Jeffrey Sumner?" I couldn't picture him as a dirty old man.

"Oh, no. His son, Joseph Sumner."

"That is strange. I thought they didn't get along."

"That's right ma'am, because Mr. Sumner made advances and it upset Mrs. Quigley."

"Thanks, Kathleen."

"There's one more thing, Miss Draper. Miss Renee is here. She's waiting to talk to you and says it's important."

"Tell her I'll be over after I check out what's going on Q & S."

"Rachel," I shouted as I neared her desk, "what happened? There's an ambulance and squad cars at the factory!" She stared at my bruised face. "I'm okay. I'll tell you later. What happened?"

"A pile of wood fell on one of the workers, Anthony Barlow. It killed him."

"What did the police say?"

"I don't know, Mattie. Mr. Quigley and Mr. Sumner were over there. They left and so did Sheriff Brown. A couple of deputies stayed behind, but nobody has been back here. The thing is, Mattie, you know that list you asked for with new employees? Anthony Barlow was the only person hired in the last year. He started seven months ago."

That stopped me. "Can you find out who hired him?"

Her quick smile reminded me why Rachel sat at the center of Q & S Design. "Jeffrey hired him. There's something else. I don't know how important it is, but Blanche from upholstery told Martha in finishing that some of the guys thought Anthony might have been the one responsible for the accidents."

"Really?" I thought of something that might explain the sudden death of their new employee. "Did anyone know that I'd asked you to compile a list of new employees?"

Rachel grimaced. "I didn't tell anyone, but Marcy, she handles employee records and payroll, is the person I asked for the names. She left a note on my desk that anyone could have seen." Rachel showed me the note.

Anthony Barlow was the only new hire I could find, Rachel. He started in February. Hope that helps. M.

"Rachel, this isn't your fault. Something's going on and it has nothing to do with you. Don't blame yourself." I went to my car repeating the words I'd told Rachel and put Anthony Barlow aside to consider the conversations I'd had in the last fifteen minutes. Why would Joe have given Diana a note, and why would she take it? It had to be the one I found. Why would Jeffery Sumner hire someone to cause accidents in the factory, and why would a lumber landslide suddenly kill that someone? Then, it came to me! The idea that latched onto my brain earlier exploded and everything made sense, including who kidnapped Diana Quigley and why.

Chapter 25

I stopped at the sheriff's office on the way to the Quigley estate and told him I was heading in the opposite direction of my intended location. "Well why don't you tell me this theory of yours, Miss Draper." He wore the smirk I'd grown to detest. With hands clenched behind my back and wearing as innocent a smile as I could muster, I told the sheriff a few phony hunches and that I was heading to the Sandburgs to talk to Renee Sandburg. "That's interesting, but I thought you said Peter Fielding kidnapped Mrs. Quigley."

"Hey, we all make mistakes, Sheriff. Luckily for me, you were smart enough to let him go. Have you been able to talk to him about the paintings?" I knew he hadn't. When they found Fielding, he wouldn't be answering questions.

"No, but don't you worry your pretty little black and blue head about that. Give us a call when you have the kinks worked out of your theories. The little things, like why Renee would kidnap her sister and who you plan to accuse next."

I wanted so badly to tell him I knew about Christina's accident, but if I did, I might not leave the office. "Sheriff, the next time we meet, you will regret ever having heard of me. I'm looking forward to watching you squirm." I had a feeling that along with falsifying an accident report, he'd have a few other things to answer for. "I figured out who kidnapped Diana Quigley and I intend to prove it." I sounded so sure even I was convinced.

Anna opened the door in a hurry and ushered me in. "Mattie, I have heard something from one of the maids. Her name is Gretchen and she works for Mr. and Mrs. Sumner."

"What did she say?"

"She has worked for them for three months. Maids don't stay long because Mrs. Sumner is…well, she is difficult. A few days ago when she went to the house, Mrs. Sumner opened the door and told her to take a vacation. She gave Gretchen a big check and told her to come back in two weeks. Then she shut the door and left her standing on the porch."

"What does this mean, Anna?"

"Gretchen said that before the door closed she thought she heard a woman scream."

"How can I contact Gretchen?"

"I will get her number."

She hurried off and I walked toward the dining room where I hoped I'd find Dave. Renee ran in, grabbed my arm, and dragged me to a wall in the library with dozens of pictures. She was excited, but sober. "What is it, Renee?"

"Mattie, is this the earring you saw?" She pointed to a photo of Joe and Sandra in a small frame.

I nearly choked and removed it from the wall, ripping the photo from the frame. "Do you have a magnifying glass?" Renee yelled the question to Anna who said she'd bring it. "Hurry!" I shouted.

Anna returned with the glass and I examined the photo closer. My eyes had not failed me. The earring I found in the clearing hung on Sandra's earlobe. "That's it! How did you see this, Renee?"

"I stopped by to see if you'd heard anything and when I saw this picture I remembered the earring you described. That's it, isn't it? That bitch!"

Something Jeffrey told me when I first met him popped into my brain. He said that if you had a successful life, someone would want to take it. Both Joe and Sandra told me they were jealous of Dave and Diana's life. They intended to have it for themselves. I realized I was carrying the shoes I found in Fielding's basement. "Renee, do you recognize these?"

"They're Diana's. Where did you find them?"

Anna stood in the doorway and I pushed them into her arms. "Put these away. I'm bringing Diana home today and Dave doesn't need to see them."

I found Dave on the phone in the dining room. "I understand. I promise there will be no police and I'll bring the entire amount." He hung up and looked at me. "That was him. He said because I messed up he wants two hundred thousand dollars instead, and if I mess up again, Diana will be killed."

"Do you have that much?"

"He's giving me until eleven o'clock tomorrow morning so I can go to the bank. I'll get a loan for the rest. I told him I want to talk to her before he sees a penny and he agreed to call at ten thirty tomorrow."

"Where does he want you to take the money?"

"The beach in Evanston, same as last time. Only this time, I'm going alone."

"If I don't have this wrapped up tonight, I'll drive you to the beach and stay back, but I intend to have Diana home. Dave, a few things have occurred and I have to ask you some questions." He stared blankly, so I forged ahead. "How is your marriage?"

His eyes widened and he fell back in his chair running a hand through his hair. "Mom told you I've been working extra hours and Diana was tired of me being at the office. We're doing okay, but things aren't as good as they could be." Lifting his head slightly he asked, "Why?"

"Is it possible that Diana has been having an affair?"

"I, I want to say no, but I don't know. I don't want to believe she'd consider something like that."

"If she was having an affair, could it have been with Joe Sumner?"

He eyeballed me. "Joe? She can't stand him. He's come on to her before and she told him to stay away. To answer your question, no."

"Maybe since you've been busy, she reconsidered and told Joe she would."

"What are you saying?"

"Kathleen recently remembered that she saw Joe slip a note to Diana the night before her abduction. I'm sure it's the one I found in the garden, and that she went to meet him in the clearing. The clearing where she was supposedly kidnapped."

"You think Diana kidnapped herself. Why? She doesn't need money and if she wanted to leave she could do that without staging a phony kidnapping."

"I don't know why she went to meet Joe, but whatever her reasons, I believe he had something different in mind. I'm convinced that Sandra and Joe are holding Diana at their house until they collect the two hundred thousand dollars. Then, they'll kill her. They have to. I also think Joe is hoping to drain you financially so he can buy you out when his father retires in two years. He's been spreading rumors that Q & S Design is in trouble. Did Jeffrey tell you why he hired Anthony Barlow?"

"He said that he was a friend of Joe's who needed a job."

"Ah, that makes sense. I'm betting he's responsible for the accidents and starting the fire at the factory. Joe was probably the one who hit me and took the earring. He came over earlier to slash your tires and make sure you didn't show up at the plant before the fire started. He must have seen me going into the woods, and followed. Later, he saw me find the earring." Dave looked at me in agony. "Joe wants the business. He wouldn't want it to go up in flames, so Sandra had to make sure she called the fire department right after Anthony started it."

"You're insane." His eyes said he didn't want to believe me, but he considered my words. "Jeffrey would never be involved in anything like this."

"Jeffrey Sumner doesn't have a clue what's going on." I pulled the picture of Joe and Sandra from my pocket and put it in front of him, then I handed him the magnifying glass. "Renee showed me this photograph. Look at the earrings Sandra's wearing."

"They're pretty. So what?"

"Do you remember the earring I found in the clearing? It was one of those. I'm telling you, Joe and Sandra have Diana, and plan to kill her when you pay them. Who recommended me to you, Dave?" I had a pretty good idea who it was.

"Joe."

"That's a little strange don't you think, since Joseph Sumner and I never met. Why would he recommend a private investigator he knew nothing about?" Dave didn't answer. "Because I'm brand new in the business and I'm a woman. He didn't think I'd be smart enough to figure out their plan. When you first mentioned hiring a detective, did he try to talk you out of it?"

"Yes. He said Sheriff Brown could handle it, but I insisted."

"When he saw you were determined to hire a detective he found a rookie that he thought he could fool. Joe said he talked to the kidnapper at the party, but it was Sandra calling from another room." Dave didn't say anything and I let out a breath. "Dave, did you ask Robert if anyone knew about his payoff to the sheriff?"

"Joe told him that he and the sheriff had been drinking and Brown let it slip, but Joe promised Rob he wouldn't tell anyone. What does Robert have to do with this?"

"Not Robert, the sheriff." I straightened and touched his hand while shoving the photo in my pocket. "I'm going to visit the Sumners. If I'm wrong, you won't be billed a penny for my time and I'll drive you to drop off the money. If I'm not back in ten minutes, you'd better call the FBI. Don't call the local cops, and you'd better not tell the feds that it's for me."

"I'll come with you." Dave didn't look like he could stand, no less help catch a kidnapper.

"No, Dave. You have to stay here and make the call." I thought he could do that.

"He can make the call. I'm going with you." I turned to see Renee at the door.

"No you're not. I'm not sure if I'm right and if I am, I don't want to put anyone in danger."

"I'm going with you."

As Renee and I left the house, I checked my weapon. I'd never used it except at the shooting range, but I'd trained myself from day one to be able to if necessary. Frankie told me never to draw it unless I could shoot. I hoped it wouldn't be necessary to test that, because I knew I could.

When we arrived at the Sumner house, I saw a familiar car parked off to the side. I couldn't place it and told myself to forget the car and focus on what I was doing. I sent Renee to the back of the house to find a window and check out activities inside. I told her to be careful.

Through the French doors that covered one side of the living room, I saw Sandra by the bar. I didn't see Joe. Then I felt something hard jammed into my back and decided I could stop looking. "Hi, Joe."

Chapter 26

"Hello, Mattie. Apparently I wasn't as smart as I thought to recommend you to Dave." Joe coaxed me forward with the gun barrel. "Now, very carefully hand me your gun and we'll go inside and have a chat, though it may be short. When I couldn't talk Dave out of hiring a private investigator, I checked around for a new agency and was delighted to find one that belonged to a woman. Guess who that was?"

"That would be me." I'd been right that Joe didn't think I'd figure it out.

"That's right. Your gun please." I handed it over wondering, as he pushed open a French door, where Renee was. "Inside."

Sandra stood at the bar, pouring herself a drink. "Did you get her?" She turned and smiled. "Thank you for finding my earring, Mattie. It wouldn't have been good if the police had found it instead of you. My, you do look bad. I told you this wasn't a job for a woman."

"For your information, Sandra, if Joe hadn't knocked me out to get that earring, we might not have caught on to your little plan. Everyone believed it was Diana's and that she lost it in the struggle. Renee Sandburg found it in this photo of you and Joe at the Quigleys'." When I waved it in the air, she sauntered over and took it from my fingers.

"Renee saw this? Oh, my. We'll have to take care of that little problem. I'm sure we can get her to drink herself to death in a hurry." She tore the picture into pieces and threw them in the air. "Do you have anything else to say?"

"Where's Diana?"

Sandra brightened at my question. "Oh, you want to see the princess. Sure. Joe, take the detective to see Diana. She doesn't look a great deal better than you."

After tying my hands behind my back, Joe pushed me toward the doorway of a large den where I saw a woman gagged and tied to an overstuffed chair. I almost didn't recognize Diana's bruised and swollen face. She was a mess, but alive. She showed little reaction to my arrival with Joe, but when Sandra joined us, Diana's entire body stiffened. It was clear who'd been smacking her around. "The beautiful Diana Quigley isn't very attractive right now, is she?"

I looked at Sandra in amazement. "What did you do, Sumner, beat her while she was tied, gagged, and defenseless? You're one hell of a brave lady."

I flashed on a brief image of my brother. No, I still haven't learned when to keep my mouth shut. She grabbed my hair and yanked me to my knees. "Listen, you bitch. Open that mouth again and you'll be in even worse shape." She slammed her fisted hand against the side of my face but didn't release her grip on my hair. That was the only thing that kept me from falling over. "Joe, give Diana another injection. She doesn't have to say anything until her farewell to her dear hubby tomorrow."

Sandra yanked me to my feet. I stood helplessly watching Diana shake her head as Joe pressed a syringe in her arm. It worked quickly. I wondered if it was the same drug they gave me in the woods. I had no doubt that it was Sandra who beat me, but someone else had their arm around my neck. Neither Joe nor Sandra had arms that thick and the strength, although Sandra had a pretty mean right.

When Joe finished with Diana, Sandra, still gripping my hair, shoved me at him. "Make her comfortable on the couch. At least until we kill her."

Joe was quite the obedient husband. He put me on the couch where I was anything but comfortable. My theory had been right on target, unfortunately. "Sandra, you're supposed to be Diana's good friend. How could you do this to her, and to Dave?"

"Get real, Detective. Do you have any idea how difficult it is living next door to the Prince and Princess of Lake Oak? I pretended to be Diana's friend so she'd introduce me to the people I needed to know. She's a boring, mousy woman who I wouldn't choose as a friend."

I looked at Joe. "You arranged to meet Diana at the clearing. How did you talk her into joining you? I saw the note you gave her and it didn't say anything except to meet you."

"Where did you see the note?" He said with no real interest.

"I found it in the garden, but until this minute, I was only guessing as to who wrote it. Why would Diana agree to meet you?"

"Actually, we have Robert to thank for that."

I was sure Robert had nothing to do with Diana's kidnapping. "What did Robert do?"

"Our original plan was for Sandra to invite Diana over here and we'd put something in her coffee, but we thought it might be too risky if she told someone where she was going. We hadn't come up with an alternative plan until at Dave's birthday party, Rob and I were having a cigar on the back porch and I noticed Diana standing near the door. Rob was blathering on about bad marriages and I could see Diana was listening. It gave me an idea. I pretended I didn't see her and mentioned to Rob that I thought I'd heard Dave telling my dad he was tired of his marriage and planned to get a divorce. Robert was three sheets to the wind and didn't even hear what I said, but Diana did. She came out and wanted to know more. Before I could say anything else, Dave and his dad joined us on the porch. On my way back inside, I whispered to Diana that we should meet and I'd tell her what I'd heard. I gave her the note later."

I was relieved that Dave had been right, and that Diana had not cheated on him. "If you met her in the clearing, why was Vagabond tied to the tree in the woods?" I swung around to see Sandra's smug grin. "You must have tied him, because Joe was terrified of the horse. Did you and Diana ride together at Jeffrey's house when Dolly was still alive?"

"We did, and Vagabond didn't dislike me quite as much as he did Joe."

"And you tied the rope across the path after to make it look like a stranger abducted her." Sandra nodded. "Why did you bother to tie Vagabond?"

"I didn't want to take a chance that he'd go to the barn before we had Diana safely tucked away."

"That makes sense. Then the two of you brought her here."

"Well, that's not quite accurate, but you have the idea. Who would have thought that a brand new female detective would have figured out our little plan?"

I really wanted to slap her. "You'd been planning to kidnap Diana for a while. Long before the first time Joe hit on her at the party. Joe, from what I heard at Q & S Design, you get a lot of rejections from the ladies. I'm surprised you didn't figure that into the equation beforehand."

Two seconds later, I was on the receiving end of Joe's right, which was actually not as impressive as the one from his wife. He stepped back and smiled, taking Sandra's drink. "Sandra's right. Dave and Diana are a shining example of the perfect couple and they have everything they've ever wanted. It's been quite entertaining watching them suffer. We wanted to draw out their agony as long as we could, but, honestly, it's getting a little boring now, and we have plans of our own."

Sandra slammed her fresh drink on the bar, "Plans that are finally going to happen despite your pathetic efforts. He promised me we would have that business and I'd have anything I wanted." She picked up the glass and pointed toward the den, spilling a large portion. "She doesn't need the money. When Q & S belongs to us, I'll have everything that Diana once had, but she won't be around to care."

"How will the business belong to you and Joe? Dave and Jeffery might not agree."

If our eyes really are the windows to our soul, the cold blackness I saw in Sandra's suggested that any light of humanity faded long ago. "Once Dave pays the ransom, his job will be finished. He'll never see Diana's money, because he'll be in prison for her murder." Sandra pulled a cloth bag from behind the bar and opened it enough to show me a gun. She never touched it and I figured I knew why. "This is Dave's," Sandra said. "I borrowed it the night of his birthday party. His prints are the only ones on it and it will be near enough Diana's body that even the Lake Oak Sheriff's Department will be able to find it. They will try and convict Dave for kidnapping and murder. When he's gone, Jeffrey will own the entire company, and Joe is his only heir."

"Jeffery may not want to retire right away. You could have to wait a few years," I suggested.

"We won't have to worry what Jeffery wants for much longer." Joe appeared surprised at Sandra's words, but said nothing.

I wanted to keep them talking to delay whatever plans they had for me until the posse I was praying for arrived.

"What's the matter, Joe? Didn't Sandra tell you her plans involved getting your dad out of the way too?"

"Don't listen to her, Joe. She doesn't know what she's talking about. She never does."

Sandra's wink at her hubby didn't look sincere to me, but Joe seemed convinced. I tried another approach. "Sandra, you were the one who called from another phone in the house. You made sure Joe would answer so no one knew it was you. You told him that you were going to the powder room and that was his cue. If anyone else answered, you would have hung up. Good trick. That one almost had me until I remembered there were two phone lines and anyone in the house could have made the call."

"Once again, Miss Draper, you are astute." Joe's compliment hadn't filled me with pride, but he that might not have been his goal. He continued. "Yes, Sandra made the call from a back bedroom and I answered. If you could have heard what she was saying, you would have blushed. I thought we had you on that one. The sheriff bought it, hook, line, and sinker."

"That's not exactly accurate, is it Joe? You blackmailed the sheriff. You told him if he didn't help you get me out of the way, you would reveal the $2,000 bribe Robert gave him to call his wife's suicide an accident." Just then I realized who it was that met me in the woods. "It was the sheriff who grabbed me after I left your house. Sandra, did you call him when you pretended to answer the phone?" I ignored her snicker. "You also lied about flying to New York. When I questioned you, you said you'd flown under your maiden name, but that was another lie, wasn't it?"

"Well, of course, it was. You turned out to be a real pain in the ass, Draper. I realized you and your boyfriend were better detectives than you appeared. I shouldn't have bothered with the phony trip to New York. I thought I'd be prepared with an alibi, but it wasn't necessary." She sipped her drink. "I was glad I wasn't gone when Mrs. Kendall called asking me to approve the arrest and termination of our curator at an emergency board meeting. Of course, that termination was only to fire the poor fellow. The other came later."

"I didn't know you were a board member until recently. When I asked you about the meeting, you said you had no idea where Diana was going, but you were familiar with the activities of the art museum. That's how you knew Peter Fielding and how much he hated Diana. You knew he wanted her out of the way as badly as you did."

"If you must know, Peter and I came up with the plan and I filled Joe in later. We had a mutual hatred of Diana Quigley. Peter didn't want money at that point. He wanted her out of the way. Joe and I wanted the money and eventually the business, so it worked out well for all of us. Actually, not that well for Peter, I suppose. After Joe and I kidnapped Diana, we took her to Peter's house in case someone decided to check here. Things were fine until you messed them up, Draper. He was afraid to keep her."

"He brought her here in the trunk of his car." I said it out loud, but I was talking to myself.

"Yes, in the trunk of his car. We knew she'd be dead soon, so we threw her in there," she pointed to the den. "She'll live long enough to have one more brief conversation with Dave."

"Oh, I get it. When Peter brought Diana, you told your maid to take a vacation. That's Fielding's car parked outside. I didn't recognize it because the garage was dark when I saw it. Where is he now?" I suddenly understood what her earlier comment meant and stopped. "You terminated him."

Sandra feigned boredom, but she was absolutely delighted to describe her successful deception. "I suppose it's your business to be nosy. Yes, Peter has gone to that big art museum in the sky, but I doubt he's a curator. He wasn't very good at his job."

Sandra might have been one of the coldest people I'd ever met. "You planned to get rid of him from the beginning."

"That was our plan," she said, pointing at Joe and herself, "but Peter didn't know. I doubt he would have gone along with it." She threw her head back with a maniacal laugh, but Joe seemed not to notice that his wife had clearly gone over the edge. Then, just as sudden as the outburst of laughter began, Sandra became calm and continued. "When he brought Diana, he wanted us to take those horrid paintings. We told him to get rid of them himself. Later, Joe thought it might be better for us to dispose of them at the same time as Peter and Diana. Peter was going to bring them back, but unfortunately, you interrupted and the police returned them to the museum.

Joe took over. They were like a macabre vaudeville team. "Then, also because of your interference Miss Draper, things got a little uncomfortable for Peter. After he lost his job he decided to leave town, but he wanted part of the ransom money. We invited him to stop by for a drink and told him we'd give him some cash before he left town."

If I stayed alive, their boastful confessions were enough to nail them. They didn't tire of regaling me with their criminal genius, so I egged them on. "Since Peter wasn't interested in the money, how did you keep him from killing Diana?"

Sandra almost choked on her drink. "Peter was a wimp. He couldn't kill her. He couldn't even stand to hear her cry. He gave her food and water the whole time she was there. When he saw her here, he was shocked to see how quickly her health had deteriorated. He starting shouting that we should call it off. I gave him a shot to quiet him down. It was a drug you've recently encountered, but he had a tad more."

She was a cold-blooded killer, and her husband wasn't much better. "Joe, did you push lumber on your old pal, Anthony Barlow?" I asked.

"Mattie, you really are quite amazing."

"The plant accidents were to make Dave crazy, and the arguments you two have been having around town were to convince people that your marriage was falling apart. You couldn't possibly work on anything together, especially something as complicated as a kidnapping. When you pick up the money tomorrow, you'll dispose of Diana and send a tip to the police to find the body and Dave's gun."

"That's correct, Detective." Joe smiled. "And now that you've complicated matters, we'll have to do the same thing to you. Dave will have killed you because you uncovered his plan. It's too bad you have to die, Mattie. I like you, although Sandra doesn't care for you much."

"I'm sorry you don't like me, Sandra, and I hate to burst your bubble, but once I figured out your little game, I told Dave and left him with instructions to call the cops if I didn't return." I thought I sounded convincing, but Sandra looked doubtful.

She turned to pour another drink and didn't turn back to respond. "The cops don't believe a word you say, Mattie, and as you mentioned earlier, the sheriff has been very supportive of Joe and I."

I watched smoke rise over her shoulder from a freshly lit cigarette. She'd killed Peter Fielding, Joe had killed Barlow, and they planned to kill Diana and me. A split second after that depressing thought, I heard a loud thud and a groan.

Frankie stood behind Joe's collapsed body holding both Joe's and my guns. Renee and Josh stood behind him. "I finished up the other job a little sooner than I expected, Mattie. I hope you don't mind me stopping by."

Chapter 27

At the sound of Frankie's voice, Sandra turned from the bar and dropped her glass. I was much happier to see him than she was. "You do pick the best times to make an appearance," I told the grinning detective. "Would you mind untying me and we can call the feds?"

"Dave called them. They'll be here soon." The gun stayed on Sandra as he cut the ropes. When I stood, he gave me my gun and a kiss. I chuckled at the look of disgust Sandra wore.

While Frankie and Josh kept an eye on the Sumner gang, I grabbed Renee and ran to the den. She almost fell over when she saw the condition of her sister, but pulled herself together and kept talking to Diana while untying the ropes. We were still at it when Dave came in. Diana did look a little green around the gills after spending a week drugged and the last few days enduring physical abuse and a lack of food and water. She was alive, but Dave didn't know that.

"Is she, is she...?" He dropped to his knees in front of the chair and held her. "Oh, God. Diana, I'm sorry."

She came to at the sound of his voice. The drugs still had a tight hold and she could barely speak, but she managed one thing. "I love you." Her head fell to his shoulder.

"Everything will be fine, Diana. Everything will be just fine. We'll have plenty of time together." He turned to me. "We need to get her to the hospital."

"I called for an ambulance," Frankie spoke from the doorway. Seconds later, I heard squad cars arrive and watched most of the Lake Oak Sheriff's Department burst in waving their guns. They all ended up pointed at Frankie. Sheriff Brown led the pack.

I had little patience left for local law enforcement. "Put your guns down. Those two are the ones you want for kidnapping and attempted grand larceny. There will probably be a couple of murder charges, too. Make sure they tell you where they put Fielding's body. He worked with them and that's his car in the woods. They might have deposited him in the trunk. You remember that trunk, Sheriff. The one I told you Peter used to bring Diana Quigley from his house."

Joe sat on the floor, numb, but Sandra wasn't ready to give up. "Sheriff, you know this woman is a fake. She's after Dave's money. She set us up. She kidnapped Diana, brought her here, and called you." Sandra must have realized how dumb that sounded and that no one, including the sheriff, was buying. She looked at the faces in the room, and finally at Joe. For the first time, they seemed to realize that their new home would be a prison.

"They've been drugging Diana and she needs to go to the hospital. I'm sure when they compare the drugs that were found in my system, they'll be the same as what they gave Diana, and no doubt, used to kill Peter Fielding." As I said that, paramedics rushed in with a gurney, which they used to push the sheriff out of the way.

He hadn't moved since he entered, but when the medics came in and pushed him aside, he landed in front of me. "The FBI called to say they were on their way, Draper. Someone called them instead of me. Was that you?" I shook my head, but the sheriff was on to his next question. "I thought your big plan was that Renee Sandburg took her sister and that's where you were going. Did you lie to me?"

"Yes, I did. I had to make sure that you didn't make a mess of things."

A noise that sounded like a growl escaped before he responded. "What about Fielding? Did you lie about him, too? It's a damn good thing that Mrs. Quigley wasn't killed or you'd be held responsible."

"Did you hear what I said, Sheriff? Fielding worked with them. I found a necklace in the trunk of his car that belonged to Diana Quigley. I also found her shoes at his house in the place beneath the stairs where he kept her. You had the person holding her two days ago and let him walk."

His face turned painfully red. "I'm arresting you for withholding evidence."

"I don't think so, Sheriff. You'll be so busy trying to stay out of jail you won't have time for me. Robert Quigley told me about the $2,000 he paid you to cover up his wife's suicide." The sheriff's mouth moved, but nothing came out. "Joe found out that Robert bribed you, so he and Sandra threatened to tell all unless you accosted me in the woods. You almost killed me!"

"I did not. I knocked you out with the chloroform and Joe gave you a shot. He said they'd leave you there with a note so you'd quit investigating. You were passed out when I left."

I turned to Sandra. "Somehow I knew you were the one who kicked me while I was unconscious. You're a pathetic creature." I couldn't look at her any longer and turned way shaking my head.

No one had been paying attention to Renee, but she'd left Diana when the medics arrived and when she heard the conversation, moved in front of Sandra. I saw by the look on her face what was coming, but before I could stop it, Renee's clenched right hand landed squarely on Sandra's jaw. As Sandra fell, Renee climbed on top of her. I pulled her away. "Renee, save your energy to help Diana. She'll need your support. They'll take care of Sandra." Josh took Renee's arm and led her to a chair. I looked at the sheriff. "You might want to write your letter of resignation before the feds get here. You're part of the kidnapping."

"I didn't know they kidnapped her! They told me they wanted you out of the way because Dave had to stop believing Diana would be coming home. They said she was probably dead and you were giving him false hope to make money." He pointed at the unhappy Mr. and Mrs. Sumner. "I didn't know about the kidnapping or Fielding. It was that one who gave the orders."

Not surprisingly, his finger directed our eyes to Sandra who was sitting up with a hand held over the imprint of Renee's fist. She glared at Renee but turned away when she saw her leave the chair. It was then that Sandra decided whose fault everything really was and she directed her defiant eyes at Joe. "You fixed it, didn't you, Joe? You found a brand new woman detective that would never figure things out. You still think men are smarter than women, don't you? You stupid ass!"

The sheriff had been quietly making his way toward the door when two FBI agents came in. "You can stay right there, Sheriff Brown. We'll need to have a chat." The agent looked at Joe and Sandra. "Since you two look the least glad to see us, I'm guessing you get to chat with us, too."

I smiled at Sandra and wondered, if she and Joe managed to avoid a death sentence, how much shopping she'd do in the next twenty to thirty years at the prison canteen.

Chapter 28

That was the Quigley case. My first big job and one that brought as many challenges as it did rewards. Jeffrey Sumner paid for a good team of lawyers and Sandra and Joseph Sumner got off with twenty to life. They both made parole after twenty. Sandra filed for divorce while still in prison and after her release, moved in with an aunt in Chicago. Joseph inherited his dad's house, but sold it to pay remaining legal and divorce fees. I wondered if they had ever once imagined what would happen if their plan failed. They might not have, since they didn't think for a minute that a rookie female PI would figure it out.

Jeffrey Sumner sold his share of the business to Dave for half its worth and retired immediately. He'd have given him the entire thing for nothing to make up for his son's crimes but Dave wouldn't take it. Jeffrey visited Joe during his incarceration, but never forgave him and died ten years before his son's release. He did buy a few horses and spent his retirement riding through the woods on and around his estate.

Josh worked for Dave and Diana until last year. He never spent anything and used his savings to buy a piece of land near my sister Mary Anne in Kenosha. He helps handle her tougher horses. Mary Anne's husband, Rick, passed on, but she still keeps a few. She told me she was the same as me—too ornery to die.

Susanne is a grandmother too many times over to count, and my brother Bill is a cantankerous old curmudgeon who I still love to pieces.

Anna died at the age of ninety-two. Frankie and I visited her often when she retired. She cooked us dinner right up until the last visit. I still marvel at the people we met on that case. Some, like Anna, and Dave and Diana Quigley, became a permanent part of our lives.

Robert Quigley sold Christina's family home and went into an expensive treatment facility to get off the booze and get help with his grief. Dave hired him a lawyer and somehow managed to keep him out of jail for defrauding the insurance company. He moved in with his parents in Kankakee, and eventually used the rest of his money to open a small diner on the river. He's a content guy these days, and they say he makes the best coffee in town.

Sheriff Brown lost his job and faced conspiracy and fraud charges. He never did any jail time, but he never did much else, either. Frankie suggested I not ask him to pay for my busted taillight.

They found Peter Fielding's body in the trunk of his car. The autopsy report showed he died of an overdose of the same drugs used on both Diana and me.

Dave cut back on his hours at work and they bought another horse. He didn't plan to let Diana go for morning rides with only Vagabond to watch her.

The Dowlings were frequent dinner guests and Dave and Diana spent more time with the kids than Chet and Linda. They didn't mind. It was Linda who recommended to Diana an infertility clinic that her sister had used. It didn't take much to convince her, and three years after her kidnapping, Diana Quigley gave birth to a beautiful baby, Lauren Marie Quigley. Today, Lauren has her mother's beauty and two children of her own. Frankie and I still see them, because we're regulars at Quigley gatherings.

Renee Sandburg helped her younger sister survive and move on from the horrible event, and it gave her the strength to change. She never went back to the mind-numbing drinking she did and began taking art classes. To her surprise, she found she had a real talent for painting. One of Diana's biggest disappointments was that she didn't see the right hook Renee gave Sandra.

Mr. Quigley paid me far too much, but he said he was ready to spend two hundred thousand dollars, so why not? Frankie and I were married right after Lauren's birth. Eventually, we had two of our own and juggled our schedules so we could both work our cases and be part of our kids' lives. We did okay, and although we never said it to one another or the kids, we were pleased that our daughter, Anna, and our son, Josh, never expressed any interest in being private investigators.

And that was how, with a little help from Frankie, I solved Mrs. Quigley's kidnapping.

"What do you mean a little help? Tell me you could have done it without me."

"I could have done it, Frankie, but it wouldn't have been nearly as much fun."

Books by Jean Sheldon

An Uncluttered Palette
After an accident destroys her hand, art teacher Rayna Hunt begins the long journey to recover her skill. Her quiet, safe world is further disrupted when an anonymous call to the police draws her into a case of forgery and art theft. She and a group of friends and students work to prove her innocence and solve the crime.

Flowers for Her Grave
When a young woman shows up in Raccoon Grove claiming to be a missing girl from a 20-year-old murder, the local gossip columnist and gardener team up to discover the truth. Accidents threaten to put a stop to their investigation and to the garden party where they plan to reveal what really happened. No one could have guessed the truth. Neither will you in this surprising whodunit.

The Woman in the Wing
A historical mystery that takes place in a defense plant. Although fictional, the well-researched book offers a glimpse into the lives of women who served at home during World War II, Rosie the Riveters, and sheds some light on the seldom told stories of the women who ferried military planes from plants to air bases around the country—Women Airforce Service Pilots—WASP.

Mrs. Quigley's Kidnapping
When Mattie Draper opened her Chicago detective agency in 1968, she was one of a handful of female Private Investigators nationwide. For three months, her greatest challenges were finding lost pets and wayward spouses—until someone kidnapped Diana Quigley. In a race to find the missing woman, Mattie tries to untangle the helpful information supplied by a growing list of suspects.

She Overheard Murder A Nic & Nora Mystery
On October 29, 1945, Nic Owen made her debut appearance as a radio detective on the new show Inez Ingalls, Private Eye. Hired only weeks earlier to read ad copy and work as an understudy, the murder of the show's star, Carolyn Park, propelled Nic to the lead role and a top spot on the list of suspects. Cecil Park, husband of the murdered woman, wants answers. As does Nora Hahn, Carolyn's 'special friend' for fourteen years.

She Overheard Murder introduces characters from the new Nic and Nora Mystery series—mysteries solved by lesbian amateur detectives in post-World War II Chicago. Finalist 2014 Lambda Literary Award.

Puzzled by The Clues A Nic & Nora Mystery
The second Nic & Nora Mystery, 'Puzzled by the Clues', follows both the blossoming relationship of Nic and Nora and that of Anna and Allen. Characters at the heart of the Owen gang and those on the perimeter, offer humor, wisdom, and the belief that there is always hope. As Anna points out, "Maybe after two World Wars, people are beginning to understand the insanity of hate."

Persistent
A Collection of Poems

We are all on a journey that can, on occasion, require that we travel alone. Those times of quiet reflection bring us peace, direction, and answers to questions unheard during the hurried, noisy days of lives. This collection shares one voice on one part of her journey. Jean Sheldon writes from the deeper parts of her being and helps us look at those places in our own lives with courage, hope and even humor.